1 3 JUL 2022

Richmond upon Thames Libraries

Renew online at www.richmond.gov.uk/libraries

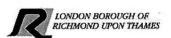
LONDON BOROUGH OF
RICHMOND UPON THAMES

D1464567

90710 000 454 579

For Lucas, Jakob and James

STRIPES PUBLISHING LIMITED
An imprint of the Little Tiger Group
1 Coda Studios, 189 Munster Road,
London SW6 6AW

www.littletiger.co.uk

First published in Great Britain by Stripes Publishing Limited in 2020
Text copyright © Emma Young, 2020
Cover copyright © Stripes Publishing Limited, 2020
Cover images used under licence from Shutterstock.com

ISBN: 978-1-78895-034-3

A CIP catalogue record for this book is available from the British Library.

Printed and bound in the UK.

The Forest Stewardship Council® (FSC®) is a global, not-for-profit organization dedicated
to the promotion of responsible forest management worldwide. FSC® defines standards
based on agreed principles for responsible forest stewardship that are supported by
environmental, social, and economic stakeholders. To learn more, visit www.fsc.org

2 4 6 8 10 9 7 5 3 1

EMMA YOUNG

HERE LIE THE SECRETS

LITTLE TIGER

LONDON

PROLOGUE

Again, I go to look at myself in the mirror. This silvery jersey top is far too clingy. I peel it off and toss it behind me, on top of literally three-quarters of my meagre wardrobe. I'm meant to be going to Freja's house in about fifteen minutes. That should be plenty of time. Except that I've been getting ready – only getting no closer to actual readiness – for over an hour now.

At school yesterday, Freja filled me in on the final plans. Her parents have agreed to visit some friends and stay out until 11 p.m. They've also bought in some light beers and two bottles of white wine for her twelve sixteenth-birthday-party guests. Not that I like wine. Or light beer... Not that I drink, in fact. Or go to parties. Or put on anything other than my school uniform or jeans or leggings and baggy T-shirts and jumpers. It was Mum who got me the silvery top. "Freja's birthday! It's special," she said, by way of explanation. And, since Freja is now my closest friend, yeah, it is special.

It's also complicated.

My nerves have nothing to do with the people she's invited. There's no guy in our class I'm hoping/terrified will be there, or some girl whose super-confidence would send me shrinking into my shell.

The problem is Holly. And I just don't know what to do.

I run a critical eye over the few remaining clothes in my wardrobe. There's nothing else. It'll have to be the silvery top. As I shake it out and pull it back on, I tell myself I'll go for an hour or two, then I'll slip back home. It's not like Freja won't understand.

On a shelf by my wardrobe is my detangling brush, a comb and my straighteners. I look away from the mirror for a moment, to pick up the hot tongs. When I turn back to it, I drop them.

A sudden rush of adrenalin has just drop-kicked my heart. My body's shaking. My legs feel hollow. I want desperately to look away. But I'm too scared to move even my eyes.

I knew Holly wouldn't like it. I *knew* I should've said no.

Because there she is – standing behind me, watching me intently in the mirror. Her dark blond hair is loose around her thin shoulders and her expression is one I know well by now: deep sadness, laced with scorn.

PART ONE

PART
ONE

1

There's something about waiting to go through American immigration that always makes me feel a little nervous – even when I have no reason to be.

I think it's all the harsh lights. The uniforms. The holstered weapons. The uneasy fidgeting of the people waiting to be called forwards to explain their plans. We are guilty until proven innocent. But this time – as I stand here in the straggly line of travellers who've just hauled themselves off the 1.10 a.m. arrival into JFK – I do actually have a secret to conceal.

At last I'm waved forward. The immigration officer is a monumental guy with a scrubbed pink face. After making brief, scrutinizing eye contact, he flicks through my passport and scans my border-control form. Using two forefingers, he types something on his keyboard. Then he frowns at the screen. His deep-set eyes swivel up to my face.

7

"So you're here on vacation?"

"I'm visiting my aunt. She lives in Brooklyn." All of that is completely true.

"Have you visited with her before?"

The information on his screen has surely told him that I have.

"Last summer, and the summer before... Maybe five times in total."

"And you want to stay in the United States for two months?"

I nod and smile.

"You have the financial means to support that?"

I'd been anticipating this. They asked me the exact same question last year – the first time I came to stay with Sadie without Dad. I was seventeen. Now that I'm technically an adult, I guess it's an even more reasonable thing to ask.

"I've been working weekends in a restaurant. I've saved up some money, and my mum's given me some, and my aunt looks after me." Yeah, I'm gabbling but this is *all* true.

After what feels like forever he glances back at my form and stamps my passport. "Welcome to New York."

*

Baggage carousel three is already crowded. The belt is juddering along but empty. I slip between an elderly

8

couple and a woman in uncomfortably tight-looking jeans. My own jeans are sticking to my thighs. My hair, which I re-dyed dark red, straightened and tied back yesterday morning, is half down and frizzy.

I rummage in my bag for my phone. After wiping the screen on my sleeve, I switch off flight mode and listen to the bleep-bleep of messages welcoming me to the United States. There's also one from Freja:

U there? So jealous! xx

I quickly type a reply.

Head still feels like it's over Atlantic. Body seems to have made it xx

Then I message Tamara, my best – and only – friend in New York.

Here! x

It's Tamara that I have to thank for the not entirely legal element of the reason I'm here. Actually not legal at all. Three weeks' cash-in-hand work, all off the books. That's the deal we were offered. And there was no way we couldn't take it, Tamara argued … and I agreed.

Next I text Dad.

> Arrived. Love you xx

Then I think about what to write to Mum. She's spending the summer as the yoga instructor at a mid-range spa hotel. It must be about 8 a.m. in Greece. I know she'll be waiting to hear from me but I can never just dash something off to Mum. I have to really think about what I write because she can twist a meaning like it's the plot of one of those Nordic noir novels that she loves so much.

The woman in tight jeans turns suddenly, jabbing me in the arm with her elbow. She doesn't apologize. Maybe she didn't even realize because the energy around us has just soared. The first cases are coming out. But I have to text Mum. Or she'll worry.

> Arrived safely. Hope hotel good.
> Will definitely get cab. Love you.

Then I add three kisses. Never more. Never fewer. Or she'd read something into it.

The elderly man to the other side of me shuffles forward. He reaches for the worn handle of an enormous brown leather case. But he's too slow. I lunge for it and, though my palms are sweaty, I manage to drag it off the carousel, nearly taking out the woman who elbowed me.

Karma, I think. The man smiles gratefully at me. I smile back. And I notice out of the corner of my eye my own battered old purple case with a red ribbon round the handle judder on by. *Not karma…?* Or maybe my good deeds still don't outweigh the bad.

2

Sadie did offer to meet me at the airport but considering the time, and the fact that Mum had given me the money for the cab fare, I told Sadie I'd see her at the apartment.

The FDR is no good, my cab driver says, as he lifts my case into the boot. There's been a three-vehicle pile-up. So we take what he calls the "streets way", via Queens. Though it's past 2 a.m., it's still hot so I lower my window halfway. The sky has an unnatural orange tinge.

I text Sadie.

> In cab but no FDR – will be a while x

I reread Mum's response to my text.

> Let me know when you with Sadie. Be safe. xxxxxx

(Six kisses tell me that she's OK but concerned.) Then Tamara's.

Yes!!! At market tomorrow. Come find me! Have news from Gunther.

Gunther, who runs the Ecco! Theater in Midtown is the guy who's giving us the job.

I reply to Tamara that I'll see her there tomorrow, throw my phone into my bag and watch New York speeding by. Smiling to myself, because it feels so good to be back, I notice what I always do in the first day or two – the clunky traffic lights, the all-night stores, LED signs on shopfronts rippling through the darkness.

Then I think my gaze must blur as I get caught up in thoughts of Tamara and the job at the theatre, and the road trip we have planned for later in the summer. Because suddenly we're slowing sharply – and I've lost track of where we are.

The taxi stops. Blinking, I peer hard through the window. The scene outside has a familiar effect: it's like a balm to my brain.

*

We've arrived at Sadie's building. It's a four-storey, nineteenth-century townhouse, with another on the left and a gap of wasteland to the right.

I dig around for my purse, and extract three twenties. After pocketing the cash, the driver jumps out and lifts my case out of the boot. Once he's driven off, I stand there for a few moments, just feeling what it's like to be back.

Over the broad road is a monumental church. It looms like a friendly spaceship. I can hear a Chinese TV station from one of the modern row houses behind me. There's a screech, and a hiss. Two cats are standing off behind a parked car.

When Sadie bought her apartment with her then-boyfriend, Levi, nine years ago, Bed-Stuy was pretty run-down. Now Levi has gone, and gentrification is here.

I switch my gaze from the cats to the low-walled patio area out front, with its built-in bench seat. Then to the imposing front door, veneered in patterned pressed tin. And up, over brick painted a brownish colour, and narrow sash windows, to the top floor – to Sadie's apartment. A soft white glow drifts from her bedroom window.

Yeah, so Levi has gone and Bed-Stuy is changing. But for me, since the first time I came here with Dad, when I was ten, Sadie's place has always been the same. My urban lighthouse across the ocean, signalling not danger, but safety.

*

Clump.

I drag my case up the final grimy, mosaic-tiled step. My bag's been vibrating, and I'm pretty sure it's Sadie trying to get hold of me, to see where I am. But I want to walk in and find her, to add a tiny element of surprise.

Now sweat's running down my back, and my strappy top is stuck to my skin. But I've made it up to Sadie's landing. Like the rest of the communal areas, it's not exactly clean. Dead mosquitoes are splatted against the hospital-green walls. The greasy, bowl-shaped light fitting cradles a dry soup of dead insects. No one could argue that objectively this is an uplifting environment. But what I'm feeling is definitely joy.

Using my key, which Sadie gave me last year, I let myself in.

There's an intense flowery smell. I take a few more steps and hear the door swing shut behind me.

The L-shaped living-dining-kitchen area looks exactly how I remember it. Sparkling white fairy lights zigzag along the bare brick walls. Opposite me, in clear frames, are two of Levi's now-fêted sound paintings, generated from the vibrations of people crying, laughing, applauding, screaming. Gifts to Sadie. To the left, around the open folding door to Sadie's bedroom, white candles are flickering in little alcoves within a living wall of jasmine and ivy. That jasmine scent is powerfully sweet.

I drop my shoulder bag to the scratched bare floorboards and flex my right hand, which aches from lugging the case. I can't hear anyone.

"Sadie?"

No answer.

A twist of movement beneath a side table catches my eye. It's Marlowe, her Burmese cat, slinking out from a wicker basket. He arches his back against my leg. "Hey." I rub the soft milky-coffee-coloured fur under his chin.

As I pass the kitchen units, Marlowe glued to my leg, I notice something. There are *two* plates with the remains of what looks like a couscous salad and fish by the sink. Two pairs of knives and forks are resting on the top plate.

Above the black sink is an open window, which is grilled. The bars jut out to create a rectangular space meant for an air-conditioning unit. In that space is a chipped, flower-patterned plate holding a mango, and also a pair of walking boots that are far too big to be Sadie's.

"Whose are those?" I whisper to Marlowe as I pick him up, careful not to dampen his beautiful coat with my sweat.

I walk along the corridor that connects Sadie's studio, the bathroom and the spare bedroom – and notice that the door to the staircase up to the roof is open. Only the inner screen door is closed. I hear slow-beat hip hop.

After giving Marlowe a quick kiss, I put him down, and climb the external, meshed-cage, ironwork staircase to the roof. The thick layer of silver floor paint has someone's boot prints in it. Tin stovepipe chimneys stick out all over. There are a couple of satellite dishes, one obviously broken. As I turn, the Manhattan skyline slides into view, the Empire State Building lit up in electric blue.

Backdropped by the skyscrapers of lower Manhattan are

two heads, sticking up from deckchairs, which have their red-and-white-striped backs to me. Between the chairs is a wooden table carved to look like an oversized champagne cork. On it are glass tumblers, a pillar candle in a jar and a music system, which explains why they haven't heard me.

Sadie is on the left. Her thick black hair is streaming down the side of the wooden frame. Angling from the other chair are two hairy knees and large bare feet.

"Hey!" I call loudly.

Sadie's head twists. "*Mia!*"

Is there anything harder to get up from than a deckchair? And Sadie isn't fit – at least I've never known her to be. Or – at that particular time, I guess – especially sober.

By the time she's up, I'm already beside her. Her emerald-green tunic is the same shade as her eyes, which are beaming right into mine. She looks excited – and indignant. "I've been calling! Why didn't you pick up – or buzz me? I'd have helped you get your bags up!"

Nine years in New York, and her Leeds accent is as strong as ever.

She flings out her arms. I step into her soft, warm hug. It's like falling into bed. A relinquishing of all responsibilities. I feel myself start to properly relax for the first moment since leaving home.

"I managed," I tell her, my voice muffled by her neck.

Squeezing me tighter, she says. "*Mia cuore!* I'm so happy you're here!"

Mia cuore…

To be grammatically correct, it should be *Il mio cuore*. My heart. Masculine. How do I know? Because the first time I remember Sadie calling me this, when she still lived in England, and Mum and Dad were still together, I also remember Mum, who studied modern languages at university, correcting her. "But her name's not Mio…" Sadie had said, making us both laugh. Then I'd noticed the look on Mum's face.

But I just don't share Mum's grammatical qualms. Hearing these words is like a shot of hot strength to my heart.

Still holding on to my arm, Sadie half turns to the guy in the other deckchair. He's watching us with what I think is an amused smile.

"Mia, meet Rav. Rav, don't even look at her, just, like, the air around her, because I swear if you look at her in a way I don't like, you will be *out*."

She's joking. Obviously. And I'm smiling but now mostly because I'm a little embarrassed. I'd guess that Rav's maybe twenty-one or twenty-two, and he's good-looking enough for me to feel slightly nervous around him even without Sadie's comments.

He does look at me. He has warm, very dark, almost black eyes. His black hair is knotted back. Faded khaki shorts and a charcoal T-shirt hang on his lanky frame.

I resist the urge to smooth my messed-up hair and to

wipe the sheen of sweat from my face and try to return his friendly smile.

And I think: *Two plates by the sink. Men's boots in the air-con space. What Sadie said to him: "You will be out"…?*

Sadie's thirty-three, fifteen years younger than Dad, who is actually her half-brother. (Same father, different mother; Sadie's is from Naples.) She has a heart-shaped face and the kind of full figure that Victorian painters would have fought each other to use as a model for a mortal desired by a god.

Then realization dawns. Actually, it dawns about a millisecond before Sadie says, "Rav is my lodger… I told you, right?"

I'd totally forgotten. In an email maybe six months ago, she said she was thinking of taking in a lodger. Someone to help pay the bills. She hadn't mentioned it since. And I hadn't asked. I wonder suddenly where we'll all be sleeping.

"Hi," he says, still with that friendly smile, showing even white teeth. American, then.

"Hi," I say back.

"Good flight?" he asks.

I guess he reads my expression because he smiles and says quickly, "Dumb question. Rum – and what was it?" He glances at Sadie.

"Lime, clove and vanilla," she says.

He smiles, nodding. "That eternal classic. Rum, vanilla, lime, clove cocktail? With Coke."

"It's one of the best I've ever made," Sadie says. "Not too strong. It's all about the flavours."

My head's pounding dully. My top has dried a little in the gentle rooftop breeze, but my jeans are still sticking to my legs. I need a shower. A litre of water. A couple of ibuprofen. Sleep. But I can't say no when Sadie's so pleased with her concoction.

"I'd love one," I say.

Rav jumps up from his chair. Grabs the empty tumblers from the table.

"Are you hungry?" Sadie asks me. "I've got Kalamata olives, jams, and this incredible goat's cheese from a little farm in Long Island. And a mango. But it might not be quite ripe."

I shake my head. "Thanks. I'm OK."

From over by the stairwell, Rav says, "You overdid the gourmet delicacies on the plane, right?"

My stomach, which is bloated from the flight, seems to swell even further at the memory of the shredded-cardboard salad and gloopy mac 'n' cheese. "Yeah, all that caviar... I just couldn't eat another thing."

His smile broadens a little. As he disappears down the steps, Sadie says, "Come, sit."

She drags a third deckchair over and positions it beside hers. I ease myself on to the rough, warm canvas.

The sky, which is dusted with stars, is no longer actually shifting above me. I'm technically still for the first time in so many hours. But my brain seems to be having trouble processing the fact. I feel like I'm still juddering.

"I totally forgot about you getting a lodger," I tell her. "I'm so sorry."

"Sorry for what? Like it would stop me having you to stay?"

"But where—"

"I'm putting Rav in my studio while you're here."

"Doesn't he mind?"

"It was either that or a tent in the basement. And I think we might have a rat…"

"But where will you work?"

She smiles at me over the arm of her chair, and changes the subject. "Remember the first time you came? I offered you wine and your dad went nuts."

"To be fair to him, I was only ten."

"I only meant like the French do. A little wine, with water, so you weren't *the child*. You were totally part of us."

I nod. I understand. Maybe I understood even then.

Certainly I remember that summer in fine-grained slow motion. Mum and Dad explaining that they'd made the difficult decision to separate and that Mum was moving into her own place. Being allowed whatever I wanted to eat at the airport, and feeling sick from the caramel doughnuts. Levi telling us – considerately, I now realize – that he had to go visit his parents in South Carolina. Sleeping with Sadie in her carved orangewood bed. Waking every morning to

21

the solid weight of her arm draped over my waist. Feeling sad, of course, and confused – but not devastated. I was so much closer to Dad.

"You're looking great," Sadie says, bringing me back to the present. "Leaving school must agree with you!"

"I'm doing OK," I say, half smiling and half meaning it.

"And your dad?"

"Absolutely no different." I take a breath. Trying to mentally sweep the past away, I meet her warm gaze. "Down to the coat hangers labelled 'Monday' to 'Friday', with his identical shirts for the week. I still haven't asked him why."

She smiles. "And your mum?"

There are things that maybe I'd like to tell her about Mum, but I've just got here, and Rav will be back any minute. And she's clearly had a couple of cocktails. So I say, "Fine, and how about *you*?"

Sadie smiles. "I'm always good, remember." Keeping her eyes locked on mine, she says, "So, should I be expecting you to be on your phone all the time to some desperate, pining boyfriend?"

I roll my eyes and try to keep the blood out of my cheeks.

"Uni in a few months," she says. "Best to go with an open heart."

"…Yeah."

She twists further towards me. "Mia, is this seriously where I tell you again that you have no idea how amazing you are, and you tell me I'm biased because we're related, and this goes on till eventually I get so frustrated, I shout, 'Just own your awesomeness, girl!'"

For the record, she shouts it.

"Yeah, OK, I'll just *own* it, American aunt," I tell her, with an expression that's meant to let her know I'm being good-naturedly sarcastic.

She reaches for my hand. "Like my hairdresser, Giuseppe, says when he's frustrated, *sheesh*!"

The gentle slap of bare feet on the roof makes me turn my head. I wonder how much Rav just overheard.

He comes over with a wooden tray of tumblers clinking with ice, and squats beside the little table. A blue halo shines round his head, courtesy of the Empire State.

It's hard not to watch him – the lean muscle in his arms, the dark burnt caramel of his neck. Around his narrow right wrist I notice a bracelet of woven silver, with a blue thread twisted through it.

Rav passes Sadie a glass. Hands one to me. It's beautifully cold. "Thank you."

"You are very welcome." He drags his chair round, so now we're in a rough circle. "It's good to finally meet you, Mia," he says and I realize that Sadie must have talked to him about me. About what exactly? "Here's to a—" He breaks off. "What kind of summer would you like?"

I don't have to think too hard. "Hot. Interesting. Relaxed."

"Hot … yeah, that's a given. Interesting – what exactly are your plans?"

"I'm going to be working with a friend at this theatre," I tell him. "Helping to create the set for an immersive performance. Then we're going to use the money to fix up her mum's car and drive out to Burning Man in Nevada."

"Tamara, right?" Rav says.

"You know her?"

Sadie says, "She may have been to a seriously wild party here last month…" She gives Rav a look I can't quite translate.

"So, interesting," he says quickly. "But *relaxed*? You do realize which city you're in?"

But that's how I feel here – at least relatively. In New York, I'm not quite the same me that exists back in Sheffield. Out here, I can leave so many things behind. "There's *something* about the Empire State in the skyline that gives it away."

He smiles. "OK … well, here's to all that for you. And to a hot, interesting, relaxed … new man for Sadie."

She pulls a face. "Whoever said I wanted a new man!"

He looks surprised. "Well, you…"

She shakes her head vigorously.

"How long have you been living here?" I ask him, to change the subject.

"Since February. I kinda had to leave where I was staying. A fine arts friend who'd done a course with Sadie said she knew an artist who was looking for a lodger—"

"And we met up for tacos at La Lupe," Sadie says, still looking put out, "and he seemed too serious to be the kind of guy who'd invite a hundred friends back to make my parties even wilder… But I said yes anyway." Now she sighs and smiles.

He smiles back.

I take a sip of the cocktail. It's fruity, sweet, sharp … odd. But in a nice way.

"What about you?" I ask Rav, lowering the glass. "What kind of summer do you want?"

He looks like he's about to reply, then remembers something. "Sadie says you're starting a degree in psychology this fall."

I take another sip of the cocktail. "If I get the grades."

"I just graduated in psychology from Gessen College. Now I'm enrolled in a masters programme, and I'm focused on some ongoing research. It's become kinda addictive. It'll take up my summer, and more probably."

"Rav's at the Parapsychology Research Institute," Sadie says.

I feel my forehead crease. "Parapsychology – what, like ESP, moving stuff with your mind?"

He leans forward. "Do you believe in ghosts?"

I stiffen. It feels suddenly like my blood's been cured, like some kind of glue. "No," I say automatically, hearing my voice as though it's not quite mine.

His eyes narrow. "That's pretty definite. Most people,

when they say no, actually mean, well, I don't know but I don't think so, though there are things surely that science can't explain, et cetera."

I don't say anything. Don't even move. The skyscrapers glitter sharply behind him.

"So," he says, "this study is to investigate why some people see ghosts. Twenty-eight per cent of American adults report having had some kind of ghostly experience. Forty-two per cent believe ghosts are real. In the UK, the percentage is more like fifty. That's a *lot* of people."

"Fifty per cent of people probably think NASA faked the moon landings," I manage to say, though my mouth feels so dry.

"Oh," Sadie says. "She has you there. Unless NASA did fake them—"

"She doesn't *have me* anywhere," Rav says, his tone not irritated but firm. He focuses his gaze on me. "You know what, we could do with more non-believers for the study. Why don't you volunteer? It'd be good experience for college. I could talk you through the protocol afterwards. You'd just have to wear this VR headset—"

I shake my head quickly. "Actually, I don't think parapsychology's on the course I've applied for—"

"*And* you get twenty bucks."

I open my mouth, but before I can say no he's talking again.

"The study itself runs for up to fifty minutes. With the

initial briefing and inventories and the exit questionnaire, total involvement runs to one hour twenty. How about tomorrow, maybe? Ten? Eleven?"

I shake my head again. But this time more definitely. I take another sip from my glass. The dull buzzing in my head that was there before I even started drinking or talking about ghosts intensifies. "I'm meeting Tamara. But anyway I don't think so. Sorry."

Rav slumps a little in his chair. "If we can just run five more non-believers, we'll have enough data for the statistical analysis."

"I'll ask at my class tomorrow," Sadie says. "You'll get them. Don't worry." Then she looks at me. "I'd make some rubbish joke about that being as big as the Lincoln Tunnel, but actually I think it was bigger."

For a moment, I'm confused. Then I realize she's referring to the fact I just yawned.

"Mia, honey, go to bed," she says. "The spare room's all ready."

Go to bed … yeah. I'm exhausted. And it would get me out of this conversation about the study, and ghosts.

But, as I get up, Rav says hopefully, "Sure you won't change your mind?"

Sadie says: "You're the psychic research guy. Can't you read her thoughts?"

He cups a hand to one side of his mouth and in a loud whisper says to me: "I don't actually read thoughts."

Before I can tell her not to get up, Sadie's out of her chair and reaching for a hug. She squeezes me tight. Still holding on to me, she says, "I have to give some classes tomorrow. But I could wake you at what – nine thirty?"

"With a Roberto's?" I say hopefully but not wildly hopefully. Sadie waking me with a mug of coffee made from ground Nicaraguan Bourbon beans from Roberto's stall at Prospect Park market has become a summer tradition.

She grins. "Mind-reading, right here on my roof. Proven. Beyond doubt!"

Rav shakes his head. "As your hairdresser Giuseppe would say, *sheesh*!"

3

I wake in darkness.

Because of the rear fire escape, which angles up against the tiny window, and the north-facing aspect, Sadie's spare room is gloomy even when the sun is blazing and the blind is open. Now it's closed. Is it still night? I'd check on my phone but it's on charge, over by the chest of drawers, and I don't really want to throw off the sheet and go and get it.

As I lie here, on a futon, feeling like it can't be morning yet, I hear Rav's voice in my mind: *Do you believe in ghosts?*

I squeeze my eyes shut but it's too late. I'm totally awake. My mind is flooded with images. Holly in a booth at Sundaes, smiling as she scrapes out a dish of ice cream. Holly peering out suddenly from my mirror—

I think: *Peace on the outbreath.*

It's how I try to get myself back to sleep. When your thoughts begin to boil, you have to try to keep a lid on them while you breathe in. Then, as you exhale, you say silently, *Peace…*

Do you believe in ghosts?

I clench my mind as hard as I can.

Peace.

Peace.

Peace.

Peace.

Eventually I must fall asleep because I'm back home, sitting at the kitchen table with a mug of hot chocolate that I can't bear to drink, watching my unrecognizable reflection in the dark window above the sink. It feels like everything I know has been kicked upside down. Myself included. It's the night of the day that Holly died.

Holly. My best friend. We're thirteen years old. And she is dead.

Suddenly I'm in town, half blinded by sunshine and water spray. I can hear a voice – a man's – angry, insistent. I see his wiry fingers clench her shoulder. Then she's running—

I wake suddenly, my heart pounding.

I haven't dreamed about Holly for at least a month. I force myself to take a deep breath. It's still dark.

My mouth is parched. I'm desperate for water. I push off the linen sheet and get up unsteadily. My sweaty hand fumbles for the door handle, but at last I manage to get out into the hall. At once I see that the door to Sadie's studio is ajar, and the light's on inside. Rav must still be up. I'm about to pad on, past the studio, to the kitchen, but, as I get close, I hear something from inside that makes me stop.

Tap.

Silence.

Tap. Tap. Tap.

It's like someone's banging a radiator with a metal bar. There are no radiators in Sadie's apartment.

Silence.

A raspy, muffled voice says something unintelligible.

Tap.

Silence.

Tap. Tap. Tap. Tap.

While I'm standing there in the hall, the studio door suddenly flies inwards. Rav. He looks surprised. Quite reasonably. "Hey," he says.

"I— Sorry. What're you doing?" I keep my voice down. Surely Sadie's asleep. "Those tapping sounds," I say because he looks like he doesn't quite understand me.

"Oh. Yeah." He nods. "I'm on the Spontaneous Cases Committee of New York City."

"The what?"

"If someone wants a haunting checked out by a reputable investigator, they contact us."

My heart races faster, and I try to hide how I'm feeling with a casual tone. "That's, like, an actual job?"

"Unpaid," he says. "Jared, the head of the institute, he got me on to it. I'm a junior member so I get the grunt work.

31

But that's OK. Ghosts are kinda my thing. So it's all good."

"What was the tapping?" I ask, my mouth feeling even drier.

"I'm just analysing the echoes in a recording that someone's sent us."

"A recording?"

His dark eyes brighten. "You can't get anything useful from a photo or a recording – audio or visual. There's so much software out there that'll let you make something you've added look or sound real, and it can be hard to tell the difference. But there is an argument – which I'd like to put to rest – that sounds made by spirits create different echoes to sounds made by living people."

"But that isn't true."

"Right."

"So you're still up at – what time is it?"

"I don't know. About five thirty."

"So you're still up at five thirty, listening to faked spirit tappings to try to prove that they echo like normal tappings."

He nods. "You wanna come in and listen?"

I wrap my arms round my waist. "I was just getting a glass of water."

"Coincidence!"

He smiles, and then steps past me into the corridor. A few seconds later, I hear the tap in the kitchen whoosh on and then off. He comes back with two tall, dripping glasses of water.

I take one. "Thanks. So people genuinely say there's a difference between real and spirit echoes?"

"People genuinely do." He smiles and pushes the studio door wide.

Right away, I see that Sadie's cleared out almost all her old stuff. A chest with about a hundred drawers that used to hold her little found treasures has gone. Along that wall now is a single bed with a white frame. And in place of a ceramic plant stand is a little white desk with a plain wooden chair. Did she have to buy this furniture because I was coming to stay? I feel bad.

Rav's laptop is open on the desk. As he goes over to it, I hear myself asking: "Do *you* believe in ghosts?"

He deposits his glass on the desk and sits down. "Whenever an experimental subject asks me that question, I say that I'm agnostic."

My voice tight, I say, "What do you say to other people?"

Another pause. I get the impression he's weighing something up. "Everyone has stories, right? Either something that's happened to them or someone close to them... So take my dad. He grew up in a house that had been in the family for four generations. Two aunts and an uncle had died there, and his grandmother, and a great-grandfather, and perhaps other family members he didn't even know about. When he was fourteen, he went through a really bad time. Bullied badly at school. One night he woke up, and it was still dark. He couldn't move, and at first he was scared. Then he felt someone stroking his arm. Softly. From his shoulder to his wrist. He says he knew it was his grandmother. That his grandmother's spirit was there, trying to make him feel better. Which it did."

I force my lips to unstick. "And you believe him?"

Rav looks tired suddenly. He rakes his fingers through his hair. "I tell him that of course it was his grandmother – because why would I take that away from him? But there is research that makes me think that what he experienced could have been sleep paralysis, and hallucinations induced by darkness, and the breeze, maybe, from an open window… The point is there are thousands of people out there with these stories. But you know how many *psychologists* – actual academic psychologists – are studying reports of hauntings and ghost experiences, to try to investigate what's going on?"

I shake my head.

"A *handful*. Globally. My professor at the institute – he's one of them. Anyway, that's why I want to become an academic parapsychologist."

I nod slowly.

With a sensation that I'm slightly outside of my body, I hear myself saying, "I think I'll go back to bed."

He sighs and flexes his arms, as though they've been working and now they're aching. "You're not really like Sadie described you."

"Sorry?"

He shakes his head. "No, I'm sorry. Ignore me.

Go get some more sleep."

"Seriously?"

He smiles. Nods.

If I'm not going to argue with him – which I'm not –
I should go. And so I do.

Not like Sadie described me…?

In the cramped bathroom, with its familiar shimmery
blue shower curtain and copper-coloured tiles, I look in the
mirror. My cheeks are creased from the linen pillowcase.
The bags under my eyes are massive. I hear Freja in my
head: *So big you'd have to check them into the hold.*

I go back to the futon and pull the sheet up to my chin.

How *did* Sadie describe me? Of course I want to know.
But that's not the thought that's banging hardest inside my
skull.

I have seen Holly outside my dreams. At a club, and at
school, and even in my bedroom. After she died.

After she died, I have seen her.

Tamara and Freja are the only people who know. So when
Rav asked, 'Do you believe in ghosts?' what else was I meant
to say? I'd never tell him anyway. Partly because I'm not even
sure what to think. I don't *know* what it is that I see.

I hurl myself on to my side. No way will I get back to
sleep… Again, though, eventually I do because I become
aware of a heavy, faintly bitter scent.

My eyes flicker open. Sadie is kneeling on the floorboards
beside me, Marlowe draped over her right shoulder.

Her shiny hair is startlingly black against her fuchsia silk blouse. She's holding a white mug.

I blink at her.

The air con is gently rattling. Sunlight is doing its best to break into the room.

She smiles a deep, warm smile. "Good morning, *Mia cuore*. Here you go. I made strawberry jam with all this gorgeous ripe fruit from Mr Kiwi's. You have to try some with a bagel for breakfast."

Blearily, I shuffle into a sitting position, and take the mug. "*Thank you.*"

I take a sip. When I swallow, it's like rays of sunshine are spreading through me. Then I remember talking to Rav last night, and the tapping sounds, and what he said about sleep paralysis and hallucinations, and ghosts.

Putting the cup down, I reach for my bag and extract the gifts I lugged over from England: Yorkshire Tea and a family-sized bar of Galaxy.

Sadie grins. "I'd say you shouldn't have ... but thank *you*." She holds them to her chest. "Really – thank you."

"It's not exactly much," I point out.

"*Classic* case of mistaking cost for value," she says, still smiling. "Now, I did tell you I have to teach classes today, right?" She looks like she feels bad about it. She also looks completely fresh, like she wasn't up till at least three, drinking cocktails on the roof. "I have to go in, like, two minutes."

I nod. "It's totally OK. I'm going to catch up with Tamara."

"And I have a gallery event tonight. But I've got you for five weeks, right! You're not starting at the theatre for a few weeks yet?"

"Yeah."

She grins. "So we'll have plenty of time to hang out."

As she gets up, Marlowe digs his claws into her shoulder, to steady himself. She winces and lifts a paw with her free hand. Makes it wave at me. Then makes it blow me a kiss.

I smile. Blow one back for each of them. I rest on my elbow so I can drink the coffee more easily. I listen to Sadie moving around in the kitchen, and then the front door gently shutting.

Given that Rav was awake at 5.30 a.m., I imagine that he's still asleep. But, when I finally head out into the hall, I see that his door is open, and the grey duvet has been pulled up over the pillow. The bathroom's empty and I can't hear any sounds from the kitchen. Unless he's up on the roof, he's already gone.

For a few moments, I stand in his doorway. I take in a creased grey shirt on the back of the chair, and books on the shelves, which I hadn't noticed last night – *Paracoustics: Sound & the Paranormal*, *Varieties of Anomalous Experience*, *The Lost Memoirs of Edgar Cayce*.

I stand there, and I look, with an uneasy, greedy kind of feeling. But, like an uninvited vampire, I don't go in.

4

I pedal fast on Sadie's spare road bike down past Prospect Park Zoo. Squinting through my sunglasses, I take in the intense blue of the sky, the snow-white of the fur of a Samoyed being groomed by a guy in a polo shirt. Then I catch the scent of the market. Or rather the stink.

I know exactly what it is. There's a composting service here on Saturdays. Locals bring their organic waste to dump in special bins, which are stacked high by the path in from the park.

When I reach the bins, I jump down, wheel the bike over to a stand and lock it up. Ahead of me is the broad, curved back to Grand Army Plaza. The farmers' market stalls are laid out beyond it. My nostrils twitch at the smell of yeasty bread – or maybe it's the home-made pet food. Over on the steps of the Brooklyn Library, a woman in a red dress is singing R&B.

It was here that I first met Tamara, two summers ago. Her mum, Misk, has a stall selling tubs of spicy beans, chicken fritters and stuffed prunes. Tamara was standing behind a pyramid of bulbous purple biscuits and a sign reading *Mis-fortune cookies – $1*. How could I not buy one?

My mis-fortune turned out to be an intricate pen-and-ink drawing of a purple butterfly caught in a net. It was so sad. And so beautiful. When I told Tamara what I thought, she said quietly, "You are literally the first person all day who has not been totally disappointed when they didn't get some lame joke about the future."

As I weave my way towards their stall, it's Misk who sees me first. She's tall, slim, with almond-shaped eyes, her hair up in a pale green head covering. "Mia!" She waves.

I wave back, smiling, and there's Tamara. Petite, like Misk, but wearing a clingy opalescent top, a long blue skirt and a pearl nose ring. It's all this in combination with the fact that she's dyed her shoulder-length hair silver-blue that makes me say, "You look like a mermaid!"

She grins. "*You* look like a girl in need of a nectarine in the sun!"

Smiling pre-emptive thanks at the woman behind the neighbouring stand, she grabs two huge red-golden nectarines, and embraces me in a huge hug. Then she takes my hand, and pulls me over to one of the stone benches set into the wall of the plaza. We sit cross-legged, facing each other.

"You're here!" Her grin lights up her whole face, just like

Sadie's did when I found her on the roof. A warmth that has nothing to do with the ambient temperature settles inside me.

"I'm here," I echo. And I grin, too.

Holly, Freja, Tamara. The three friends that really mean something to me.

Freja is complicated because she was close to Holly, too. I think the reason she managed to step out of the shadow of Holly's death is because she wasn't there; she didn't see it happen. It wasn't seared into her mind.

Tamara is also special, in a different way. She's like a butterfly flying way too high for any net to reach her.

Being here, in New York, with Tamara … it's like a glimpse of a life without those fractures and pressures. I know I wouldn't be able to keep it up forever – and I know that Holly doesn't like it because I can feel inside me that she doesn't. Even when I don't see Holly, I can often feel her. But here, in this city, far away from home, her grip on me isn't as strong.

Occasionally I feel guilty when I'm with Tamara – like I'm pretending to be someone I'm not. But I think that what I'm really trying to be is me *if* Holly hadn't died. And yes, maybe without all those years worrying about Mum.

"Gunther is very excited that you're here," Tamara says. "He is, like, totally, literally thrilled. *Literally*, and I quote, 'thrilled'…"

I smile. "No pressure then." I take a bite of the nectarine.

I'm still full from Sadie's gorgeously sweet strawberry jam and bagel, but it's delicious.

Tamara takes a bite of hers. "But he's saying now that he'll need a hundred postcards."

I almost spit out my mouthful. "That's double what he said! It takes me, like, four hours to make *one!*"

She nods. "He says, and again I'm quoting, *I will need an abundance of postcards for the effect I desire.* I was meant to be drawing a silhouette of the Paris skyline on the walls, right? Now he wants detail. *Detail, Tamara!*" She imitates a man thundering: "*Detail!*"

I shake my head, wondering how I'm going to manage it.

Last summer, I found a Victorian postcard in an antique shop back home. A woman's full skirt had been embroidered in rich red and gold thread. Even the irises of her eyes had been stitched in delicate blue. The Gothic text reads *Greetings from Scarborough*.

Using a sewing machine fitted with embroidery hoops in the art room at school, I made a version to send to Tamara. A girl – me – sewn into the cardboard in fine red and black thread with the words *Greetings from Sheffield!* in my finest calligraphy underneath.

Tamara had met Gunther at an art show at her school at which his niece was also displaying some work. He'd loved Tamara's ink drawings and – when she accidentally dropped it out of her bag – my postcard. Enough to make Tamara promise that she'd do some weekend work for him at the theatre, and that we'd both work on the set for his next full production. I'm still not really sure what it's about. All I know is what Tamara told me: he wants postcards with a 'decadent Wild West' theme.

"He still wants us to do it all in three weeks?" I ask her. She nods.

"And he still wants us to start in—"

"One week Wednesday. They're using the space for something else till then… Have faith in Gunther," she says brightly.

"Do you?"

She laughs so loud that a couple emptying a tub into a composting bin turn and stare. "Some. But I have faith that we'll get paid whatever. Dee, who handles the paycheques, has already got our cash put aside." She takes another bite of her nectarine. Through a mouthful of orange flesh, she says, "Dee likes me."

"Good," I say.

"I got her on to this study your aunt's lodger's running and she loved it."

"I met him last night. He said he knew you."

She lowers her nectarine to her lap and arches a perfect black eyebrow. "In what sense?"

Her question surprises me. I try to read her expression. "In how many different senses might I mean it…?"

"So, maybe a month ago, I agreed to meet him at Barcade, and I thought he meant with some of his team, but it turned out it was a date. Anyway, I beat him at *Donkey Kong* and we had a drink." She brushes a shimmering strand of blue hair from her face. "He's OK. I do kinda like him. He's just … serious. Anyway, he was looking for volunteers and I said I'd ask around. I did tell Dee not to get too drawn in because he's totally obsessed with all this weird ghost stuff—"

She stops. She'd been talking so quickly, her train of thought powering along when it hit a bump. I feel the heat of blood in my cheeks.

I watch her try to work out whether it'd be better to try to brush over the moment or say something. I think I know which way she's going to go before she does.

"Not that I think it's weird for other people to believe in ghosts," she says intently.

I let my breath out in one long go. "I told Rav that I don't."

Everything around us feels suddenly muted. It's like there's a ringing in my ears.

"Why?" she asks.

"Because I didn't want to talk about it. And I don't want Sadie to know."

"You still see Holly?" she asks quietly.

I meet her gaze. Nod.

"Recently?"

I don't break eye contact. Nod again.

She exhales hard. "I think you should tell him." I shake my head.

"Mia, he actually knows about this stuff. I mean, like, really *knows*. His professor, Jared Robertson, he's meant to be some kind of world authority on hauntings. Maybe they could help."

"*How?*"

I hadn't meant to sound sarcastic or harsh – but I have a strong suspicion that I did. It doesn't seem to bother Tamara, though. "She died five years ago. You still think you see her—"

"I *do* see her."

"OK," she says evenly, "let's say you do see her. It has, like, this *hold* on you. The fact she hasn't gone."

I shift my gaze away from her, to the blur of stalls. I'm looking, not seeing. My mind is moving back in time.

It feels so terrible now – but it will *get better, I promise.* That or some version of it is what everyone said to me after Holly died. And three months after. Even a year after.

It's not like everybody else forgot her. There were still moments at school when something would happen that would remind someone of her, and their tears would be catching, and the teacher would stop whatever we'd been doing and let whoever wanted to talk about it do so. But I never volunteered anything, because it's not like these were out-of-the-blue reminders for me. My everyday existence felt like a constant opposition to the fact of her absence.

A few weeks before the first anniversary of her death, Dad sat me down and, as gently as he could, suggested that it was time to move on. "You can't let what happened to Holly affect you like this, after *so long*. It's not right."

So long… And that was four years ago.

In some ways, yeah, it has got better. Occasionally I can even go a full day without thinking about her. But if I ever start to believe that maybe I could leave her behind, and maybe I *could* go to a party with Freja, or even go out on a date, I feel her suddenly close, and I know she's watching me and that she's not happy—

Tamara scratches her arm, setting the thin metal bangles on her wrist jangling. The singing and the voices all around us are suddenly loud.

"Did Rav tell you about his study?" she asks.

I nod, my head feeling heavy. "Did *you* do it?"

She shakes her head. "I did my bit. I got three people from the theatre to do it. But I think they still need subjects."

When I don't comment, she goes on: "I guess he asked you. So far as I can tell, he asks everyone."

"I said no."

She tilts her head up at the sun. Squeezes her eyes shut then looks back at me. She leans closer. I can see the burnt copper flecks in her irises, the tiny glistening pores in her skin. "I'm gonna tell you two true things. Afterwards, I have to go back to the stall, and I promised I'd help Mom with the cooking tonight cos she's got three days of big lunches for some group to prep for… But I could come out for a bit first. Anyway, so, if you

45

believe what I'm about to tell you, then meet me at Barlow's – that pub near NYU – at six. If you don't, then I'll call you tomorrow. OK?"

I nod.

Not taking her eyes from mine for a moment, she says, "The first thing I have to tell you is that for *your sake*, even if you don't do that study, I think you should talk to Rav, and you should ask him about what he knows because I truly believe that power comes through knowledge, and you need power over this situation. The second thing is that I love you. And, while I don't believe that anything happens for a reason, I also believe that if you pass up an important opportunity, it's like an offence against *life*. OK, so that was three things but they're definitely related." She swings her feet down to the ground. "I left my phone at the stall. I'm gonna text you Rav's number."

Before I can even think about how to respond to any of that, she's off, slipping in among the shoppers. When she passes the home-made pet-food stall, I lose her.

I feel fuzzy now. Shaky, and strange. Mostly, of course, because of what Tamara just said but also because of the ripe fragrance of my half-eaten nectarine and the stink of composting vegetables. Just as I'm wondering if Tamara is going to send me Rav's number, my bag vibrates with an incoming text.

5

The raised Myrtle Ave/Broadway subway station was built in 1888. I know this because I once looked it up while I was waiting for a train. It's all massive iron girders and oversized rivets. Like some kind of urban shipwreck, it provides shade and sanctuary for the stores below. As I start up the metal steps, I'm glad to be out of the sun. It's about midday now, and it's sweltering.

Rav sounded surprised but definitely pleased that I'd decided to do the study. He suggested that I leave the bike back at home and take an M train all the way in. When I come out on to the platform, I'm in luck – an M is just pulling in.

I squeeze myself on to a bench seat between a body-builder type and a tiny woman with a yellow snake in a clear plastic container on her knee. We head into and out of Williamsburg, the sunshine strobing through the struts of the Williamsburg Bridge. Then the train tunnels down through Lower Manhattan.

The car was perfectly air-conditioned so I'm not quite prepared for the heat. But as I climb the steps up to 4th Avenue it hits me. A blast of oven-wind makes me cough.

Rav texted me the address:

Parapsychology Research Institute. 127 DeLancey Street. You'll find it interesting. I promise.

When I get to DeLancey, I find that it's a major road, running long and straight. I can hear construction noise. Car horns. Engines. The strains of a brass band over in Washington Square Park, playing jazz. I pass a local store with a sign advertising *ICE CREAMS AND UMBRELLAS*. Then ahead, on a gleaming brass plaque on the wall of a tall, narrow art deco building, I spot *127*.

I stop. The momentum of Tamara's advice and the commitment that I made to Rav to do the study have carried me this far. But at the back of my mind has been the knowledge that, when I actually got here, I wouldn't necessarily have to go in. I could always change my mind.

I peer down the road, through the dust-specked sunshine. Pedestrian lights stand at every cross-street. They all suddenly flick from showing illuminated red hands to white stick figures walking. Maybe I succumb too easily to instruction – or maybe I was just looking for a nudge –

because now my legs carry me on to 127.

The huge wooden front door is held open with a wedge. Through a second door, of heavy glass, I can see into a little vestibule. It's tiled in marble in shades of brown, with what looks to be a much bigger foyer beyond. A sign on the wall just inside the door reads *Parapsychology Research Institute* in gold letters.

Out here, on the street, is life. The thump and rumble of construction. Jazz. People. I turn my back on all of it so I have to own this decision.

I, Mia Foster, was asked if I believe in ghosts, and said I did not. And now here I am.

6

I try the glass door. Locked. I call Rav's number. After four rings, I hear: "This is Rav Flynn. Leave a message."

I end the call and decide to give him five minutes. If he's not here by then, I'll leave. I'm thinking about going back to that store I passed for a cold drink when I realize a girl is hovering just to the other side of the doorway, watching me.

She's about my age. She's wearing battered brown boots, a short, floaty purple skirt and a baggy orange T-shirt. There's a small navy bag over her shoulder, weighed down by something. Her hair's bright scarlet, with black roots. Her dark brown eyes blink out from an elfin face.

"Hi," I say. "I'm here to take part in a study." Because I feel it would be weird not to say anything, she's looking at me that closely.

"Which study?" she asks after a moment.

"To do with belief in ghosts." I sound so vague, I know. "And VR."

She nods slowly. I'm wondering if she's here for the study, too, but, as she shifts her arm, I see that the heavy object in her bag is a textbook. The top is sticking out, so I can read the title: *Power and Poltergeists: A critical analysis*.

"Oh, are you a student here?"

She clasps her hands together, fingers interlocked. The black polish on her short nails is chipped. "I lost my sister," she says quietly, her words almost lost in the background street sounds. A tear trickles down her cheek and she wipes it quickly away.

Trying to hide my surprise, I say the only thing I can think of. "I'm sorry."

"I know a spiritualist who says she talks to her. But I don't know if she really does."

If you can sense pain coming off someone, almost like a scent, I can feel hers. But I honestly have no idea what to say.

"*I* can't hear her," she goes on. "I only have this woman's word for it. I need someone—" She stops. "I think he can tell me if it's true." Her slender right hand jumps to a chain around her neck, coming to rest over a little silver butterfly pendant. "I think I can trust him," she says, half to herself.

My throat feeling tight, I say, "You mean Jared Robertson?"

Her eyes narrow. "You know him?"

51

"I just know he's a professor here."

"I don't know if I can trust anyone else." She speaks so quietly, it's almost a whisper. She glances at the glass door. "It's locked. Can you let me in?"

"I don't have a key," I tell her. "Or a pass."

She frowns. Sighs until there can be no breath left in her.

"But I know a student here," I say. "He's expecting me. Maybe he can get you in."

She looks startled. As though I've just disturbed her. But now she's digging in her bag, and pulling out a phone, which is ringing quietly. When she checks the screen, her face tenses. She swipes. Clicks it off. Glances anxiously back through the glass door, and seems to make a decision. She hunches her shoulders and starts to walk quickly away.

She's already past the store, her flat boots clacking on the pavement.

But I can't just let her go. She's obviously suffering. And I know exactly what it's like to lose someone close, only not to be sure if *lose* is quite the right word.

"Hey!" I jog a few steps after her.

She slows. Glances back. Blinks at me through the dazzling sunshine. Then a group of kids in red holiday-club T-shirts swarm up the street from behind, and engulf her. They surge into the store. After they've all jostled their way inside, I realize that she's gone.

Quickly, I scan the people on the pavements, searching

for her. A buzzing sounds from my bag and I fumble for my phone.

"Mia? Sorry, I left my cell in the lab. Are you still here?"

I do another urgent sweep of every person I can see. None of them is her. Then I look back towards the institute. If I say no, will Rav notice me from a window, walking away?

"I'm just outside," I tell him.

"Great! I'll be right down."

I feel bad that the girl's gone and I didn't do anything to try to help her. But she *has* gone, so there's nothing I can do now.

For the second time that morning, I turn away from the open energy of the street.

I narrow down all the possibilities that the city has to offer into one.

7

Rav raises a hand in an easy wave. From the other side of the locked glass door, I wave back.

In this brighter light, he strikes me as not quite so good-looking. The lines of his face are less angular. Not so strong. Actually it's a relief.

"That was quick," he says, yanking open the door. "I'm still kinda surprised you came."

He steps back to let me in, and I follow him towards the lifts. "Why?"

"You were so definite last night. I thought maybe you'd change your mind again." He's still smiling.

I can't help glancing back one last time, in case the girl has returned, but there's no sign of her.

"Well, you promised me twenty bucks. Which I'll need if I'm going to get Sadie her favourite carrot-cake ice cream from that shop by the river. You know the one I mean?"

He nods deeply. "And it's worth every cent." He hits the up-arrow button. "But I also know that she is now a huge fan of the red cherry. And I heard that carrot cake's *your* favourite."

The lift doors slide open. I guess I'm looking surprised because he says, "Full disclosure: Sadie has told me quite a lot about you."

As I walk in, I see my frown reflected in the highly polished brass interior. *Quite a lot.* What does that mean, exactly? Not Holly. She wouldn't have. And not Mum. No matter what she thinks of Mum, Sadie is loyal to her family.

I remember what Rav said about me being different to how Sadie described me. I fold my arms tightly across my ribs. "Such as?"

Pulling a pass from his pocket and holding it to the control panel, he hits the *4* button.

As the lift jerks and whirrs upwards, he says, "For example, you like to skinny-dip in rivers in winter."

"I've done that *twice*! And…?"

"Your best friend's a born-again Christian but you're not religious. How does that work?"

It's true – about Freja and me. But I'm not sure why Sadie would have mentioned it. It turns out to be a rhetorical question, anyway, because he goes on, "When you were a kid, you had this obsession with a Hungarian dancer who trained in Haiti as a voodoo priest."

"She was a *neighbour*. She lived two doors down from

us. And she was an anthropologist at the university. She also used to make me this amazing Hungarian trifle with chocolate sauce and cream. It made a change from Tesco rice pudding."

"Sadie said she was what, like, the only voodoo priest in Sheffield?"

"Sadie's never even lived in Sheffield! What would she know? Actually, you can't walk down Eccy Road without getting turned into a zombie. *Such* a pain when you just want a kebab."

His eyes crease into a smile. The lift stops.

"Sorry. I – we – talked one night after too many of Sadie's cocktails… That stuff about the skinny-dipping and the friend. The way she said it, I thought she was trying to tell me you were kind of –" he pauses – "unusual on purpose. Which would be OK. But, when I said you're not how she described, I meant I didn't understand what she was telling me. Because you are unusual – naturally. Unaffectedly unusual. That's what I'm trying to say."

"*Unusual*… Right."

He steps out of the lift into a white corridor with a grey carpet and brass-rimmed dome lights in the ceiling.

"With all the positive connotations of that word," he says as he sets off down it. "But look, with hindsight, we've all done odd things, right? When I was sixteen, I worked in the summer as a fake brother for this family rental company. I've never skinny-dipped in a freezing river but I do have a thing for chilli peppers. When I was eighteen, I came fifteenth in the All-Albuquerque chilli-eating contest. I'd hoped for top ten, but, hey."

"Fake *brother*?" I say. As I follow him along the corridor, I find myself scanning the name plates on the doors that we're passing:

DR JEANNE MEIRING, PhD, FPRI

STREDNOVA, LEE, HARRIS, FLYNN – Rav's room, I guess.

WHO YA GONNA CALL? DR PRETI!

"Well, when I say *worked*, I was on the books. Turned out there wasn't a huge requirement for fake brothers of Indian ethnic origin in the Albuquerque region. Or fake family at all, in fact… It was this Japanese student who set it up. Family members for hire is big over there."

"Albuquerque? That's in…?"

"New Mexico. Where I grew up."

He stops by a door labelled *Lab 3*. "Usually Lana, the lab technician, would also be here." He pulls a plastic pass from a pocket in his shorts. "But she has to work on something with Jared so I'll take you in. We'll go through the informed consent forms then we'll get started. Sound OK?"

I nod but I'm not looking at him. A large pinboard on the wall has caught my eye. It's covered in flyers and what look like the front pages of academic papers. Words leap out at me:

Parapsychology
Altered perception
Anomalous

There's an advert: *VOLUNTEERS WANTED: Suggestion and metal-bending.* And, pinned in the centre:

Media Madness:
The Crisis in Modern Ghost-hunting
Professor Jared Robertson, Parapsychology Research
Institute, Gessen University, NYC
Jefferson Market Library, Greenwich Village
27 June, 7 p.m.
All Welcome

That's tonight, I realize. There's a black-and-white headshot in the top right corner. It's of a man in his forties with a high forehead and hollow cheeks, his wiry black hair shot through with grey.

"My esteemed professor," Rav says. "Come on."

He raises his pass to a scanner on the wall and the door to Lab 3 clicks open.

A study on ghosts... I'm about to do a study on ghosts. While Rav isn't looking, I wipe my palms on my trousers.

He flicks on the light and we step inside. The rush of my blood in my ears is suddenly deafening.

The rectangular room looks and smells totally bland.

Which somehow makes me even more apprehensive.

At this end, there's a circular white table with a blue plastic folder on it, and four white chairs. A narrow table is pushed up against the wall, with two white storage boxes on top. Across from the table is a three-seater grey sofa, which faces an empty expanse of grey carpet. No windows. Just more of the brass-rimmed dome lights. It's almost totally silent. There's just the slightest hum, from the lights or ducted air con perhaps, because it's cooler in here than it was out in the corridor.

"Take a seat." Rav pulls out a couple of the chairs. "I'll need you to read through the consent form first."

I put my bag down on the floor and sit. The plastic is cool through my thin trousers. Rav takes a sheet of paper from the blue folder and slides it across to me. It explains that I'm about to take part in an immersive VR study.

The VR environment is designed to create an altered sense of reality. Therefore, individuals susceptible to hallucinations, delusions and altered states are strongly advised not to take part.

I reread the sentences. Am I susceptible to hallucinations or delusions? But it's just VR. It won't be real. I can tell the difference between real and not-real, right?

I don't even read the rest of the form. I just pretend to. Then I sign my name.

"Good. Now I have to fit you up with some sensors. They'll measure your heart rate, breathing rate and galvanic skin response – basically how much you sweat. They're all physical signs of how you're feeling."

He goes over to one of the storage boxes on the side table and returns with what looks like a battery pack, connected by long blue wires to four circular transparent plastic pads.

"Can you stick one of these sensors to your inner left wrist?"

I take a deep breath and do as he asks. "What about the others?"

"Then one on the inside of each ankle. Here." He points to his own bare ankle to show me where.

"The last one goes on the tip of the middle finger of your left hand." He watches me fumble a little as I wrap the pad round my finger. "OK. Now if you can clip the pack to the waistband of your pants, maybe?"

"Good. Follow me past the couch and I'll help you with the headset and fit your gloves. When you're in the VR environment, you'll see virtual hands, and you'll be able to use them to direct where you want to go. OK?"

I nod. So far so professional, so reasonable, so normal. But that line from the consent form is flickering in my mind. *Individuals susceptible to hallucinations, delusions and altered states are strongly advised not to take part.*

I am *not* susceptible – at least I don't think I am. I don't think I'm hallucinating when I see Holly because I see her so clearly. She does things. I didn't hallucinate the *sand*—

I try to tune back in to Rav. "You'll be going into a building," he's saying, "and you'll be able to open doors and touch things. All I want you to do is walk around and explore. Go anyplace you like. You may on occasion have some unusual sensations. Maybe you'll see or feel something different to normal, or how you'd expect to be feeling. If you do, I'd like you to describe it. I'll be recording everything you say. And I'm going to be beside you. If at any point it gets too much, just tell me. I'll take your arm and remove the headset. OK?"

It's VR, I tell myself again. *Like a game.*

"Unusual how?" I ask.

"That'll be up to you to decide. Unusual sensations for you."

My heart's certainly racing already. But, whatever's in the virtual building, it's a simulation. It's programmed. So it has to follow someone's rules. Which means it'll be OK.

Rav brings a black VR helmet over. As he lowers it on to my head, the lab is replaced with something so incredibly different… I've never experienced sophisticated immersive VR before. I have to stop myself saying, "Wow!"

I'm standing on a long, crumbling driveway. It's as though I'm on a film set, or in some other place that isn't exactly real, but close. It's dark. Snow is falling. Wind is howling through the branches of tall pines in dense woodland to either side of me. Perhaps thirty paces ahead is a huge dilapidated fountain, the stone basin stained and cracked. Beyond it a grand double stone staircase fronts a mansion with turrets and sharply arched Gothic windows. Some of the panes of glass are missing, the gaps boarded up. I glance down. Ice glistens in long, forking cracks, like veins, in the drive.

"OK?" Rav asks.

It seems odd to hear him out in the lab yet so close.

"Yeah." I let my breath out slowly. Take a deep one.

"I'm gonna put on the gloves," he says. "Hold your hands out straight for me."

As the soft fabric slips over my skin, two virtual hands appear in front of my eyes. They're cut off at the wrists and they seem to be floating. But, when I move my hands, they move, too.

"You're gonna listen to a narrative," Rav says, in that same calm, professional tone. "After that, go inside the building and explore as you want. I'm not gonna say anything else, unless you tell me you want to stop. Just remember: if you see or feel anything unusual, say it out loud, OK?"

"…Yeah," I say, and I shiver. *But I'm not afraid*, I try to tell myself. Because this isn't real. Yet the fake snow is making me cold.

Motion makes my eyes jump up to a window to the right of the staircase. It has just transformed into a screen showing a woman with long blond hair. She's dressed in a khaki jacket, and she's holding a microphone. Over her right shoulder I can make out the same building that I'm standing in front of, only it's in a good state of repair.

"I'm reporting from outside the Stainehead Juvenile Correctional Centre," the woman says. "Four months ago, a sixteen-year-old boy died in unexplained circumstances. Yesterday the centre revealed that two more inmates have died in their care in the past six weeks. The precise causes of death have not been ascertained."

The picture distorts as if the broadcast has been interrupted. Then the girl reappears.

"Following the still unexplained deaths of three young inmates in its care, the Stainehead Juvenile Correctional Centre has announced that it's to close."

Again the picture distorts, and resettles. Now the mansion behind the girl's shoulder looks just as it does in the VR environment.

"The Stainehead Correctional Centre was forced to close three months ago, after a series of unexplained deaths. Though no one lives here, there have been reports of strange noises coming from inside. The security guard who was hired to protect the property has quit, claiming that it's haunted."

The TV screen vanishes. With a creak, the heavy front door swings open. Candlelight flickers somewhere inside. I hear music. A song. From the hollow tone of the voice, and the scratches in the recording, I'd guess it's from the 1930s or 1940s.

Not real, I think as I walk past the mossy fountain, and up the stone steps.

I find myself in a rundown entrance hall with a high vaulted ceiling. Weak light from an iron candelabra shows a bare flagged floor. Ahead is a broad wooden staircase. It rises before turning, and stretching up into shadows and out of view. To either side of me are rusting metal doors, fitted with bolts. The music seems to be coming through the door to my left.

Rav said to explore, so that's what I should do. I guess I should follow the music.

At the touch of my disembodied hand, the bolt shoots back. The door swings open to reveal a dim corridor, its walls covered in puckered, peeling red paint. A line of dented steel doors, most daubed with graffiti, run along the left side. They all have bolts. Some have padlocks. One, about two-thirds of the way along, looks to be ajar. Is the music coming from in there?

I move slowly, cautiously.

The first door that I pass is shut. The second is open a crack. I stiffen. I don't watch horror movies but I expect something to happen as I reach this door—

It doesn't. I continue walking, hearing my feet scrape on the rough concrete floor. Suddenly – in the middle of the corridor – there's a tingling on the back of my neck. A shiver rolls through me.

"I can feel tingling," I whisper. "On my neck."

I force myself to keep walking, towards the music.

Now I can hear the lyrics clearly, I realize they're sweet. The man is singing about dancing with a woman, cheek to cheek. But in this abandoned building, and with the reporter's narration fresh in my mind, it's sad, too. If it's actually from the 1940s, then he, who loved to dance, is surely dead, like those fictional inmates of the centre.

The tingling intensifies. I twist my head. Something was there. Over my shoulder – a black shadow – just beyond the corner of my eye, behind me.

I spin round, unsteady on my feet, but I see nothing. Only the corridor, the colour of dried blood, stretching back towards the candlelight.

"I feel like I saw something," I whisper.

And I'm positive someone was actually there. I didn't just glimpse them, I *felt* them. There's a familiar tug of fear down through my body. I could call out. Tell Rav I need to stop. But this is not home, and Holly's not here. I can make myself do this. I can walk into that room.

As I get closer still, I realize that the door isn't open. Or it's not any more. The music coming through it is so loud. The vibrations seem to be penetrating my flesh and bone, taking control of my heart. I jump. I just heard something. A man's voice whispering harshly. Not the singer. Then a yelp of pain. From inside the room. A girl's desperate shout of fear.

What was that? Over my shoulder, trickling to the floor. *Sand?*

My chest contracts so much that I can't move. I'm quivering and my muscles are struggling to hold me up. *This isn't real*, I tell myself. But whatever part of me I think I'm talking to isn't listening.

*

I'm standing in Lab 3, breathing fast and shaking. Rav's just taken off the headset and the gloves, yanking me back into the real world. Now he's watching me closely, his expression concerned.

"You OK? Mia?"

I force myself to meet his gaze.

"You're out and you're back in the lab with me." That same professional tone. "You OK?"

I take a quick, sharp breath. I didn't ask him to remove the headset. "I was fine."

He looks surprised. "You seemed distressed. Your heart rate was one hundred sixty-two."

I squeeze my eyes tight shut, like it'll get rid of the images in my mind. The sand – was that really built into the virtual environment? The man's unpleasant whispering – was *that*? If I'd stayed in there, what else might I have seen and heard?

"I got plenty of data," Rav says. "You did really well. Don't worry about stopping early. I had to follow protocol. If a subject becomes distressed—"

"Doesn't *everyone* get distressed?"

He hesitates. "Apprehensive, sure. A little scared, maybe. Afraid and excited – like during a horror movie – definitely. Distressed? Not so much."

I look up at the dim dome light as if it could bleach those sensations from my mind. The sand. The man's voice. I know where they came from. I dreamed about Holly last night, didn't I? The dream that used to make me too scared to go to bed.

Rav replaces the headset and gloves in the boxes. He pushes a hank of black hair behind his ear. "I usually do the exit interview in here but maybe it'd be better someplace else. How about the park?"

I nod.

"Let me help you." He crouches down to remove the plastic sensors from my ankles, then takes the ones from my wrist and finger. My hands still trembling, I unclip the battery pack from my waistband and pass it to him. I rub my hand hard across my face.

Virtual reality. *Nothing* was actually real.

8

I have had at least one dream that came true and which (I believe) was not just a coincidence.

I believe in extra-sensory perception.

I'm lying on my front, propped up on my elbows, on a patch of scratchy brown grass beyond the reach of the spray from the fountain in Washington Square Park. I'm holding an iPad that Rav gave me. The screen is displaying a series of statements to which I must give one of three responses: 'False', 'Uncertain' or 'True'. I find myself hitting the False button hard.

I know what Tamara said: *Talk to Rav.* But I told him only last night that I don't believe in ghosts and, especially after what just happened in the lab, I'm not going to start talking about it all now. I barely know him.

What would he say to me, anyway? Would he just nod – like he must have nodded when his father told him about feeling his grandmother's spirit stroking his arm? Or, if he tried to come up with some kind of rational explanation, is there even a chance I'd find it convincing? I already know the answer to that.

I realize that by not replying truthfully to these statements I'm not helping his study. But I'm just one participant. Conclusions aren't built around single results. And I just don't know what else to do.

All kinds of statements make me pause.

- *I have had at least one vision that was not a hallucination and from which I received information that I could not have otherwise gained at that time and place.*

- *I believe in life after death.*

- *I believe that some people can contact spirits of the dead.*

But I indicate 'False' for all three.

When I'm done, I push myself up and hand the iPad back to Rav, who's sitting cross-legged a little way away from me. He hunches over the screen.

I force myself to focus on his hand, and the stylus that he's using to enter something. After a few minutes, he looks up. "You are about the goatiest of all goats."

I have no idea what he's talking about.

"Zero out of thirty-six points," he continues. "You really

don't believe in ghosts. Or anything else paranormal."

I swallow. "I did tell you."

"You're eighteen, right? The average eighteen-year-old might score, I don't know, say twenty on the Sheep-Goat Scale."

I shrug and look past Rav, who's focusing on the screen again, to the fountain. People are sitting on the edge, cooling their feet in the pool of water. I watch the jets surge with such hopeful force. It seems sad that they have to lose all that momentum, and drop. When they do, they dissolve into a shifting curtain, like a drape of smoke.

It's mesmerizing. Especially after the intensity of the lab, and having to talk through some of my experiences in the virtual environment with Rav.

After a minute or so, Rav looks up again. "When you felt like there was someone there in the corridor with you, did you get any sense of who it was?"

I shake my head.

He nods thoughtfully and turns back to the screen. Moments later, he puts the iPad down beside him. "Done."

"Why sheep and goats?"

He shrugs as though it's obvious. "Sheep are ... sheep. Goats are evidently considered to be more independently minded animals."

"So can you explain now? The protocol?"

He bends his long legs and loosely hugs his knees with his arms. "A number of different environmental factors have been associated with reports of ghost encounters. Like Vic Tandy's."

I've never heard of Vic Tandy and I guess I look appropriately blank because Rav says, "He was an engineer and an IT lecturer. At Coventry University. His story goes – and he's published an academic paper on this – that he was working late in his lab one night, but he had the feeling that someone else was there with him. He glimpsed this black shadow out of the corner of his eye, but he couldn't quite get a fix on it."

I tense, remembering what I felt back in the lab.

"He had this definite feeling that there was a presence there with him." Rav pauses. Maybe he's expecting questions but I wait for him to carry on.

"Tandy was also a keen fencer. He had a foil – you know, a really fine sword – clamped in a vice on his bench, ready to be cleaned. He noticed that the tip was vibrating. And he wondered if maybe infrasound was responsible. Infrasound's at a frequency too low for humans to hear, right? But even when we can't hear it, at certain frequencies, we can *feel* it, in vibrations, though we're not always consciously aware of it. So he goes and finds an infrasound monitor. And he discovers that actually there's a really strong infrasound source in his lab. It's coming from this new extractor fan that's been fitted to the air-conditioning system. And right next to where this fan was fitted was where he saw that black shadow and felt the presence."

I guess I'm frowning at Rav, evidently not quite putting two and two together, because he says: "He wasn't the first to make the link but he's probably the researcher best known for it. Infrasound can cause weird physiological sensations. Like shivering. Like feeling just … strange. And, at around nineteen hertz, it can create a powerful feeling of a presence."

"So in your lab…?"

He nods. "We have four infrasound generators built into the walls. Actually there's other stuff, too. But in this study we're exploring infrasound. We want to know whether infrasound, in combination with the suggestion that you're in a haunted location – albeit only virtual – can make even people who don't believe in ghosts feel like one is present."

"That's why I felt the tingling on my neck?"

He hesitates. "Yeah. So we're also interested in intensity. What level of infrasound does there have to be for people to report feeling something physical? It's randomized every time. Even the experimenter doesn't know until after a trial."

It's obvious from his tone that there's something he's not saying. "So?"

"I had a look at the randomization data before we left the lab. Your level was the lowest that we use."

"…OK"

"And you are the most extreme goat that we've run in the study."

"And that means?"

"It means you're … unusual. I suppose I could put it that way. Independent confirmation, not just my opinion." He smiles but it looks a little forced.

"No, seriously, what does it *mean*? I'm sensitive to infrasound? How?"

"How? There are spectrums of sensitivity for all the senses, right? This is no different." He pauses. "Look, there are various sources of infrasound that you might not consciously be aware of. Trucks. Heavy traffic. Certain fans – like in Vic Tandy's AC unit. So you might not know there's infrasound around, but you might feel it – maybe even in the way you felt it in the lab."

I'm thinking, *There's no heavy traffic near my house, or school. And certainly no AC units.*

I'm about to ask him if there are other common sources when a voice projects through the curtain of spray around the fountain: "Rav! Jesus, why don't you ever answer your cell?"

A lean, toned woman in her early twenties, wearing gym gear, emerges from the droplet cloud. Her hair is very light blond, long and dead straight. She looks at me, then instantly away.

"I was running a trial," Rav tells her. His tone is part friendly, part cool.

"Jared needs you."

She sounds eastern European. Or maybe German.

"For what?" Rav asks.

"The talk, of course." She doesn't try to hide her irritation.

Rav glances at me. "Mia, this is Lana, our lab tech. Lana, you've heard me talk about my landlady, Sadie? This is her niece, Mia."

"Very pleased to meet you," she says automatically. "But, Rav, Jared needs you to email him the notes relating to Borley Rectory. He cannot find them in the cloud account."

"OK."

"Like, now."

"Right," Rav says.

She exhales hard. "And you're going to be there?"

With a strained smile, he says, "Seven o'clock. Jefferson Market Library."

"So when you've finished hanging out—"

"Debriefing."

Lana looks at me with slight interest for the first time. Her eyes are a clear olive green. "Thirteen left now?" she says to Rav.

He nods.

"Perhaps we will finish the trials by the end of summer."

"Hopefully."

She spins. Takes a few steps. Stops. Turns. "I found a box of beer-bottle tops. I put it in the trash. I figured if you didn't take it with you, you didn't want it. Right?"

"Right. As always," he says, and his smile is even more strained.

After Lana passes back through the water curtain, I actually laugh. I know I shouldn't but it's like she's broken the surface tension inside me and something has to bubble out. "You used to live with *her*?"

Rav nods his head sadly. "We were together for a while. I brought those bottle tops back with me after a summer school at a university in Brussels. It really isn't funny."

"It is a bit funny," I say. "Is she always like that?"

He hesitates. "Actually no. Sometimes she's *way* ruder to me. But not so much to other people. If you'd met her without me, she'd probably have come across like a normal human being."

"So she's a lab tech? That's not a student?"

Rav shakes his head. "She used to be a student. She grew up in a tough suburb of Prague. Was top of her class. Went to Charles University at sixteen, and won a full scholarship to Gessen. Then this girl in our class accused her of using scholarship money to buy drugs."

"Did she?"

"Honestly I don't know." He picks a blade of dry, brittle grass, runs it between his fingers. "But she'd practically been promised funding for post-grad study, and the grant decisions were made about a month after the allegation. She got nothing and no one would give her a loan. The best Jared could do was offer her a job as a lab tech.

She still really wants to do a PhD. One day, I guess…"

"But was there any evidence she used that money to buy drugs?"

Rav shrugs. "This girl didn't know Lana well. There was no reason for her to have a grudge against her. It was her word about some conversation she said she'd overheard against Lana's. The university obviously decided to err on the side of caution."

"But that sounds really unfair."

"Yeah… It probably was. Life's not always fair, right?" Changing the subject, he says, "So what are you doing now? Did you meet up with Tamara already?"

I nod.

"She OK?"

"She's not only OK but rocking a mermaid look."

He smiles. "Oddly enough I can picture it."

Tamara may think Rav's too serious but I get the definite impression he's still into her.

He reaches into his pocket and pulls out a canvas wallet. "Almost forgot. Your twenty bucks."

"From your own wallet?"

"I'll get it back from the institute, don't worry."

I take it and slip the note into my bag. "Thanks."

Rav grabs the iPad and gets up. "Why don't you come to the talk tonight?"

"I'm meeting Tamara."

"What time?"

"Six … at this pub nearby."

"Barlow's?"

I guess I look surprised. He nods. "She loves that place. I'm still not totally sure why. Well, look, the talk's just at the Jefferson Market Library. You guys could have a drink, come on after. It's free but it's ticketed. I could put you on the list."

I know what Tamara said about seizing an opportunity but a talk about ghosts? "I don't know. Maybe."

"Don't decide now. You could call me later, let me know?"

"But you don't ever answer your cell," I say, imitating Lana, making us both smile.

Then he looks a little guilty. "Seriously, don't let her utter disdain for me and anything to do with me totally taint her for you. She's really not that bad."

I stand up, too. Brush dead grass from my trousers.

He's about to head off but he hesitates. "And don't worry about the trial, OK. It was all virtual, right? We manipulate you on purpose. That's how it works. It's all controlled."

"Yeah, I know," I tell him because that's what he wants to hear, and it's what I want to hear myself say, too.

But after he walks off, back in the direction of the institute, I find myself focusing on what I heard and what I saw. I'm sensitive to *infrasound*?

And I remember the red-haired girl, and what she said. And the item on the scale: *I believe that some people can contact spirits of the dead.*

*

If I'd found a medium, and asked after Holly, I wonder what they'd have said to me. But I didn't. After the first few weeks, and a few really difficult meetings with a therapist at school, I did my best never to talk to anyone about her, apart from Freja.

I told Tamara only because I kind of had to. It was a few weeks after we'd first met. We were walking through Prospect Park. She'd been talking about her mum's brave life choices, and I realized I knew nothing about her dad. So I asked. She told me he'd been killed in an explosion four weeks into the Iraq War, when she was just one. When I said how sorry I was and I couldn't imagine what it must have been like to lose someone like that, tears rushed to my eyes.

Tamara stopped walking. "Can't you?" she said, watching me try to dry my cheeks. "Are you sure?"

And, once I started talking, it almost all came out.

How Holly lived six streets away and how we became friends in the first week of Reception.

How Holly's mum was a hairdresser who worked in a salon not far from our houses, and her dad had gone off to do a construction job near Marbella and decided to stay.

How her much older sister, Lauren, worked as a receptionist at a local hospital. And how it was Lauren who explained about periods and sex, and music and false lashes, and boys and girls, because Lauren was into both.

I told her about how Lauren used to do makeover sessions for me and Holly and Freja, whom we met in the first year of secondary school. If Freja or I was in a bad mood, which I don't think happened often, Holly would tell us to take our mardy cardies right off, which always made us smile. She even told me once that I shouldn't get upset about what people said about my mum, because whose mum was perfect? Not hers.

I remember one morning, at the end of break, two girls in the corner of the classroom obviously talking about Mum. I was very sensitive to the signs and they weren't trying to hide their sniggering.

Holly walked right over to them and started laughing loudly. "Oh my God, Poppy, you're so funny! You should be on TV. Tell everyone – go on – it's just so funny, I can't stop laughing." Everyone in the class turned to look at Poppy, whose cheeks had flushed red. "Go on – tell everyone what you were just saying about your mum's bum-lift! It's so funny, I might actually explode."

Poppy was saved by our teacher walking in. I never noticed her talking about Mum again.

*

I'm standing here, in Washington Square Park, all these years later, and thousands of miles away, but the memories just won't stop coming.

I picture Lauren, when I was about twelve, telling us she was moving to Newcastle with her boyfriend, a theatre nurse. Then it was just me and Holly and Freja… Then it was *always* me and Holly and Freja.

Out on our bikes, sometimes in the Peaks, with Freja's dad. Out to Meadowhall on the tram, to look at clothes we couldn't afford. Out on foot, arms linked, to buy chips from our favourite chippy in Crosspool, and into town to vie to win our own prize for 'most bizarre topping combo' at Sundaes (when winning meant you had to lick the dish clean).

Even after Holly's mum's new boyfriend, Patrick, moved in, and lost his job and started drinking too much and everything soured at home, Holly was still laughing, still caring, always kind. Everybody wanted her to like them. But we were a tight little trio, doing everything together … except dying.

*

I press my palms hard against my eyes. In New York, these memories are normally lifted off me enough that I can breathe. Not today. I try to force my attention outside my head. I can feel a warm breeze on my skin.

Still I find myself thinking about what Tamara said this morning. Rav knows about ghosts. His professor is a world expert… And I wonder if he's ever heard of ghosts moving location. In all the ghost stories I've read, though ghosts are incorporeal, and surely not bound by any known physics, they are always anchored to a place.

Until last year, I used to think that, when I left Sheffield for good, I'd also be able to leave Holly. Then I went to an open day at Manchester Uni. I was at the tail end of a line of visiting pupils being escorted through an echoing lecture hall, and, as I turned to glance back up at all the rows of empty seats, I realized that one wasn't empty.

That was typical Holly. Getting away with doing whatever she wanted – even when she was dead.

9

"Oh my God, I love this place!"

Tamara hangs her bag off the side of a copper-coloured chair and flops down at the little corner table that I've been guarding for the past ten minutes.

She glances around her happily. The pub is all dark wood, with a pressed-tin ceiling. There's a jukebox, which is playing rock, and a curving bar at the back with a brass rail.

"You can get pints," she says. "And there's no wait staff. You have to go to the bar."

"*Oh my God*," I say, smiling, "how *quaint*. I have been here before with you," I remind her. "There was that night last summer—"

I watch realization dawn. "The band! From Vienna? Yeah!" She slaps the table and arranges her mouth into a pout. "Maximillian promised he'd message me."

"Maximillian lied?"

"He did! Damn him!"

I get up to go to the bar. "So what do you want?"

She pulls a face. "They always card you here. Better wait."

"What – till I'm twenty-one?"

She smiles. "For Rav!"

"*Rav's* coming?"

"He messaged me, like, five minutes ago to say he'll be here in five minutes."

"You asked him to come?"

"Actually he called me. He told me you'd been in to do the study."

I feel whatever smile was left slip from my face. I wanted to talk about normal stuff with Tamara, not think about the study.

"He just told me you'd been in, and you'd said we were meeting later, and he told me there's this talk he thinks we'd find really interesting—"

I interrupt her. "*We?*"

"What, like I don't do intellectual events in libraries?"

"It's a talk on ghosts."

"Ghost-hunting."

"You don't believe in ghosts."

"Not only do I not do intellectual events but I also refuse to listen to arguments that oppose my beliefs?"

My mouth opens but, before I can speak, she smiles and says, "You've obviously spent *way* too much time already with Rav. I'm kidding! How'd the study go, anyway?"

"…OK."

She squints at me, like she's trying to extract more from my face than I offered in that single word. But she evidently decides not to press me because she says, "I talked to Mom. So long as I cook up a batch of bamia at some point tonight, she's happy. Whether we go or we don't go to this talk, it's fine. I told Rav to come by and have a drink with us if he's got time. I haven't seen him for weeks." She grins at me. "Plus, he's old enough to buy drinks for us—" Something must catch her eye because her head jerks up and I follow her gaze – to Rav, who's hovering in the doorway, looking for us, I guess.

"Hey!" Tamara shouts.

The music – Imagine Dragons, I think – is so loud, he doesn't hear her. Tamara puts two slender fingers between her lips and blows. The whistle makes half the bar look round.

Rav immediately spots us and comes over, pretending to be embarrassed.

"I think I'd've heard that back in the institute… You need drinks."

"We do," Tamara says, nodding gravely and reaching for her bag. "I'll buy the first round but if you don't mind getting it?"

"No, first round's on me," he says. "What would you like?"

Tamara smiles at him. "Thank you, Rav! I'd like a glass of barley wine."

"*Barley* wine?" I ask her.

"It's, like, Icelandic or something," she says.

"I guess I'll try one, too. Thank you."

"Coming right up," he says. I watch him head for the throng by the bar.

Tamara rummages in her bag and pulls out a plastic container. "I brought these – a present from Mom." As she peels back the lid, I see that it's stuffed with fried, golden-brown, egg-shaped objects.

"Kibbeh!"

Some of the most delicious things I've ever eaten. One of Misk's specialities.

Tamara smiles. "There are some almonds and golden raisins in with the meat."

"You think they'll mind if we eat them in here?"

"Look how packed it is! No one'll even see. Oh, and I nearly forgot – I have an update from Gunther."

"Oh yeah?" I take a kibbeh and start munching.

"I went by the theatre on the way here, just to see if there's any chance we could get in to start earlier. There was this – I think they were Romanian – puppetry group, three of them, having a massive argument with Gunther, but all through a translator. So there was, like, five minutes of yelling in Romanian. Then the translator goes, 'Mr Constantin says they're not happy with the conditions.'

"Gunther goes, 'That can't be all he said!'

"The translator goes, 'Well, mostly.' Then there's another full five minutes of yelling in Romanian, and the translator says, 'The stage rotation is not working properly.' So either Romanian is the *wordiest* language ever invented…"

"Or it was ninety per cent obscenities."

She smiles. "I walk over and he looks so pleased to be interrupted. I tell him that we really need more time for all this *detail* – at least another week – and of course we'll need paying.

"He frowns, then he whispers, 'Two extra days, full pay. *If,* for the benefit of my Romanian friends, you make it look like I'm the most incredible person in the world right now, and you're so utterly grateful even just to know me—' I must've been looking like this was going to be tough, right, cos he goes, 'OK. *Three.* Deal?'"

"Here we go."

Tamara and I look up. It's Rav bearing a tray of drinks.

"Thank you!" Tamara says. "Want a kibbeh?" She proffers the container.

"Thanks," he says.

I thank Rav for getting my drink and take a sip. It's malty, with a lemony background taste. Not really my kind of drink but not awful.

"So do we have three extra days?" I say to Tamara.

She grins. "And three extra days' cash in our pockets! We start next Sunday." She raises her glass of amber-coloured wine. "To us. And you," she says to Rav.

He finishes his mouthful of kibbeh. "To you. And me... These are truly awesome. Three extra days doing what?"

"The theatre job," I say.

He nods. "Oh yeah. OK." Then he focuses on Tamara. "So Sadie told me last week about your offer from Rhode Island. You didn't say...?"

My gaze swivels back to her. "Really?" I knew she'd applied to study fine arts at various colleges, and the Rhode Island School of Design was meant to be the best in the country.

She takes another sip of her wine. "Well, I don't know yet if I can afford to go. Kinda depends on getting a scholarship. So we'll see."

"If you don't get one, no one will," I tell her.

"At least your mom supports you," Rav says. "I had to tell mine I applied for pre-med but there was some kind of mix-up, and I was put into psychology – and it was that or nothing."

"Why'd you tell her that?" I ask him.

He takes a sip of his dark beer. "For totally stereotypical immigrant-parent reasons. When I was eleven, her plan was for me to become a professional golfer or surgeon. When the golf dream evaporated, medicine was all that was left."

"Why a golfer?" I ask him, helping myself to another kibbeh.

"I was pretty good – she wasn't completely deluded –

but I wasn't good enough. She came from this town called Chandigarh in the Punjab on a tennis scholarship to study math. All the way to the University of New Mexico. She envisioned something similar for her son. Only Ivy League."

"Like a golf scholarship to study medicine at Yale," Tamara says.

He nods. "Right."

"I didn't know there was that kind of thing," I say.

"You've never heard of the famous Harvard fussball physics scholarship?" Rav asks. "Or the Stanford darts scholarship for global economics?"

I'm fairly sure he's joking but not totally...

"You're meant to smile," Tamara says, prodding me. "That was Rav being funny."

He pulls a pretend-hurt face but she's laughing now, and he shrugs and smiles.

"So who's gonna be there tonight?" she asks him.

"Well, Lana, obviously. And Yunoo and Alli."

"Yunoo's also at the institute, working towards a PhD," Rav says to me. "Alli is a year into her masters programme. Yunoo's on the SCC with me."

Tamara's forehead wrinkles. "The what?"

But I think I understand what he's talking about. "Spontaneous Cases Committee?"

Rav nods. "He works all five boroughs but he's especially interested in reports from Koreatown. And how the manifestations compare with ghost and poltergeist reports in Koreatown versus the rest of Manhattan. Actually, he's really interested in general in cross-cultural studies – how paranormal and especially ghost beliefs in some cultures and countries compare with beliefs in others."

"What's Alli working on?" I ask him.

"She's on the VR study with me. But her dad is setting up some kinda spiritual retreat. As soon as her masters is done, she'll go help him run it." He checks his watch. "I should probably drink up."

"You just got here! And it's like five minutes away!" Tamara protests.

"It's six thirty already. And I have to make sure Jared's all set up."

Tamara takes a long drink of her wine. "So we'll walk with you?" She looks at me.

Her gaze is frank but I have the feeling that I've been set up to go. Not necessarily as a shared plot with Rav – this could easily be all Tamara who has good intentions, I'm sure. But I've still been set up. And I do mind... But only so much.

I might not feel like I *want* to hear it but I can't help being interested in what Rav's professor has to say. And, now she's pushing me, it's easier to say, "...OK."

10

When I walked into Barlow's, the clouds were already darkening to slate-grey. So it's not a huge surprise when the first drops of rain splat on to the pavement.

Rav, Tamara and I are on 6th Avenue. Other people must have checked the forecast because, as the raindrops fall even bigger and bolder, the pavement becomes a sea of mostly black umbrellas.

"Just there," Rav says, hunching his shoulders a little against the rain. He's pointing over the steadily streaming traffic at what has to be one of the most unusual-looking buildings that I've seen. It's like a cross between a church and a fairy-tale knight's castle, with turrets and stained glass.

While we wait for the lights to change, I hold my bag fairly uselessly above my head. At last we hurry over and through two sets of heavy doors, into a stone entrance area.

I drop my wet bag back to my shoulder and shake droplets of water from my arms. Tamara squeezes out her hair. A woman in black trousers and a black top – either a librarian or a security guard – waves a stern finger at us.

"What's she expect us to do?" Tamara mutters.

Standing around us are little huddles of people. Over by a staircase, which is also built from bare solid blocks of grey stone, I spot the poster that I saw on the noticeboard at the institute this morning.

Media Madness:
The Crisis in Modern Ghost-hunting

Professor Jared Robertson, Parapsychology Research
Institute, Gessen University, NYC
Jefferson Market Library, Greenwich Village
27 June, 7 p.m.
All Welcome

At the bottom, someone's added in big black letters:

TODAY

Rav rakes his fingers back through his hair and reknots it. He glances up at an ironwork wall clock with Roman numerals. "I should get up there. You wanna come with me?"

"Or hang out here for more scowling from that librarian?" Tamara asks, and we follow him up the broad spiral staircase. At the top, we pass through a truly massive, ornate dark wood doorway into a cavernous room, its long walls lined with bookcases. Set into the far wall are floor-to-ceiling arched windows, streaked with rain and criss-crossed with the shadows of branches jerking outside.

"It was built as a courthouse," Rav says. "This is where the main court sat."

About seventy or so people are already seated on wooden chairs, which are arranged in rows facing a lectern and a retractable screen. More people are gathered, talking, at the back. Rav gazes out over the crowd. I think I spot Jared Robertson, over in the far-right corner, at the same time that he does.

Robertson looks five or even ten years older than he does in the photo. His hair's more grey than black but still thick and wiry. He's tall, a little gaunt, and wearing a black shirt and black jeans, with what looks to be a Ghostbusters belt buckle. Talking with him is Lana, who's changed into a green dress and spike-heeled ankle boots, and a girl with shoulder-length hair tinted in darkening shades of pink.

"I should go check on Jared," Rav says.

"Yeah," I say. "Go."

A loud voice from the back of the room makes Tamara and me look round. An overweight guy in a black T-shirt is saying, "If everybody could take a seat, we'll be starting in just over five minutes."

"There's a *lot* of black clothing in here," I comment to Tamara.

"Ghosts. The occult. Not exactly associated with primary colours. I love Alli's hair, though." She's looking at the girl standing with Lana and Robertson. "You think it'd suit me?"

"Or maybe that colour?" I jerk my head towards a woman halfway along the row closest to us. She must be seventy but her long hair is dyed a deep mulberry.

"A little too Addams Family," Tamara says. "But I want her skirt." It's emerald green and velvet.

I glance back towards Robertson, and spot Rav, who's now talking to Lana, and also another guy. He's very tall and broad, his hair as black as Rav's, but clipped short. Yunoo, maybe.

The guy in black repeats his request for everyone to sit, and there's a swell of people in from the back. More are still streaming in through the monumental door. The rows are rapidly filling. I head into the one right by us, which still has spaces.

"Stay by the end," Tamara says. "In case."

I raise an eyebrow.

"You know me," she says. "Limited tolerance. I don't want to embarrass Rav by having to climb over half a row to get out."

After she sits down, she puts her phone on silent. I'm about to do the same when I see that, while we were in Barlow's, I missed three messages.

One is from Freja:

Bday plans going well! Update to follow soon x

One from Mum:

Beautiful here. 😎 🦈 What you doing? xxx

And one from Sadie:

Heading to gallery. Hope all great xxx

After flicking my phone on to silent, I quickly reply to Mum.

Just checking out this amazing library xxx

And to Sadie.

With Tamara and Rav xxx

While I'm thinking what to say to Freja, there's a hiss of a microphone and a woman says, "Thank you, everybody, for coming this evening!"

Sliding my phone into my sodden bag, I look up. A striking older woman in an elegant silver jacket is standing to one side of the lectern. The room is almost full now, I realize.

The woman goes on: "As some of you know, my name is Mair Hudson and I am director of the Intellectual Curiosity Club of New York City. This evening I am honoured to be able to introduce Professor Jared Robertson from the Parapsychology Research Institute at Gessen University. Professor Robertson is a world authority on paranormal research and the study of hauntings. He will speak for around half an hour. After that, we will have a short break. Then there'll be plenty of opportunity for conversation and questions." She claps enthusiastically, encouraging the rest of us to do the same.

Robertson gets to his feet and heads for the lectern. For a couple of moments, he gazes out at us. His very pale blue eyes shift slowly, taking in the room. Just as the silence is starting to get a little uncomfortable, he says, "Let me start with a question: what *is* a ghost?"

I can't immediately place his accent. Transatlantic I think it's called.

Before anyone has a chance to reply, he goes on: "If I'd asked that question of an audience one hundred years ago, what I'd have got back would have been entirely along the lines of: 'It's the spirit of a dead person.' But if I ask that question now, today, I might also get…?" He looks expectantly at us.

"Energy!" a woman shouts out. He nods.

"Something created by strong emotion," a man calls.

"Pain. Love. Anger. Puberty."

Again Robertson nods.

"An entity with a desire for revenge," a guy somewhere behind us says loudly.

Robertson points over my head at him, nodding. "Right, and a spirit with a desire – a *need* – for revenge is a concept that's still very popular in certain countries. Like Korea, right, Yunoo? If you could maybe explain? Tonight does not have to be all about me." He gives us a tight smile.

The tall guy who'd been talking earlier with Rav and Lana gets up from a chair in the front row and turns to face the audience. "In Korea," he says, with just the faintest accent, "*gwisin* are spirits that remain in the world of the living because they have unfinished business. They must exact revenge – or continue caring for someone. That desire is so strong, it stops them from going to the underworld until the task is complete." He nods briefly, then sits back down.

"So," Robertson goes on, "let me ask you another question: how many of you in this room have seen or felt the presence of a ghost, or been witness to the activities of a poltergeist?"

Three or four seats down from me, a woman instantly raises her hand. As a few other people do the same, heads start turning to look. It takes a little while but soon more than half the audience have their hands up. I clench mine together in my lap. Tamara doesn't look at me.

"OK," says Robertson. "Thank you." The arms go down.

"If I were to ask the general population of the United States that question, I'd get about twenty-eight per cent of adults – *millions* of people, right? – saying they have *direct* experience of a ghost. But if you want to look for actual evidence of a ghost – whether you're the host of a TV show, or on a ghost-hunting weekend, but *especially* as a scientist – the first thing you have to determine is what *is* a ghost. *What exactly* are we talking about, and looking for?"

He pauses. The room is silent. I can feel the anticipation building.

"Now what I have to make very clear is that, no matter what anybody on TV tells you, there is actually no agreement about what a ghost *is*. Scientists, and even many parapsychologists, are very wary of getting involved in any kind of research in this area in large part because of this very issue. So, if we don't even know what ghosts are, how do we go about detecting them?"

"EMF meters!" someone shouts out.

Robertson nods slowly. "EMF… Electromagnetic fields. If you watch any *respectable* –" he makes air quotes with his fingers – "ghost-hunting show, they'll have an EMF meter. If the readout surges, then a ghost is present! Yes?" He pauses a moment. "*No*."

The tension in the room rises. I have no idea how you'd measure it scientifically, but it's there. I can sense it.

"The fact is," Robertson goes on, "*if* we are going to get

serious about ghost-hunting, we have to get deeply serious about what is scientifically justifiable, and what is not. The whole EMF detection pretence is, quite frankly, laughable. In fact, there is *no such thing* as a ghost-detecting machine."

Silence again. The kind you could slice. Robertson stands up just a little taller.

"When you look at the popularity of ghost-hunting weekends, ghost-hunting evenings, ghost-hunting shows, what you are looking at is not a modern scientific movement, but a *spiritualist* movement. These are groups that are looking for fulfilment of their beliefs. And that, I'm afraid, is the poisoned heart of the crisis in modern ghost-hunting."

A few rows back a woman is whispering loudly. I turn to locate her. She's very thin, in a navy blue suit, with long auburn hair and heavy make-up. I can't quite make out what she's saying but the man beside her, who seems to know her, is trying to shush her. Other people turn to look at her, too. She shakes her head angrily and gets up. "Stacey Disaranno, *American Poltergeist*. If I could just make a response on this point—"

I look back at Robertson. He narrows his eyes and waves an arm dismissively. "Stacey, this is not the time or the place."

"If you'll just allow me—"

"*Stacey*, thank you, but tonight yours is not the face on the speaker poster."

"*Jared*—" she starts but the man in the suit stands and takes her arm. He says something in her ear. She shakes him off and storms out of her row and towards the exit.

"To move on," Robertson says, frowning, "to the seeds of expectation that are always sown. Let's take the case of a Victorian rectory in England. Borley Rectory. Here it is—"

He glances at someone in the front row and an image appears on the screen of a double-fronted building with twin chimneys and pointed roofs.

"Victorian Gothic... It was built in 1862. And once upon a time it was billed as the most haunted house in England. In 1937, a well-known paranormal researcher called Harry Price took it over for an entire year. Here is Price, with a collaborator, in an allegedly haunted *bed* in Chiswick, London—"

There are a few laughs from the crowd. The image changes to two men in an extravagantly carved wooden bed, the covers pulled up to their chests.

"So," Robertson goes on, "Price took it over for a year, for a deep-dive investigation. He assembled forty-eight investigators, mostly students. He gave each of them a guide to all the paranormal phenomena that had been reported at the rectory over the years. *The Blue Book* it was called. But the well-founded criticism of that so-called *investigation* is that he was essentially instructing them in what to expect, and what to report, so that, when he gathered all their observations together, there'd be a compelling collection of convergent stories. And that's what he got. But he'd seeded them all. Ghost nuns. Spectral horses and carriages...

Imagine someone reporting seeing a spectral carriage today. But we might still expect to see a maid in period dress, perhaps, or a lost-looking child. What ghost-hunter goes into a building ignorant of the stories of hauntings reported within it? None. Because the set-up is key. And, once you get people anticipating what's to come, lo and behold, they tend to report it."

There's another minor outbreak but of quiet conversation, near the back, and Robertson ignores it.

"A friend of mine, a British parapsychologist, has a favourite trick. He has a torch in which he loosens the battery connections. At some point during the night's adventure – because they always happen at night, right? – the beam *will* start flickering. And someone, if not everyone, will immediately start talking about how they can feel the presence of a spirit, the cold on their neck, the chill in the air... All of that from loose batteries."

A woman near the front obviously can't contain herself any longer because she shouts out, "So what are investigators *meant* to do?"

Robertson raises a hand. "And that's what I'm coming to. What *has* to happen is an abandonment of this un-evidenced use of so-called ghost-hunting technology. Cameras – OK. Whatever you record will convince no one but you. But if you want to use them – fine. The rest? Forget it."

"So how *do* we get evidence?" someone else shouts.

Robertson frowns. I hear the rain still falling against the

windows and the fidgety impatience of the people around us. Tamara glances at me and raises an eyebrow.

"You know what," he says at last, "I was going to talk for a while longer then do questions, but let's do it your way. Why don't we take the break now – five or ten minutes? You can think through what you want to discuss, and, when we come back, I'll open the floor."

There's a general murmur in the crowd and people start talking, some quietly, some loudly. Robertson steps away from the lectern.

"That was a little intense," Tamara says. "Rav doesn't look that happy…"

He's walking our way with the girl with pink hair – Alli.

"Hey," he says when he reaches us. "Sorry, I meant to get back to sit with you, but then it all got under way so quickly. Tamara, you've met Alli, right?" They smile a greeting at each other. "Alli, this is Mia. Mia – Alli."

"Hey," Alli says enthusiastically to me. "I wanted to come meet you! Your aunt Sadie is like the sweetest person I've ever met. Though she makes the *meanest* cocktails. She's like yin and yang totally personified."

As Tamara edges round her to talk to Rav, I take in Alli's deep brown, smiling eyes and her frank expression.

I smile back. "She is a special person."

"She truly is. I bet you're wishing you're with her instead of here tonight. I feel like a literal fight could break out any moment…"

"No, it's all really interesting."

She raises an eyebrow.

"Honestly! It is. So Rav said Jared Robertson's supervising your masters, too."

She nods. "Though I'm kinda the odd one out in the team. I come at it all from a different perspective. The others are basically looking for scientific evidence that ghosts exist. Without that, they can't let themselves believe. Me, I already know ghosts exist. I'm just hoping I can help find what's needed to convince the non-believers. How about you? Are you with Jared? Or with most of the crowd?"

I blink at her. "I'm … really – I—"

She lets me off the hook with a warm smile. "Well, don't let what Jared says be the only thing to persuade you one way or the other. He's an amazing researcher and I respect him completely. But, given the level of disagreement among experts in just about every field I've ever come across, it's a simple fact that not all of them can be right about everything. I think it's OK to disagree. We don't all need to feel the same way."

She glances round. I follow her gaze – to Robertson, who's heading back towards the lectern. "And prepare for round two… Hope we get to talk more soon, Mia." She fixes her gaze on me. She's the kind of person who, when she looks at you, makes you feel that she's seeing right into you, not just letting her gaze glance off the surface. It's a little unsettling but I do like her. "I'd better get back up front. It was great to meet you," she says.

"And you," I tell her.

As Alli starts to head back up the rows with Rav, Tamara sits down with me. "Rav says sorry, he'd better go support Jared. Nice chat with Alli?"

There's something in her tone that I can't quite read.

She grins. "Seriousness face-off: Alli versus Rav. It'd be way too close to call."

"I like her!"

"I like her, too! In, like, really small doses."

"You are such a harsh judge of character!"

She shrugs, still smiling.

Someone shouts, "Quiet, please!" And I realize Robertson is talking. He's addressing a guy standing up in the third row.

"Right," Robertson says, "the biggest challenge is how to deal with the technology-wielding, hyping amateurs who say all you need is common sense—"

Then someone else shouts out, and the woman in the silver jacket, who introduced herself at the start, stands and requests respect while the professor is speaking. I feel a little bad for the TV poltergeist woman. The event seems to have descended into argument. She might as well have stayed.

"Let's have another question," Robertson says.

A guy near the front raises an arm. "Could you give us your views on the investigation of the Enfield haunting?"

Robertson frowns. "I can but I have a feeling you won't like them."

There's a minor eruption from the back left and he waves his hand for silence. "OK. For those of you who don't know it, there was alleged poltergeist activity at a three-bedroom home on Green Street, Enfield, in north London. It was first reported by someone outside the family – a police officer no less – in August 1977.

"Over the next eighteen months, neighbours, journalists, psychic researchers – all kinds of eyewitnesses – said they saw chairs sliding across the floor and even a fireplace grille moving apparently of its own accord. According to their statements, marbles and Lego were thrown around, and two girls, then aged eleven and fourteen, who lived in the house, were levitating. I do not doubt that the investigators who went into the house set out to be scrupulous, but there are problems. For example, the newspaper photographer who took the famous photographs in the girls' bedroom wasn't even in the room at the time. The camera was remotely operated. He was listening to a live audio feed and if he heard something unusual – like a bang – he'd take a photo. The girls could have been doing anything out of range of the lens."

"Even throwing themselves across the room?" a woman shouts.

"What about the levitation?" someone else calls.

Robertson raises a hand for silence. "If you take the photographs at face value, the girls did levitate. But they could have had some kind of simple lifting mechanism—"

A scoffing sound from near the front makes him break off. Someone else shouts out: "And what about the case the year before, from Long Island? The mother seeing her daughter talking to someone, and the rocking chair rocking? The mother even heard another voice – but only the daughter could see the woman in the chair?"

Before Robertson can respond, there's another shout from near me. "Do you actually believe ghosts exist?"

He waits a beat. "I believe that for the people who see them, they do exist. If you *see* it, it's real for you, right? And all our reality is subjective. We don't like that idea but it's true. But is there any convincing evidence for ghosts, in the way that there is for some other stuff we can't necessarily always see – like black holes? Then *no*."

There's an explosion of questions and outrage from the audience. It feels like a few minutes later, but it must be longer, when Robertson shouts, "Look, folks, I think we've had enough debate for one night. I suggest we draw the formal portion of the evening to an end. If you want to leave now, please feel free. If not, I'll stay behind for anyone who really wants to come ask me a question. Thank you."

The woman in the silver jacket leaps to her feet to thank Robertson, but she's almost drowned out by the noise of chair legs scraping, conversation and scattered applause. Rav's standing now, too. He catches my eye. Beckons us over.

When we reach the front, Tamara says there's someone she wants to talk to. I go to Rav. "Are all his talks like that?" I ask him, smiling slightly.

He exhales, and his body visibly relaxes. "That was definitely crazier than normal," he says, shaking his head. "Jared was in full-on combative mood tonight."

I'm about to ask why that was but Yunoo comes to join us.

"Yunoo!" Rav says, his expression brightening. "This is Mia, Sadie's niece. Off to college to study psychology in October. Mia, what can I tell you about Yunoo? He's irritatingly smart."

Yunoo laughs. He's half a head taller than Rav, who has to be six feet.

"*Not* true," he says. "But, if you think about it, everyone in our little group is irritatingly something. Rav actually *is* irritatingly smart –" Rav shakes his head – "and self-deprecating. Jared –" he glances over at Robertson – "is irritatingly brilliant and stubborn, which he gets away with *because* he's brilliant. Alli is irritatingly conscientious and organized *and* smart. And Lana…" He grins widely again. "Actually Lana is mostly just irritating." He laughs loudly, then slaps Rav's back so heartily that Rav pretend-staggers a couple of steps.

"I say that out of solidarity with my friend here," Yunoo says. "Now I hear that you're the goatiest goat yet in our study."

I look at Rav, surprised. "Isn't there, like, such a thing as experimenter–subject confidentiality?"

He holds up his hands. "I just told him by way of pre-introduction."

"Yeah," Yunoo says. "One other thing about Rav: he's not very good at following rules."

"I am extremely good at following rules," Rav says. "I just—"

"Sometimes conveniently forget them?"

Somebody else spoke those words, and we all look round. It's Jared Robertson. His very pale blue eyes rest briefly on my face then skip on to Yunoo. "Sorry to interrupt. Can I borrow you? I have someone with a question about poltergeist beliefs in Central America."

Yunoo nods. "Absolutely."

I glance past Robertson, searching for Tamara, and see that she's in conversation with the woman in the emerald-green skirt. Actually, judging by their gestures, it looks like they're talking *about* the skirt. When Robertson and Yunoo have gone, I ask Rav, "What's with the Ghostbusters belt buckle?"

Rav shrugs. "I know his ex gave it to him. I guess at first maybe it was meant to be a bit of a joke. Knowingly semi-ironic. Maybe he thinks it suggests he doesn't take himself too seriously."

"Only he does."

"He certainly takes his work very seriously. So what did you make of his talk?"

I try to think how to sum it up. If I'd been hoping for answers about Holly, I'm not sure I got any. Though there was something that has stuck in my head. "When he said if you see something it's real for you, what do you think he meant? Hallucinations are *real*?"

"I think he meant there's no such thing as this external objective reality that is passively reproduced in our minds," Rav says.

I frown, trying to work my way through what he just said. "But—" And I stop because Yunoo's back.

He drapes a massive arm round Rav's shoulders. Smiling, he says, "Do *vous* remember me?"

Rav grins. Obviously, there's something going on here that I'm not getting.

"She said she wanted to know about poltergeist beliefs in Central America," Yunoo says, his voice maybe as quiet as he can make it, which isn't very. "But she actually wanted to ask about poltergeist *letters*."

"Do *vous* remember me…" Rav says to me. "It's a classic line from a letter purportedly written by a poltergeist called Donald, who claimed to be a French prince."

"Only his French was about as good as mine." Yunoo grins.

"It was also at about the level of the fifteen-year-old girl who was around when the poltergeist allegedly manifested. I'll leave you to draw your own conclusions."

"Rav! Yunoo! We've got to go!"

We all look round. Lana is grabbing a green tote bag

from under a chair in the front row. Alli is behind her, reaching for a denim jacket slung over the next seat.

"Go where?" Yunoo demands.

"It's *on*," Lana says, her tone again so urgent that it almost sounds angry. "*Tonight*. There's a meet. And *she's* going to be there."

"For sure?" Yunoo asks, his expression suddenly serious.

Alli nods. "I just saw the alert but it was sent, like, ten minutes ago. We have to hurry."

Lana slings her bag over her shoulder and pulls her long hair back over her shoulders. "Jared says we must go immediately."

Along with Yunoo and Rav, I look over at Robertson, who's still surrounded by people, and talking to a guy in black jeans. But I guess he registers our gaze in his peripheral vision because, without looking away from the other guy's face, he jabs a finger in the direction of the exit.

Alli says something I don't catch to Lana, who nods.

"Meeting point is Jacob's Ladder Playground," Alli calls to Rav and Yunoo. "Williamsburg. On Kent Avenue."

"You really sure she's gonna be there?" Yunoo says. "I had plans…"

"That ass-hat Eric cannot contain himself," Lana says. "If she isn't, his reputation will be shit."

"It will be *shot*?" Yunoo says helpfully.

She frowns. "*Shit*."

Lana and Alli hurry off down the central aisle.

Yunoo goes to retrieve a small grey backpack from under a chair in the front row.

"What's going on?" I ask Rav.

"I may have to explain on the way."

"…What?"

"You should come. I think you'll find it interesting."

"*What?* Who's the *she* you're talking about?"

"Rav. Seriously, man." Yunoo is waiting, one eye on Robertson.

I don't move. Rav says, "Hold on." He dashes off to Tamara, says something in her ear. She looks round at me, her expression thoughtful. I know they're talking about me, and now I definitely do mind. She leaves the woman in green and comes over.

"I have to get home to cook the bamia. But I've heard of these people. If I was you, I'd go."

"But—"

"Rav, I'm leaving…" This is Yunoo.

"You don't have to trust him," Tamara says, taking my hand and jerking her head towards Rav. "But trust me."

"I should go?"

"You should go," she insists. "Knowledge is power, right? And this could definitely be an opportunity for knowledge. Call me later. Or in the morning. I wanna hear about it. Go."

11

The pavement's slick with rain, and there's no tread whatsoever on the flat soles of my sandals, so I have to walk carefully, trying not to slip. Yunoo and Rav are already at the door of the cab that they just hailed.

As I reach it, I notice something out of the corner of my eye. Just past a huddle of people outside the library. A flash of scarlet hair.

I tense. She's moving quickly, her neck bent. Her thin skirt is clinging to her legs. The girl I met outside the institute, I'm sure of it. She has to have been at the talk. How did I miss her? She must have been among the crowd at the back.

"Mia!"

Rav's at the open door, waving me over.

I want to go after the girl, talk to her again, see if I there's anything I can do – but I have no real choice but to get in beside Rav. When I do, something strikes me. "They didn't wait to share a cab?"

"Lana and Alli?" he says. "They'll be on their bike."

"Their *bike*?"

We pull out into heavy traffic.

"Lana and I shared this apartment with another girl," he says. "After I moved out and the girl went back to Canada, Alli moved in. She brought this tandem with her from home. Apparently she and her dad used to ride it."

Yunoo is gripping his phone. He brings up a map app.

"So what's happening?" I ask Rav, feeling slightly nervous now.

"OK. There's a local group called Manhattan Manes." He pronounces it '*Man-ess*'. "Manes is what Ancient Romans called the spirits of the dead." The cab swings left. Rav presses a palm against the driver's seat, to stop himself falling against me. "About four years ago, a couple of guys from Bushwick started up Manhattan Manes."

"Eric's really the ringleader," Yunoo puts in.

"Right," Rav says. "So they organize pop-up ghost hunts. At least that's how they bill them. You pay to subscribe to a closed list. When they have an event, they send an alert. It's always really short notice. There'll be a place to meet in, like, thirty minutes. If you turn up, you're in – and they take you on to wherever the hunt site is. If you're not there on time, you miss out."

Anxiety makes my stomach tighten. "A *ghost hunt*?"

He nods.

I swallow, trying to get a grip on my nerves. "I thought Jared Robertson just said there's no way to detect a ghost."

"He said there's no such thing as a ghost-detecting *machine*."

"And he doesn't believe in ghosts."

"He said he has no proof," Yunoo says.

"We're actually going on a ghost hunt?"

Rav nods. Obviously he can see I'm not wildly happy about the idea.

"What did you say to Tamara?" I ask him. "Why did she come over and say I should go?"

"She just told me she couldn't make it. But she thought you should come."

I stare ahead, through the windscreen, not actually seeing anything.

"You don't believe in ghosts, so there's nothing to worry about – right? Mia?"

Yunoo leans forward. "You'd better take East Houston and the FDR," he calls to the driver, eyes on his phone.

Tamara told me to go. She said to trust her. But I'm struggling to understand why she would think this is something I should do. Rav's study, even the talk – OK. But *this*?

"Look, if you really don't wanna go, we can drop you by transport," Rav says.

Yunoo flashes him a look. "Of course – but after we've been dropped."

"I promise you it'll be interesting," Rav says. "Group psychology, suggestion, the power of charisma – I expect it'll all be on show."

"Who's charismatic?" I ask. "Eric?"

"No, there's a girl," Rav says. "She's seventeen. From Flatbush. Her name's Regan Martin. She doesn't call herself a medium but a lot of people do."

Yunoo nods. "Generally we pay little attention to so-called mediums. But Lana's seen Regan in action once before. She's convinced that Regan's really worth checking out."

"And she's convinced Jared," Rav says. "Possibly because one of Lana's most irritating traits is being often right."

"So why isn't Jared coming?"

"He publicly disses ghost hunts," Yunoo says. "In his position, it's not the kinda thing he can easily go to. For us, it's different."

Rav doesn't exactly look at me – we're too squashed together – but he glances round briefly. "So you think this could be interesting?"

What do I say? The main reason I told Rav that I don't believe in ghosts is because, if I said I *do*, he'd no doubt have asked me why, and if I'd had any kinds of ghost experiences. Which I wouldn't have been able to answer.

My head still full of what they just said about Regan

Martin, I find myself thinking about what the red-haired girl told me about a spiritualist who claimed to speak to her sister.

"When people say this girl's a medium, they actually think she can communicate with spirits?" I ask quietly.

Yunoo says, "We don't know exactly what's going on. But, if it's hard to explain, it's interesting for us. Anomalous incidents are what we live on." There's a thrum of excitement in his voice. "Like Rav said, for non-believers it's really interesting cos you also get an insight into the psychology of people who do believe."

The cab swerves, and we're up on the Williamsburg Bridge. Little lights sparkle all along the suspension cables. I try to peer out at the river but all I can see are those flickering lights.

Yunoo's looking again at his phone. "There may be a little leeway on the time," he says hopefully. "There's no subway station near the meet point. Only buses. And the South Williamsburg ferry terminal."

When we're finally over the river, we pass one, two, three, four streets running south. The one-way system means we can't take any of them. At last the taxi takes a right. We cross a junction and make another right. In the near-distance, the downtown skyscrapers are dense columns of glitter.

"Almost there," Rav says. "What do you wanna do?"

The cab slows and stops, and before I can change my mind I say quietly: "I'll come."

Yunoo pulls a note from his phone case, hands it over and we get out. My legs are a little shaky but I've made my choice. If Regan Martin really is a medium, I want to see what she does.

Right now, we're by a long, empty playground with apartment blocks on three sides. Over the road there's a high chain-link fence. On the other side is what looks to be a wide strip of wasteland along the bank of the river.

"Where are they?" Rav says, peering around.

I shiver. Though the air's warm, the breeze is strong, and my clothes are still damp from the rain. There's a dank smell – stale water and rot. The only sounds are of invisible traffic behind the tower blocks and muffled clunking noises from the direction of the river.

Rav's phone buzzes with an incoming message. "Lana. They're at the naval yard."

"They're inside already?" Yunoo asks urgently.

Rav shakes his head. "But we might have to run."

12

We jog together, following the line of the chain-link fence. After a few minutes, we come to a warehouse, set on the street and locked up with a huge rusting chain. I glimpse a peeling yellow sign in Hebrew plastered to a window. Two figures appear ahead, out of the shadows, coming from the other direction. As we get closer, I realize that they're Orthodox Jews, the man with long ringlets, the woman in heavy make-up and a loose black dress, her head covered with a felt hat. They glance blankly at us as we jog past.

Then Yunoo stops. We've reached a wide gate in the fence. Its crossbars mirror the stripes of the Union Jack flag. He grabs it and shakes.

"Locked," I say, noticing a heavy padlock on a chain at the base.

Through the gate, I can see a vague path through scrub and rundown buildings – old warehouses by the look of

117

them, and a rickety shed on a high tower. I guess it was once the cab for a fixed crane.

Rav looks uncertainly at Yunoo, who says to him, "They must have gone in already. We'll have to go over."

"It's gotta be twelve feet," Rav says.

"You think they climbed it?" I ask.

"They'd have got hold of a key somehow, and locked up after themselves," Yunoo says. "That's the way they work. No damage. No sign that they've been there. It's like a thing with them." He crouches and interweaves his fingers, palms up, to make a platform. "Who's first?"

Rav looks at me.

Scaling a twelve-foot fence. Breaking into the Brooklyn Navy Yard. If anyone sees us, and calls the police, I could be deported. And for what? A *ghost hunt*.

Yet I'm surveying the gate, trying to work out how best to climb it. Some part of me does want to be here. I look around for CCTV. "What if we're on camera?"

"I seriously doubt anyone's watching live," Yunoo says. "And, if someone does see us on video later, how would they know who we are? Come on."

I take a deep breath and plant my right foot on Yunoo's palms. One hand gripping his shoulder, I'm hoisted as high as he can carry me. The hexagonal gaps in the wire are just big enough for me to get a toehold. When I get to the top, I don't look down. I focus completely on the position of my body. I swing my right leg over, then the left and, very

118

carefully, I start my descent. When I'm halfway down, the gate shudders. Rav's coming up the other side.

After jumping the last metre or so, I flex my fingers, which are sore. A minute later, Rav's beside me. Then there's a thud. Yunoo.

I can't see any security guards around. Or guard dogs. Just rubbish – crumpled paper bags, mostly – blowing over the weeds. And an abandoned car, minus wheels, its windscreen splattered with blue paint. There's a loud creak from the shed up on the tower. Its door just swung open and now it's rattling in the wind.

"I don't see them," Rav says.

"I've done surveys here before, remember?" Yunoo says, setting off diagonally to the left. "I've got a pretty good idea where they'll be."

"Where?" I ask.

"There's a building in here with a reputation," Rav says grimly.

"What kind of reputation?"

"It doesn't matter right now," he says. Which isn't remotely a satisfactory answer, but I don't push it. Partly because I'm afraid of what he might say.

"Just up here." Yunoo points, and we take a gravel path in between two low warehouses. Their windows have mostly been smashed. Strewn over the weedy ground are discoloured wooden planks sprouting rusty nails. From pallets, maybe, that were left to disintegrate and rot.

Yunoo stops suddenly, waving at us to do the same. I can hear hushed voices up ahead. There's a white flash. Then another. Phone torches, I guess.

Yunoo nods, and we set off again, walking faster. Then I see them properly: a line of phones snaking towards a rectangular block of a building. It's much bigger than any we've encountered out here so far. Red brick. Four storeys. Bars on the windows. Undecipherable graffiti on the walls. Through a window on the third storey, I see a light moving.

Rav's phone starts buzzing. "Yeah?" he says quietly. "OK." He slips it back into his pocket. "Lana and Alli are already inside. Regan's here."

*

As we walk in, I'm apprehensive, obviously. But with all these other people around, most of them chattering to each other, my nerves actually start to subside.

The air is heavy with metallic-tasting dust. After my eyes adjust to the dim light given off by a scattering of LED lanterns, I realize that we're in a huge central atrium that soars all the way to the roof.

To my left is a metal spiral staircase. It leads up to gangways that run along the inside perimeter of the first storey, providing access to a series of doors. This layout of metal doors, linked via gangways that are accessed by a spiral staircase, is repeated on each level. It looks like we're inside an old prison. The pale green paint on the walls is peeling badly, I notice. Maybe what I'm tasting is old paint.

I take a step, and something crunches under my sandal. Quickly, I dig my phone from my bag and activate the torch. The floor is of pockmarked concrete. It's strewn with broken glass and rusty nails and also – less predictably – red-and-yellow paper lanterns, dirty and torn. I must have just stepped on a lantern.

Rav's over by the wall, bending over something. As I get close, I realize it's a battered blue icebox. He kicks off the lid, sending it clattering to the concrete. A couple of empty cans bob in dirty yellow water.

"Beerlao," Yunoo observes, joining us. "Someone's had a party in here."

Rav frowns. "I'm not sure I'd want to party in an abandoned hospital."

"Hospital?" I ask.

"Not just any hospital," says another voice, making us all turn.

A thin guy with short black hair is walking past, lugging a black case. He takes it over to a folding table just past the staircase.

"Eric?" I whisper.

"Jayden, his partner in crime," Yunoo whispers back.

"What kind of hospital?" I ask, feeling uneasy. "For quarantine?" All those doors, and the peeling paint, and the broken padlocks… It reminds me more than a little of the VR correctional centre.

Rav calls suddenly, "Lana! Alli!"

I look up, and there they are, over past the table. Alli raises her hand in a wave of recognition. They come over, Lana's spike heels wobbling as she picks her way through the rubbish.

"Hey!" Alli says brightly when she sees me. Judging by the tight expression on Lana's face, I guess she's not happy that I'm here. She looks like she's about to openly complain to Rav, but then a horn – like a car horn – makes us all freeze.

Into the echoing silence a woman shouts: "Everyone, let me have your attention!"

There must be forty people now in the atrium, and I can't immediately work out who just spoke. But the phone lights begin to converge on a short woman with a shaved head and a sleeve of tattoos on her right arm.

"Who's she?" I ask Rav, my ears still ringing.

"That's Bella. Their operations director."

"What a location, right?" Bella calls. "We're just finishing the set-up. When everything's ready, I'll sound the horn again. Until then, please continue exploring. But watch your step."

Someone near us whoops.

Yunoo says to Lana, "So you've seen Regan?"

She nods. Lana takes his arm, and, with Alli, they move away a few steps and start talking quietly. Maybe they don't want me to hear. Which is understandable. I'm not part of their group. I turn to Rav. "*Why* did you think I should come?"

"Hot. Relaxed. Interesting. That's what you said you wanted your summer to be, right? Surely this counts as interesting?" He smiles but there's a slight edge to it. When I don't return it, his own smile fades. "Look, I also think that the reasons why so many people believe in ghosts and what traits or environmental conditions contribute to ghost reports is desperately understudied. You're gonna be studying psychology. I would like to see more people get into this field—"

"*Clear the floor!*"

The yell came from somewhere above us. My head jerks up. I can't see anyone. Only the grille of the gangway above us.

The same voice – a man's – yells: "Back up against the walls *now*!"

Rav and I are already fairly close to the wall but we stumble against it, my heart racing again. Everyone else scatters outwards, too, making me feel almost like we're shockwaves from a bomb that is yet to explode...

And then it does. Something drops and smashes to the ground with a crashing *clang*. Dust billows up, making me cough.

A woman yells: "What the fuck?"

There's a laugh, from up high, out of the cloud of dust, and darkness.

Waving his arm, to try to clear the air in front of his face, Rav aims his phone at the drop zone. Most other people have the same idea. The beams illuminate a mess of crumpled metal, splintered wood and leather.

Dizziness sweeps through my brain. I stare. And I stare.

Cracked brown leather covers the back and seat pads. There's a leather mouthpiece. An unbuckled ankle strap trails into dust. It's a restraint chair from another era.

"What kind of hospital?" I whisper, because I have to hear someone say it.

"It was a psychiatric hospital," Rav says and my body sags.

"It's not been used for decades," he says. "I didn't realize they even had any old kit left in here… Mia? Mia, did something hit you?"

Not literally, I think.

Very slowly, I shake my head.

13

I remember very clearly the first time I heard the word 'psychosis'. I was eleven years old, and it was Mum who explained it to me.

We were walking, just the two of us, round Redmires Dam. It must have been early spring. The wind was gusting and I was wearing boots.

"There's something I want to talk to you about," she said. "My voices."

Ever since I can remember, Mum has heard voices. There are about six that she hears regularly. Some are helpful. If she's at the shops, they might remind her to buy something she'd have forgotten otherwise. There's one that often tells her that she's a good person. A couple aren't helpful, at least not from my point of view, or Dad's, but they're not mean to her.

"I just—" She hesitated. "Other people – kids at school

– they might say things. And I don't want you to worry about me. I want you to know that I've talked to Dr Lee." Dr Lee was our GP. "For some people who hear voices, it's to do with an illness. It's a psychosis, and they lose touch with what's real, which can make life really difficult. I don't have a psychotic disorder. I don't have schizophrenia. I just want you to know that. In case people say things."

"But whose voices are they?" I asked her.

She stopped walking and pulled her long hair from her face. Looking at me intently, she said: "I think of them as my guardian angels. And who's to tell me that they're not?"

This type of voice-hearing isn't necessarily a problem, then – unless you're a kid, and your mum's at the school gates, talking to no one. Except for when she's working, she usually wears her hair down. When she's talking while she's walking along the street, or in a shop, I imagine most people assume she's wearing a wireless earpiece and she's on the phone. But the other mums worked out that wasn't what was happening, and so did the kids. And, though I don't think the voices are unpleasant about her, they have led her to believe things that aren't true.

The reason she moved out, I learned later, was because one of them insisted that Dad didn't love her the way he should. It told her that she should find someone new, move on. She did move to her own two-bedroom flat – where I've stayed almost every other weekend, and on Monday and Tuesday nights. But so far, anyway, she hasn't found anyone new. And Dad, I know, is still sad about what happened. One afternoon, just a few years ago, I came home from school and found him in tears. "She's convinced I don't love her," he said to me. "But *that isn't true*."

*

"...to tell you..."

A woman – Bella, I think – is shouting somewhere over the other side of the atrium. I concentrate hard, to try to bring my mind back into focus, to the hospital.

"...responsible has been escorted out. Now we're going to get on with our evening!"

There are a few coughs, and a subdued "*Yeah*" from over by the spiral staircase.

I take a deep breath.

Mum has never been in a psychiatric hospital. She's never been anywhere close in time or place to a chair like this. But I can't help thinking: in the past, in less enlightened times, if she'd been in New York, might she have been taken here? Held in one of these cells?

The thought makes me feel like I'm sinking. As though I'm underwater, I hear Bella's voice, echoey and distorted: "We are so lucky tonight to be joined by one of the most talented mediums this city has ever known! Before I ask her to come forward, I need agreement that we will give her the mental space to do her thing. Which means quiet. And respect. Agreed?"

A few more *Yeah*s echo round the room.

I can't get thoughts of Mum out of my mind, and I'm not sure I can hold my own weight any longer. I squat. Close my eyes so I can't see that broken chair. When a hand falls flat and firm on my back, I almost fall forward. Trembling, I look up.

It's Yunoo. "Hey. You OK?"

I lick my dry lips. Nod.

Bella is still talking. "We have the equipment ready. But first we want to go pure. Acoustic. *Old school*. Lovers and fighters, it is my incredible honour to introduce Regan Martin!"

Whoops ring out.

"Sure?" Yunoo's voice is close to my ear this time. He's squatted down beside me.

"I just felt a little queasy... I think it's the smell."

He sniffs a few times. "Could be lead paint. My best advice is to try not to breathe. At least not too much."

He smiles, and the warmth of it gets through to me. I take a shallow breath. Nod. Feel a little better. He holds out a massive hand to help me up, and I take it.

When I'm standing again, I realize people are moving to congregate at the bottom of the staircase.

"Good," Yunoo says, watching them. "Maybe now at last we'll cut to the chase."

Trying my best to avoid looking at the chair, I search out Rav. And I spot him, in the mix of people, in conversation with a couple of girls. I guess, given what he does at the institute and with the Spontaneous Cases Committee, he probably knows quite a few of the people here.

Then, as the crowd shifts, I make out a slender girl in a black sundress at the foot of the steps. Her brown hair is very long, and cut with a short fringe. Her eyes are shut. She's pressing her palms together, her fingers aimed at the ground. This has to be Regan Martin.

"Do *you* think ghosts exist?" I whisper to Yunoo.

He looks down at me with a smile but it's an awkward one. "Even if we could agree on a definition, that's not exactly a polite question for a parapsychologist. Depending on the audience for your answer, you're damned if you do and damned if you don't."

"*I'm* the audience," I say, feeling a little frustrated, because no one ever seems to give a straight answer. "Only me."

I focus on Yunoo's face. I'm still waiting for him to respond.

Then to himself, more than to me, he says: "What *is* she doing?"

*

"Follow but don't touch her!"

Bella's holding her arm in the air, to indicate to everyone gathered behind where Regan is, I guess.

"Keep together now!" she shouts. "Watch your step!"

She flicks on a torch and its powerful beam jerks up the staircase.

"What was she doing?" I ask Yunoo.

"She was holding her face like she was in pain… Then she just marched for the steps."

When we reach the staircase, I concentrate on carefully placing my feet.

At the top of the first spiral, we walk out on to the gangway. Two people can just about fit side by side, so we're forced into pairs. The railing's at about my waist height, with vertical bars beneath. I can't help feeling glad that I'm next to the wall – even though that puts me by the doors. They all seem to be shut, with busted padlocks. Every time I reach one, my pulse quickens, like I'm expecting something to jump out. But nothing moves … apart from us, squashed up together, our feet crunching curls of old paint.

I turn to Yunoo, and realize he isn't beside me any more. The line next to me seems to be moving a little faster. He must be just up ahead.

Bella's voice comes back along the lines: "Quiet, please!" And we all come to a sudden stop. "We're going to rotate you. But Regan needs silence."

I feel definitely uneasy, hemmed in by people I can barely see. I listen hard, trying to catch what's happening at the front.

Someone – Regan? – is whispering.

I glance past the guy to my right, into shadows.

Somewhere on the floor below is the restraint chair. I find myself imagining the people who might have been strapped into it. They have yellow skin. Starved bodies. Terrified eyes.

Imagined faces, I tell myself.

From the front of the crowd, a word makes it back. *Fire*. The adrenalin alarm goes off inside me. But no one seems to be panicking, or trying to fight their way back. Perhaps it wasn't 'Fire' after all.

I don't know if it's the blood-taste of the old paint and the squeeze of all these people, or my mental images of those faces, but I'm feeling nauseous again. A roll of it suddenly unfurls through my stomach. I take a stumbling step backwards, and it's like I'm falling through sand. The slightest touch, and the people somehow find space to part, until I'm right at the back, near the spiral staircase.

I'm sweating and I'm breathing fast, and I have to keep swallowing. But the surging in my stomach has eased. I can't hear Regan, or see Rav or Yunoo, Alli or Lana. The air is so thick here, it feels hard to breathe. I'm by the wall. My fingertips brush across the rough, uneven surface, and hit metal. A door – to a cell that used to hold a human being. I find myself pushing. When it swings silently inwards, I hold my breath.

*

Though my feet move, I have the odd sense that I'm not in control. As they walk me inside, something cool touches my cheeks. I stiffen but it's just a breeze. Using my phone torch, I see that the far wall of the narrow room holds a barred window, its glass long gone. A cloud must shift because moonlight suddenly drifts in. It snags on smashed shards of mirror on the concrete floor.

Scanning the bare walls, I take in a small once-white ceramic sink, stained and cracked. In the wall above it are four holes, which must have held the fixings for the mirror.

My heart jumps.

In the far corner, away from the window, is a rusting single bedframe. Most of its sagging, blackened springs are broken, corkscrewing to the floor. Yellow skin.

No. That wasn't real. But fear stabs through me. Something's moving. My head twists.

A black shape. Something's in my hair. I grasp at it, shake it. Someone's in here. There's something in the room with me.

Where?

A metal tang makes my tongue curl. I smell burning and I cough. The air stinks. Like scorched fabric. I spin, my eyes pulled to the darkness behind the door.

Now something's brushing my ankle. I jump back, my sandals slapping on the concrete. Quickly I bend down to swat at it.

An insect. No, *insects*.

I can feel them scuttling over my feet, under the straps of my sandals, up my trouser legs, on my shins. I can even hear the tiny scratching of their legs on my skin. My heart thumping, I jump on the spot, trying to shake them off. My hand leaps to my stomach. There's something in my belly button.

I'm too scared to shout out. My breathing ragged, my fingers frantic on my stomach, I stumble out of the room. Blindly, I take the metal steps down to the atrium as fast as I can, every slip of my sandals sparking fresh panic through me.

I run unsteadily, holding the wavering light in front of me. My left foot skids on something. I realize it's the ankle strap from the chair. Nausea rises again, right to the back of my throat, but I keep going – and I'm through the door, hurtling into a rough patch of moonlight.

My cheeks are wet. I'm crying, I realize.

The rancid breeze from the river makes me dry-heave. My breathing's coming so fast, I feel dizzy. Then I register that I can't feel the insects any more. Shakily I aim the torch at my feet. They're filthy but there are no bugs. I lift each trouser leg in turn, as high as they'll go.

Nothing.

My heart jittery, I grip the bottom of my vest and raise it. I touch the skin around my navel. It looks undamaged. I was afraid – I was convinced – something had burrowed in.

I shiver. I remember the smell of burning and I spin round. I can't see any flames in the windows. Or smoke. Through the first-floor windows, I can make out the flash of phone torches. But they're moving steadily, purposefully.

No fire. The smell of burning wasn't real. Were the insects real?

I blink out over the shifting black river, towards the downtown skyscrapers. Lights are still on. Traders over on Wall Street are still working. The regular world is still going about its business.

And I want to be back in it.

*

I don't even think about trying to message Rav. I just need to get out. I'm prepared to have to scale the gate again, but, when I get there, I find the padlock hanging open. Then I remember that whoever pushed the restraint chair over the gangway was removed from the event – by someone who didn't secure the lock properly afterwards, I guess.

The gate's heavy. I have to shove it hard to open up a gap big enough for me to squeeze through. As I turn to close it, I notice a figure jogging towards me along the path between the warehouses. It stops for a moment near the derelict crane tower. Scans the wasteland.

"*Mia?*"

Rav.

I take a breath. It sounds like a gasp. I raise my arm and wave stiffly until he sees me.

He jogs over. Twists his body through the gap in the gate. He's looking concerned. "Hey. Lana saw you run out of the hospital. What happened?"

My hands still trembling, I hook my hair behind my ears. "I just … had enough. You should go back in."

"What happened?"

"*Nothing.*"

I let my breath go. Folding my arms tight across my chest, I glance back along the street. It seems like forever since I saw that couple, in their Orthodox Jewish dress… If they were actually there. But they were. They *were*. And the insects? I squint down at my dirty feet.

Rav says, "Mia, look, I think of Sadie as kinda like family. So, by extension, that makes you kinda like family, too. And I'm the one who brought you here."

I look up at him. But really what can he say, or do? I don't even know what happened.

"What made you run out?"

I don't answer.

"I'm going to … go home," I say as steadily as I can. "But you should definitely go back in."

"I don't need to go back in. Lana and the others can report to Jared."

I blink, and look up. I don't see stars. Just the flashing lights of planes, and a helicopter sweeping over the river, heading north. My gaze on the sky, I say, "I felt like insects were crawling all over me. But I don't think they were."

"…OK."

I shake my head. *Not OK.*

"I went into one of the cells. Something touched me. There was something in there."

Tears again. They roll down my cheeks. I hurriedly wipe them away.

"Why did you go into the room?" he asks.

I don't answer.

"When you felt the insects on your skin, it was what – like a tickling sensation?"

I nod.

"And in that room, what you experienced, the feeling of presence – was it anything like it was in the lab?"

"Something was *in there*." I rub at my cheeks. And I get that sense again of not being sure that I can bear my own weight. So I sit down heavily on the kerb, knees bent, my feet in the gutter, which is still wet and sludgy from the rain. Rav sits down beside me, mirroring my position.

I have a choice. Tell him. Don't tell him.

Don't tell is the rule. But, like Tamara said, he has knowledge of these things. And, after what happened in the hospital, I'm *scared*. If I don't say something now, when will I?

"Two things," I say, feeling both exhausted, and electric. "When I told you I don't believe in ghosts, I don't think that's actually true. I don't know—"

I stop. He waits. I'm so knotted up inside, I'm not sure it's going to come out. But I manage to say, "My best friend died when we were thirteen. I think I've seen her. And heard her."

"You mean…?"

"Her ghost? I don't know." I press my palms over my eyes.

"Seen her where?" he asks quietly.

I look not at his face but at his long legs. And his arms, which are loosely hugging his knees.

"The first time was a few months after she died, and I had to go back into an old classroom, to get something for my history teacher. It was empty. Then I *saw* Holly on a chair in the corner. Watching me."

"OK," he says.

"Maybe a year later, the middle of the night, I was asleep, dreaming about her. We were running, I don't know where, then suddenly she pushed me. When I woke up I was half way across the floor and I heard her voice right behind me saying, 'You can't lose me.' I heard *her voice. She* pushed me out of bed. I know she did." I fall silent.

"Any other occasions?" he prompts.

"I was fifteen. Getting ready for a party. I couldn't find anything to wear. I looked bad in everything. I was looking in the mirror and suddenly she was there, standing right behind me, with this look on her face that said yeah, everything about me was *wrong*."

Rav doesn't say anything. So I keep talking.

"Another time, it was two weeks after my sixteenth birthday. A boy in my class asked if I wanted to go to a club called the Leadmill because a friend of his was playing guitar in a band. But, when we got there, a group from the sixth form was in there and he hardly spoke to me. I pretended I needed to go the toilet – and she was there, by the sinks, just looking at me."

I swallow. "Last year I was on my own at home. I went downstairs to make a sandwich. When I came out of the kitchen, I heard stuff moving upstairs. Things being scraped across the floor. Drawers banging. It went on for ages… In the end, I made myself go up. As soon as I got to my room, the sounds stopped. I went in and the only thing that was out of place was one drawer. I kept my swimming stuff in it. It was open. I went to shut it –" I take a deep breath – "and there was sand on my swimming costume."

"Sand?"

I nod. "It meant something – between us."

"You think she somehow put it there?"

I nod again.

"And when you went back to the drawer later, the next day?"

"I haven't opened it since then."

"What, ever?" He sounds surprised.

"I told Dad I'd forgotten to bring my swim bag back from the pool and it wasn't in lost property. He bought me new stuff."

Rav's silent. I guess he's thinking about what to say. I listen to his breathing and all the other faraway sounds of the city.

"A few months after that, I went to Manchester Uni for an open day," I tell him. "She was in an empty lecture theatre, sitting on a chair."

He frowns. "You think it was Holly's ghost?"

"I don't know if it's her *ghost*, or some kind of energy, spirit – I don't know – and the way I experience it is by seeing her. Hearing her voice. Or—" I stop.

"Or?" he says after a moment.

I was thinking about Mum and her voices. I don't tell random people about Mum, either. But I've just told him about Holly. My biggest secret. The locked box in my mind has already been opened. "Has Sadie said anything to you about Mum?"

I look round at his face. There's a smear of dirt on his right cheek, green paint flecks in his hair. He's watching me closely. "I'm gonna have to say, about what?"

I prepare myself. "Her voices?"

The slightest frown crosses his face. He shakes his head.

"She's heard them since she was fourteen. She says they help her."

"OK," he says carefully.

"She calls them her guardian angels. She told me once she thinks they might even be the voices of spirits."

He nods slowly. "We had a guest lecturer give a talk last year on hearing voices. There are people who hear them and they welcome them."

"Yeah. But she *hears voices*. So – what? – she's *actually* hearing dead people, or she's—" I stop. I'm thinking of the insects. Of what I saw and felt.

"I'm just a student, right?" Rav says. "But I don't think it's as a black and white as she's hearing the voices of dead people or she's having auditory hallucinations out of nowhere."

I stare at him. "What else can it be?"

"Is that what you're worried about? Seeing Holly. Feeling insects on your skin and someone in that room with you? You're worried that either it's real or none of it's real – and, if none of it's real, then you're hallucinating … and that's not necessarily less scary than ghosts existing?"

I don't answer. My heart thuds so hard I feel my pulse in my throat. At last I nod.

He fixes his gaze on me. "Mia, that hospital – there's a reason it's got a reputation for being haunted. It's a bit like in the lab. Only it's not infrasound."

He shifts his position so he's angled towards me.

"Jared pioneered the work on this. He surveyed the hospital a few years ago. Yunoo mentioned he'd been here before? He was on the team. The exterior is brick but some of the rock that was used to build the walls is magnetic. Like Jared said in his talk, electromagnetic fields don't indicate the presence of a ghost. But they can make people *feel* like there's a ghost with them. For some people, exposure to certain EMFs induce feelings of presence and even hallucinations."

I stare at him, trying to work through what he's saying.

"Remember your lab results? You're, like, the most infrasound-sensitive subject we've ever had. Maybe it's the same with EMF. That's what made you feel like there were insects on your skin, and like someone or something was in that room with you."

My mouth is so dry. No way can I speak.

"I should have told you before we went in. But I didn't imagine you'd have that kind of reaction." He pauses. "We suspect that Regan's also unusually sensitive to certain environmental signals, and that's why she has these medium-like experiences. It's not that she's *lying*. She just doesn't understand what's actually happening. Jared wants to know more about her because, if she is hypersensitive to environmental signals associated with paranormal-type experiences, she's interesting. And maybe useful."

I've been focusing so hard on his face, I think I've forgotten to blink. My eyes are stinging. I swallow. "What about Holly?" I whisper.

"I don't know." He shakes his head. "I can suggest things… I don't *know*."

"What things?"

"There's no way I can tell you for sure."

"Maybe she really is haunting me."

"…I don't know."

He glances over his shoulder. Another helicopter is sweeping low over the wasteland by the river. It's passing over the warehouses close to the hospital.

I sit up straight to get a better look. "You think someone's reported seeing people in there?"

Rav pulls his phone from his pocket, swipes and taps. I hear ringing at the other end. It stops. "Yunoo, there's a helicopter out here... Yeah, I'm with her. OK." He ends the call.

"You really think it could be magnetic rock that made me feel all those things in there?" I ask him.

He looks up from his phone. At that moment, his dark eyes seem infinitely readable. "In *there* – yeah. A hundred per cent I do."

14

When Rav and I get home from the hospital, Sadie is still out.

My phone has been on silent since the talk in the library, and it's only when I now check it in the kitchen that I see I've missed a string of messages.

The first was from Sadie, telling me that she was going on after the gallery event for drinks with a few friends.

Then there was one from Mum:

What you doing in the library? xx

And another, ten minutes later:

Mia, come out of the books and talk to me! xxx

An hour after that:

> Everything OK?? xxxxx

Followed by a missed call from her. And then a text from Sadie:

> Mia, can you call your mum? She's worried xx

"Everything OK?"

While I've been checking messages, Marlowe rubbing himself up against my leg, Rav's also been on his phone. Now he's leaning against the worktop by the sink, looking at me.

"Just Mum. I had my phone on silent."

"I guess it was tough," he says, "growing up with your mom hearing voices."

After a moment, I nod. "She told me not to worry about her. But I did worry that she'd be taken away, even though she was sure she wasn't ill. I thought some doctor would decide she needed sectioning."

"Did other kids at school know she heard voices?"

I feel my expression morph into disbelief. "Right, cos kids are *so* slow to pick up when people are different?" I realize I sounded harsh. Take a breath. "Sorry... I know she tried not to talk back when she was around school but she couldn't always help it."

He shakes his head. "No, I'm sorry... I didn't mean to pry."

He rakes a hand back through his hair. Yawns. He looks totally exhausted. It isn't that late but I guess he hardly had any sleep last night. And I feel like I could just collapse.

"I might just send some messages and go to bed," I tell him.

He meets my gaze. "I think sleep is definitely a good idea right now. But we can talk more about the hospital, and your friend, tomorrow if you want to."

I nod. "OK."

He gives me a tired, but I think meant to be reassuring, smile and heads off into the corridor. A few minutes later, I hear the electric shower spurt into life.

I think for a while about what to tell Mum. Finally, I send:

> Sorry!! Went to a talk and forgot to take phone off silent. All good. Love you xxx

There's a kind of pang in my chest when I write *Love you*. Now I'm older, I truly understand that she's happy about her voices, and anyway there's no such thing as *normal*, and no one will take her anywhere. But it took me a while to get to this point.

The message shows up as 'Delivered', but it doesn't shift to 'Read'. Maybe she's gone to sleep.

After Rav finishes up in the bathroom, and I hear the door to the studio click shut, I go into the steamy bathroom and take a long, too-hot shower. In my bedroom, I pull on the loose jersey shorts and vest that I wear to sleep in, and do the one final thing that I know I have to do if I'm to have any chance of sleeping.

I lie on my side on the firm futon mattress, propped up on my elbow, the sheet pulled over me, against the AC. And I call Tamara.

It rings four times before she picks up. "Hey!"

"How's the bamia?" I ask her.

"Apart from burning the onion, so I set off the smoke alarm and had the woman upstairs banging the floor and had to start again, I think it's about acceptable." Pause. "How was your evening?"

I take this as a cue to launch into the question that I've realized I most want to ask her. "What did you say to Rav – after the talk, when they all said they had to go? He went to say something to you and you came over and said you thought I should go with him."

She doesn't answer right away. So I say, my chest tight, "You didn't tell him about Holly? I mean, you haven't told him?"

I'm not explaining things well. But it's hard to even get these words out.

"No," she says quickly. "I haven't told him anything about Holly!"

"So why did he go and talk to you?"

There's a pause before she says, "He came over and said

there was a Manhattan Manes event that he thought we might both be interested in. And I said I couldn't but I thought you should go."

I get the sense she's holding something back. "That's all?"

She sighs and a wave of adrenalin rushes through me. She *did* tell him?

"He said he was really glad I'd called to meet for drinks cos he'd thought that after I didn't call after Barcade I wasn't interested in seeing him again—" She stops.

As I comprehend what she's telling me, my anxiety, my indignation suddenly fade. "He wanted *you* to go with him... I was like a collateral invite."

She starts to protest: "No—"

"No," I interrupt her. "It's OK. That's *good*." I let myself fall back on the mattress, the phone still pressed to my ear.

"I wouldn't have told him anything about Holly. You know that, right? I thought you *should* go because I thought if you could see what a manufactured *show* these ghost hunts are it might help to convince you that ghosts aren't actually real."

"You've been on one before?"

"I may have watched a few on YouTube. My neighbour's kid's into them... It *was* a total joke, right?"

I blink. In my mind, I see the restraint chair smashing to the ground, feel the insects on my skin. I flick my eyelids open. Try to focus on the white wall. "I don't think there were any ghosts," I tell her.

"So, see…? You're glad you went, right?"

I think about the conversation with Rav on the pavement. I am glad I went but not for the reasons Tamara's thinking. I hate to feel like we're running along a different mental track, but I'm so tired now – almost too tired to talk, never mind explain.

"So sleep well," she says. "If I can get up early to help Mom, I could be free to meet some time in the morning. I'll call you. *Layla*, Mia."

I surprise myself by smiling. *Layla*. One of the first words in Arabic that she taught me. It means 'night'. When I once said *layla* to her as we parted ways after dinner, she grinned and told me I was totally misusing her native language.

"*Layla*," I tell her back.

15

The next day is one of those perfect summer days. Hot but not burning. The sky a bright, pure blue.

Tamara did call. We cycled together to Coney Island. She didn't bring up the ghost hunt right away. Instead, we talked about the Ecco! Theater's summer programme, about the famous professors at the Rhode Island School of Design, her puppeteer friends, about Burning Man – about Freja, even.

Over a lunch of hot dogs and thick chocolate milkshakes, I explained about Freja's plans for a weekend in Brighton in September to celebrate her eighteenth birthday. There'll be me, I told her, plus two other girls from school and her boyfriend in an Airbnb flat for a few nights.

"So it'll be fun," Tamara said brightly.

I squinted at my reflection in the mirrored lenses of her sunglasses.

"You *are* going?"

I frowned at my hot dog.

Tamara pushed her sunglasses up on her head. "This has got to stop, Mia. *This summer*. It *has* to stop."

She understood what I wasn't saying. That I know Holly won't want me to go.

Her black eyes narrowed even more. "She was your *friend*. I still don't get why she wouldn't want you to have fun… You haven't ever seen her in New York?"

I shook my head.

"So I'd love to say the answer is to stay here forever. But that's not the solution, right?"

"I guess not…"

Then I told her about last night, and what Rav said to me about the magnetic rock and even about hearing voices. I *was* glad I went, I told her.

After wasting coins in the arcade machines, we hit the rides. I'm not a huge fan of rollercoasters but I love the Wonder Wheel. It's a big old Ferris wheel that looks like it was put together by a geometrically-minded spider. As we reached the zenith, Tamara smiled at me. She spread her long arms out across the top of her seat. Behind her head, Manhattan was hazy with sunshine and distance.

"The fact is, our lives are pretty amazing," she said. And I had to grin back, not because her insistent enthusiasm was so infectious, but because I love her for it.

About five, I got a message from Rav:

> You coming home soon? No problem if not. Sadie planning a bbq. She's wondering how much tuna to buy.

I replied:

> Back soon

About five thirty, Tamara and I started back along Coney Island Avenue, and on and up through Flatbush, where we both got a drenching from a gushing fire hydrant. After we skirted the boundary of Prospect Park, she peeled away, one arm held high in farewell.

Now the sun has turned the buildings gold, and the temperature of the air seems to match that of my skin. It's giving me the strange and lovely sensation that my body is at one with the city.

After wheeling the bike to rest it against the low wall of Sadie's building, I pull my bag up over my head and peel my sodden top free from my belly. My denim shorts are still heavy with water.

"Guess number one: you fell in the East River."

The voice makes me jump.

It's Rav. He's sitting, shoulders hunched, on the bench in the paved area out front. But he's not alone, I quickly realize. Jared Robertson is beside him, in black jeans and a black T-shirt, his eyes concealed by wraparound sunglasses.

"Mia, hello," Jared says. "I'm sorry I didn't introduce

myself yesterday. I just came by to … um … talk something through with Rav."

"Hi," I say uncertainly.

The happy ease that I'd enjoyed most of the afternoon starts to fade.

"So not the East River?" Jared says.

"You'll have to guess again."

"There was a freak rainstorm and you happened to be right in it," Rav offers.

"Not even close."

"You went swimming," he says, "but you forgot your towel. And your swimsuit. And the fact that swimming in the McCarren Park lido in anything other than approved swimwear is prohibited."

Normally this kind of comment would make me smile. But there's something about Jared Robertson's presence that keeps my face straight. "Fire hydrant."

"They can be tough to avoid," Jared says, nodding.

"Actually it was impossible to resist," I tell him.

Rav smiles. "So you've had a good day?"

I nod. "Sadie home?"

He leans back against the wall. "She went back out for something she forgot for her cocktails. But listen, it gives me the chance to talk to you about something."

Of course, I immediately wonder what, but he still looks relaxed. And the atmosphere out here on the street is so positive, so energized. A couple of kids are shrieking happily. Chinese pop's playing from one of the row houses. The scent of a barbecue drifts over from further up the street.

At that moment, Jared feels for his jeans pocket and pulls out his phone. "I have to take this. Excuse me." He gets up and strides out on to the street.

I sit down beside Rav. "What did the others say about Regan? Is that why he's come to see you?" I glance at Jared, who has his back to us. He looks to be deep in conversation.

Rav turns to look at me. He looks tense now. He's rubbing the silver bracelet on his wrist. I feel my own body stiffen.

"I told you Jared took a team to survey the hospital a few years ago? They made a map of the magnetic hotspots, but they didn't publish the data. Yunoo was on that team, and he was the only person there last night who knows where they are. Lana – and Jared – were hoping Regan would feel like she had to do her thing in the areas where they'd had the highest EMF readings. But she didn't. Where you were – on the first floor, back near the staircase – that's where they recorded the strongest hotspot. She didn't get anything there at all."

"Near the staircase…? So it really could have been a magnetic field?"

"Causing what you felt in that room? Yeah."

I nod slowly. It's a little hard to accept but how I felt in the lab seemed pretty real, too. "That's good to know."

I move to get up but he says, "That wasn't what I wanted to talk to you about."

I relax my legs again. But I don't know if I'd call any other part of me relaxed now.

"Many times in public," he says, lowering his voice, "Jared's rejected the idea of *ghosts*, as in observable supernatural entities that could be said to exist outside the mind of the observer. But there is one location, a property he visited years ago, that still makes him wonder."

Rav pauses. I feel like the air is cooling right around us. I glance over towards Jared, who's now a little way down the street, still talking into his phone.

"Makes him wonder … what? Whether ghosts might actually exist?" A shiver rolls down my arms.

"He didn't get the chance to do a full investigation. And he's always wanted to go back. But the owner wouldn't permit it. Now the property's passed to a relative, and she's been in touch, and he thinks there's a possibility he'll be allowed back in. If he is, we'll go with him – me, Lana, Yunoo, Alli. But the new owner is insisting on having a medium on the team. Jared was hoping that Regan might be the right kind of medium. Only after last night it doesn't look like it."

"Wait – Jared Robertson believes ghosts might actually be real?"

"He's never ruled it out."

I think back over something Yunoo told me in the hospital. "But he doesn't think mediums really talk to the spirits of the dead? Right? So why not just take Regan anyway?"

"What he wants – what he needs – is someone who could reasonably present themselves to the owner as a medium, *and* who is highly sensitive to environmental signals that he has previously linked to ghost reports. We'd take in EMF meters. Infrasound detectors. Cameras. Everything. But say we record high infrasound in a room where there have been ghost reports. It would be useful to have corroborative physical testimony of anomalous physical sensations in that room. To link the science to the subjective experience. If we can. Because the null hypothesis for this study would be that there is no ghost present, right? So the new owner wants a medium, and Jared wants that person to be someone who is environmentally sensitive, and so who could be useful to the investigation. And someone he can trust. Now Regan is out…"

He's looking at me intently. Realization suddenly hits. "*Me?*"

"You're the most infrasound-sensitive person we've ever tested, and, going by what happened at the hospital, you're highly sensitive to magnetic fields, too."

My heart is racing now. "I'm not a medium!"

"Mia, there are people who see and hear things that are hard to explain. And you are one of them."

Suddenly I feel sick. "You told Jared what I told you about Holly?"

"No. *No.*"

"And *Mum*?"

"*No.* I didn't tell any of them any of that. I *wouldn't* tell them."

I rub my hands over my eyes. Let them drop back to my lap. "But the owner wants a medium. If you don't tell her what I told you, why would she even begin to believe that I am one?"

A look that I can't quite read comes into his eyes. Is it guilt?

"In her defence, she was there to work. For Jared."

Now I'm even more confused. "*What?*"

"Lana saw you," Rav explains. "She knew about your infrasound data. When you slipped to the back of the crowd, and you went into that hospital room, she followed you. She videoed what happened on her phone."

I feel the blood drain from my face.

"She was outside," he says. "Not in the room. On the walkway. Filming through the open door."

My voice so stiff it doesn't sound like mine, I say, "I didn't see her."

"It was dark. And she wouldn't have wanted you to see her."

I clasp my hands in my lap. "Maybe it was *her* I felt."

"But you said that was inside the room?"

I stare at him. "Have you seen this video?"

After a moment, he nods.

My mouth dry, I ask, "Who else?"

"Yunoo. Jared. Alli. That's all."

I raise my feet up to the bench seat, hug my knees to my chest. My blood is rushing. The thought of someone watching me while I was in there makes me feel so sick, and angry. "That was a total invasion of privacy."

"I know. And I'm sorry. I had no idea she was going to follow you, or film you. Seriously. *None*. Or I'd have stopped her."

"But she did," I say quietly. "And you've all watched it."

He looks uncomfortable. "I know. I really am sorry."

I'm feeling angry when I say: "And now – what? – Jared's asked you to talk to *me*?"

Rav takes a deep breath. "He asked if I thought you might consider it. I said you're going to be studying psychology at college, and you were interested in our research, and maybe you might."

"But given what you know – what I've told you – why would I want to go to some property that he thinks might *actually* be haunted?"

He's very still. There's another squeal from the street. And a hiss. It sounds like a jet from a water pistol.

"Can't you think of a reason why?" he asks.

The way he says it, it's clear that he can. And yeah, I guess I can think of one, too.

"Apologies. I had to take that call."

We both look round. Jared is pocketing his phone.

He flips his sunglasses up on top of his head and looks from Rav to me, and back to Rav.

"Rav has explained to you what's happened?"

I swallow. "You mean Rav's explained to me that Lana videoed me without my permission and showed you all? Then, yeah."

Jared nods slowly. "I do understand that you must feel really angry about that."

My chest burns. "Oh, you do! It's *understandable* that I'm angry?"

He blinks. "If it's any consolation, I know Lana feels very bad about it."

"But she *did* it!"

"Because she knows how important it is that we find someone with your kind of sensitivities," he says, his voice low. "Look, we all sit on spectrums for these things. No one's ever done a proper study but it wouldn't surprise me at all if mediumship springs from environmental sensitivity: some people are aware of things that the rest of us just don't feel. You fall into that category. We hoped Regan Martin did. But, judging by what happened in the hospital, she doesn't seem to be responsive to magnetic fields. And you do." He comes a little closer. "I came partly to talk to Rav but also because I hoped to meet you. There's a property. Has Rav already mentioned it?"

I don't say anything, so he goes on. "A private house. In Southampton. Long Island. Not that far from New

York." His forehead furrows. "Quite a few years ago now, an investigation that I was able to start there was cut short. I was barred from returning. But in all the years I've been surveying hauntings—" He stops. His pale eyes look troubled. "It's the one place I *have* to be sure about."

I swallow. My anger seems to have dissipated. Now I'm not sure what I feel. Cold inside. Worried. Unmoored. Like my world is shifting too fast, and I'm close to losing my way. "Sure that ghosts don't exist?" I whisper.

"Sure that I've done *everything* I can to investigate it. I've waited a long time to be allowed back in. Now I have the right team, and all the equipment that wasn't available back then. And I'm acquainted with someone who could – who *would* – be the ideal missing piece for the project. If I can get final clearance from the new owner, I'd really like you to join us. Obviously you don't have to give me an answer now. I just wanted to come here in person to ask you."

Despite the heat, goosebumps break out on my bare legs. "What's so special about *this* house?"

He hesitates. "There's a kind of abundance and congruence of eyewitness testimony that I've never come across before. And—" He stops again. "There's something else. But, for the results of an investigation to be truly meaningful, there are some things I have to hold back, some expectations I just can't seed in you." He glances at Rav. "In any of you."

Pale eyes fixed back on me, he says, "There's a document

159

that contains a little of the background. I'll email it to Rav, and he can send it on to you." He turns to Rav. "That call was concerning the property. There are some things I need to attend to. I'll see you tomorrow." Then he switches his gaze again to me. "Mia, it was good to meet you properly. I really am sorry about the video. We all are. Genuinely. I just ask you to think it over."

He holds out his hand. When I take it, it's cool and dry.

Rav raises a hand in farewell. "I'll be in early."

"Then you'll find me in my office."

Jared walks away, turning left towards the subway. And I flop back against the wall.

Neither of us speak for a minute. Then Rav says quietly, "I think if he can run a full investigation and come out certain that there's nothing supernatural in there, it'd be a bigger relief than he'd even admit to. When he says there's no such things as ghosts, I think he ninety per cent believes it. But that ten per cent of doubt is hard for him to carry."

I look at Rav. "What if he does the survey and he still can't be sure? Or what if there *is* something supernatural in there?"

He doesn't answer right away. Squeals and music from down the street barely break through to my consciousness. I'm focused so intently on his face, and how he's going to answer my question.

"How could a verdict either way be worse than where you are now?" he says at last. "You're scared of the possibility of something supernatural, and that's totally understandable. But whatever, Holly's *with* you. Not just on those occasions you talked about. In the background, right? She's haunting you in all kinds of ways. And if you do experience things in that house that are hard to explain, but we can pin them to environmental signals and expectations, then that would suggest to me that that's what's going on with Holly. In that case, I'd be encouraging you to see your experiences as being psychological, not paranormal… Not *ab*normal but originating in your own brain, which gives you a degree of control."

I don't say anything. I think I understand what he's saying. But I don't know if I agree.

"Look, worst-case scenario, I think, is that a supernatural explanation is the only one that works. Well then, Jared will know that ghosts are possible – and so will I – and so will you. And then we'll come up with a plan for how to deal with that."

"A *plan*?"

He nods. His dark eyes are serious. "I do get that uncertainty might seem preferable to a difficult truth. But actually I don't think that it is." He hesitates. "Friday night, when I was listening to the tape recordings and I told you about Dad's experience with his grandmother, stroking his arm… It wasn't actually Dad."

I realise at once what he's saying. "It was you?"

Now there's confusion in his eyes. "I know why I say

what I say – that I believe people think they're telling the truth when they tell me their experiences – but I don't think those experiences are *super*natural, because it's the most rational thing to say, and I trust Jared's investigations over the years. And I know that there's an absence of proof, and I want to be rational, right? But honestly? I'm not sure what I believe."

I find myself remembering something Sadie told me once. I know it came from her Italian mother. "There's a saying in Naples: *I know it's not true but I believe it anyway.*"

He nods slowly. "I have heard that precise phrase from Sadie's lips."

He blinks over at a young girl who's cycling past, ringing her bike bell. I wonder if he's said everything he wants to say. But then he goes on: "If I go to this property and I come out *knowing* there's nothing there, I've decided I won't think about believing it was actually my grandmother any more. Which will also be a kind of comfort. Just different from the one I think I needed as a kid…" He looks at me. "And, if that's how it plays out, neither should you. Believe she's literally haunting you, I mean."

I force my eyes to stay on his. "You think it's possible to be sure?"

After a moment, he says, "I think we have to set our own boundaries in our minds. This will be mine… Look, like Jared said, you really don't have to decide now. Take some time. Think it over. Talk to Sadie?"

"Sadie knows my best friend died. She doesn't know the rest."

He nods. "Maybe talk to Tamara, then?"

"I already know what she'd say."

"It's all made up, ghosts don't exist and it'll be a waste of time—"

I shake my head. "She told me to go last night, didn't she? She would tell me to go. She believes in facing your demons."

"It's an admirable belief," he says at last.

"If you're strong enough."

"Are you worried you aren't strong enough?"

I look down at my hands, unsure how to reply.

"Look, I know I don't really know you. So I'm not going to come out with some pseudo-insight into your inner personality. But I believe that we are all stronger than we generally think we are."

"…It's an admirable belief," I tell him.

His eyes crease into a smile that seems wistful more than anything else.

"When would you go?" I ask him.

"Jared said it could be as soon as Wednesday."

"I'm starting at the theatre with Tamara next Sunday."

"It shouldn't take more than a few days."

"…I need to think."

"Of course."

But, sitting there on the bench seat, I'm not actually sure

what else I need to *think* about. Maybe I just need to let it all sink in a bit more.

And, a little after four the next morning, I make up my mind.

*

I wake suddenly, my mouth parched.

The embers of the fire of the chilli, ginger and lemongrass that Sadie pummelled and mixed into vodka, with fresh lemon juice, are still smouldering on my tongue. It's dark. I have no idea what time it is but I'm desperate for water.

I drag myself up and into the kitchen, which still reeks of ginger. I take a tall glass, fill it from the tap, drink, refill it. A little unsteadily, I carry the glass back to my room.

The barbecue had been fun, Sadie in the mood for celebration. The owner of a well-known gallery in Williamsburg, whom she'd met at the event the night before, wants to review some of her work for potential inclusion in an exhibition. I know it's been a long time since she's shown anything at that kind of level.

I spent a lot of the evening genuinely not thinking about the ghost hunt, or the video, or the property in Long Island and Jared's proposition. But as I sit on my bed, taking cool sips of water, I think: *If I don't go, will I always regret it? Or if I do go will I always regret it?*

I'll talk to Tamara. But it's too late now – or too early. As I'm looking at my phone, I think of Jared saying that he'd email a document to Rav to send on to me. Now I see that Rav messaged me at 1.43 a.m. Not long after we all went to bed.

He's sent me a link to a document. I click on the link and a PDF opens.

16

SPONTANEOUS CASES COMMITTEE
OF NEW YORK CITY

Halcyon House, 223 Whalers Bay Road,
Southampton, Long Island

INVESTIGATING OFFICER: Dr Jared Robertson,
Research Fellow, Parapsychology Research
Institute, Gessen University, NYC

SUMMARY

This imposing nineteenth-century property
belongs to the actress Franca Ambler and the
musician Jon James. I was approached directly by
Mr James after their six-year-old daughter, Hanna

James, fell to her death from a first-floor window. The death was ruled accidental but it could not be satisfactorily explained. According to Mr James, a poltergeist occupies the house, and he fears that it may have been involved in his daughter's death. Since the 'accident', at least three independent witnesses have reported seeing Hanna's ghost, as well as experiencing poltergeist activity, presumably caused by the original entity.

These are therefore the questions that I set out to answer:

- Does a poltergeist occupy Halcyon House?
- If so, was it somehow implicated in the child's death?
- Is Hanna James now also haunting the property?

After being invited to Southampton, I began by interviewing employees. Their stories, I maintain, are compelling. Two witnesses in particular – a housekeeper and a gardener – have been deeply affected by their experiences. In fact, not since the Enfield poltergeist has such a body of contemporaneous, vivid and consistent eyewitness testimony of poltergeist and non-poltergeist haunting activity been assembled.

That's all there is.

I reread the text, and realize I've been holding my breath. I check my phone. It's 4.22 a.m. What now? No way can I wait.

I go out into the silent corridor and to the studio. I knock gently. "Rav?"

I knock again, not necessarily wanting to wake him, but wanting him to be awake.

Then I open the door a crack. "*Rav?*"

I hear someone moving. The rustle of a sheet. I push the door open a little wider. In the dim light coming in along the corridor from the kitchen, I can make out the bed and Rav's prone form. "*Rav?*"

He jerks up suddenly. The sheet, which was over his shoulders, drops to his waist. He squints at me through a mass of black hair. "Mia?"

"Can we talk?"

"What time is it?" he mumbles.

"About half four."

He rakes his hair back from his face with both hands. Licks his lips. "Too much ginger in those cocktails, or too much vodka? That is the question."

Holding the sheet over his lap, he reaches for the anglepoise lamp on the little desk, flicks the switch, and winces a little at the sudden yellow light. He grabs a glass of water by the side of his bed and takes a long drink.

Leaving the door open, I go to sit cross-legged on the

floor, my back to the wall, across from the bed. "I looked at that file. Where's the rest?"

He rubs a hand over his face and blinks. "There is no rest."

"But there must be. What about the interviews he did?"

Rav takes a deep breath. "OK. When Jared sent me the file, he also said if you had questions, and I knew the answers, I could tell you. So the father, Jon James, had heard Jared talk about his investigations at some Long Island paranormal convention. This is going back a long time, to when Jared was still a post-doc. But I guess James was impressed."

"Right, and?"

"And, after Hanna died, James went directly to Jared, and brought him in, without telling his wife, who was away. Staying with relatives, I think. When she came back and found out, she went—" He stops himself. "She was upset. Jared was told to leave and to forget he'd ever been called in. He'd already roughed out a draft of the first part of his executive summary, which you've just read. But he did as he was asked, and didn't write anything else up from his notes, didn't talk to anyone about it. I don't know what it had to do with it, beyond the fact of Hanna's death, but, a few months after Jared went in, James moved out."

"I think I've heard of Franca Ambler."

"She did a bunch of movies. Mostly supporting roles. The best friend's sister. Nanny to the comedy supervillain's kids. You know who Jon James was?"

Was? "Is he dead?"

"About six months after Hanna. Prescription opioid overdose."

I shiver. "Was he in a band?"

"Shrivener."

I frown. The name means nothing to me.

"Cello-metal. Their biggest hit was this song called 'Vanquishment'. The weird thing is they use it in the Psychology Department. It's validated. If you want to induce an angry mood in study participants, you can play them 'Vanquishment'."

"*Cello*-metal?"

"They were big in Holland. Anyway, he was into the occult, black magic, numerology, all that. They bought the house just after Hanna was born. Franca's older sister, Amy, came to help out with the baby and she had some weird experiences in the house, and so did Jon James, and the housekeeper. Poltergeist-type activity. I don't know the details because Jared hasn't talked about them much. Yet."

"And Hanna's death was ruled accidental."

Rav nods. "There was no evidence – or reason – to suggest that either of the parents or anyone else associated with the house was responsible. Jared says everyone described her as a happy, loved kid. There were no marks on her body except those consistent with the fatal fall."

"I feel like I'm hearing a *but*."

"But the upper-floor windows had been fitted with

safety locks, so they couldn't be opened more than a few inches. After Hanna died, Franca Ambler took the company to court, claiming that her daughter must have unlocked the ones on her bedroom window herself. She lost the case. They argued, successfully, that it would have been essentially impossible for the locks to be accidentally opened."

He finishes his water, puts the glass back on the table. "Whatever actually happened, Franca Ambler lost the case. And a lot of their money. But she kept the house, and she stayed there. But she wouldn't let Jared or any other investigator back in. Then, about six weeks ago, she died. Bowel cancer," he adds quickly. "Ownership of the property passed to her sister, Amy Ambler, who actively wants a comprehensive paranormal investigation. She got in touch with Jared. She must have known he did the initial survey."

"Why does she want it?"

Softly, he says, "I guess she, like Jared, just wants to know the truth."

"But why didn't he find the truth when he first went in?"

"He had to stop before he could get to an actual investigation of the property. And, all those years ago, he had nothing like the knowledge or the equipment that we have now. Things have changed a lot."

"But he said there's no such thing as a ghost-detecting machine."

"Right. But there is tech that allows you to control environmental factors that investigators didn't know about back then… And there are some in the paranormal research community who argue that ghost or poltergeist witness testimony should be weighed the same way as testimony presented in a court of law. Take someone who's saying they witnessed a murder. If you can't put them at the scene with forensic evidence or video footage, you can't prove that they were there. But, if the details of what they say they saw agree with the details of another independent witness, then maybe you can start to build a case. If you can gather enough corroborating testimonies, maybe you can even convince a jury that the person in the dock is, beyond reasonable doubt, the murderer."

"But that's never been done – proving the presence of a ghost beyond reasonable doubt?"

"Some people would argue that it has. Jared mentioned the Enfield poltergeist in his talk."

"But he's not convinced about it."

He shakes his head. "But the Enfield case was back in the 1970s. I'd like to see a case like that examined using modern methods."

"But that's what you do? When you check out a house, or whatever, with the spontaneous cases group? Put together a dossier."

He nods. "I've heard a lot of stories that sounded convincing, in that I believe the individual involved was telling the truth as they saw it. But I don't think I've heard enough to secure a conviction."

"Why does Amy Ambler even want a medium in the house?"

"It's not unusual for a medium to be called in to a suspected haunting."

I remember the scuttling feel of insects on my skin and I have to force my hands to stay where they are. "You really think that video will convince her that I'm what she wants?"

"I reckon, if you allow Jared to show it to her, he'll be able to convince her. So what do you say?"

I try to think. But I already know which way I'm going to go. I have to let this take me where it takes me. If I back away now, I feel sure I'll regret it. "OK," I say. "Yes."

PART
TWO

PART
TWO

17

The silver minibus pulls out into the heavy Manhattan traffic. Drake's playing on the sound system, and the beat's in my chest. The sun's so intense that when I look out of the window I have to squint, even with my sunglasses on.

"Can't you put the AC up?" Lana shouts from behind me.

"It's on!" Yunoo calls back. "Be patient!"

"Turn it up!" she tells him.

He shrugs, turns up the volume and pumps his fist in time with the music.

"*Yunoo!*" she yells.

He twists his head to flash her a grin and turns it back down.

He's behind the wheel of the departmental sixteen-seater, Rav beside him, fanning himself with his hand. I'm on a double seat behind Yunoo. Lana and Alli are sitting a little further down, nearer the back. Yunoo had asked if anyone else wanted to drive but Lana only gave him a look that I took to mean: *Why would anyone want to drive through Manhattan?*

When I arrived at the institute, to my surprise it was Lana, hurrying along the pavement in bright orange cut-off jeans and a matching T-shirt, who was first to greet me. She pushed up her sunglasses and fixed me with an intense stare.

"I have to start by apologizing for the video," she said, and she at least looked like she meant it. "I know you probably feel now like you can't trust me. So I have to try to work hard to make up for that. But I want to say I'm really glad you're on the team. We're very lucky to have found you."

"…I'm glad I'm on the team, too," I mumbled, struggling a little to assimilate her words, but glad that she was being friendly.

Her face relaxed into a small smile. "Video aside, maybe you know that Rav and I have history. And unfortunately he brings out the worst in me. But I should try harder…" Moving briskly on, she says, "Come, we're basically all packed up and ready to go."

Somehow, we found space for my bag in the boot area, which was already piled high with gear. Along with black plastic crates of kit were bagged rolls of sleeping bags and pillows with the dry-cleaning tags still attached and everyone else's bags.

"Where's Jared?" I asked Yunoo.

"Ah, he's driving himself," he said. "We'll meet him there."

I felt relieved to hear this. I still wasn't quite sure what to make of Jared.

It's Wednesday – the day Rav thought we could be heading out.

On Monday morning, he called from the institute to say that Amy Ambler had approved my membership of the team. On Monday afternoon, I had to clear it with Sadie.

She had questions, obviously.

I concentrated my answers into one main thread: it'll be an amazing opportunity to witness an academic investigation and will no doubt be really useful for my degree course. She wanted me to check in with Dad. Since he knows nothing about what I've experienced with Holly since she died, he had no objections.

In the end, against my expectations, it was Tamara who was hardest to convince.

"But this is a house where a girl died." She said it so bluntly and with such force that I was a little stunned.

I explained that this was me trying to seize my life chance, like she'd told me to.

"But you actually *want* to do this?" she asked, scrutinizing my face.

"I want to do it," I told her.

"I have to help Mom with this catering job or I'd come with you," she said.

"It's OK. I'll be fine," I reassured her.

"You have to call me every five minutes to let me know it's all OK."

"Every *five*? You think that'll be often enough?"

She ignored my attempt to lighten the mood. Just looked concerned. "You're really sure about this?"

When I finally convinced her that I was, she said: "If you decide you want to get out of there, call me, OK? I'll come get you."

"What, in your mum's car? It'd never make it."

"I could take the bus!" She squeezed my hand. Let a glimmer of a smile into her black eyes. "The public bus is a *very* underutilized vehicle for emergency person extraction."

*

A jolt of the minibus brings me back to the present. Yunoo's hauling us round a corner – and I do a double take. An athletic-looking woman in a sleeveless dress with very long dark hair just emerged from a café, and I feel sure I recognize her. Then I realize she just resembles Amy Ambler, in a photo that I found online.

The caption read: *Amy Ambler, sister to tragic Franca, takes time out from her private dining business to attend her niece's funeral.*

Alongside that photo was one of Franca and Jon

gripping each other's hands. Jon, a big, broad man, was dressed in a narrow-fitting black suit. He looked grief-stricken, or angry, or both. Franca, willowy and tall, was in a long white lace dress, oversized sunglasses and a broad-brimmed black hat.

As the minibus continues to stop-start its way through midtown, I get out my phone, and I do another search on the family.

I click on images. There's Amy, in the same clothes as before, but this time with a man who bears a striking resemblance to Jon James. He's holding a baby and isn't identified in the caption but he's clearly James's brother, or another close relative.

I also get plenty of promotional stills of Franca in movie roles, and even more of Jon James with his band. Some are of the band playing but a lot are staged; James always looking a little incongruous beside his classical cello.

I jerk forwards in my seat. The knots in the traffic suddenly seem to have loosened, and it starts to flow. Before long, we're on the interstate, heading out of the city, into the dazzling green-and-sunshine-gold of Long Island.

The music is so loud, I'm effectively isolated here in my seat so I turn my attention to Jared Robertson.

The first result is a page from the institute website. It lists his research interests: *Hauntings and Ghost Beliefs*, and recent journal publications. Flicking back to the search results, I find several conference listings with his name as a keynote speaker, and also interviews about ghosts published in magazines, including one in *New Scientist*, and another, a Q&A with *New York Today*, which I quickly start scanning.

Q. How did you become interested in the paranormal?
A. As a kid, I was fascinated by ghost stories. I got into it all through fiction. Then I started to put together my own compilations of stories I collected from friends of my parents, kids at school, magazines, books. By the time I was twelve, I had a stack of these folders probably four feet high. I guess you could call it an obsession.

Q. But you yourself had never witnessed paranormal activity?
A. No. But here were all these people, including my own mother, who did report these experiences. It fascinated me.

Q. So you have never had even a hint of something like that?
A. I've had feelings. Chills. A sense of foreboding, even dread. Coincidences. Nothing I haven't been able to explain in other ways.

Q. I have to ask: your ex-wife is now a high-profile member of the poltergeist circuit, if I can call it that. She clearly believes.

A. Stacey is of course entitled to her own beliefs. And we are no longer together. I am not going to comment beyond that.

Stacey? That name sounds familiar. Surely not…

I search '*Jared Robertson Stacey Disaranno*'.

Up comes a photo of the two of them in black tie at some reception, holding hands. His hair is still black. He's wearing the Ghostbusters belt buckle. I wonder if they've always had clashing beliefs. Is he so harsh on ghost-hunting shows partly because *she's* his ex?

I glance up from my phone, out of the window. Trees are spreading, apparently unending, to either side of us. It's like the road is somehow pushing its way through a green sea. Then I glimpse the actual sea, sapphire-blue and dazzling.

My phone, which is still in my hand, buzzes. It's a message from Freja.

Dad's offering to pay for dinner out for us all on the Saturday. Japanese or Italian…? What do you think? xx

She's talking about Brighton, of course. I look back out of the window, as if some kind of answer lies there, and see

183

that the trees have given way to low buildings. A sign by the road reads *Manorville Town Center*.

In the end, I only manage:

> That's really generous. Promise to let you know if
> I can definitely make it soon as I can xx

I feel guilty – of course. Brighton is a long way from Sheffield. Before what happened at Manchester Uni, I'd have been fine about going. Now, how can I be?

"Caffeination!" Yunoo calls suddenly. Then he shuts the music off and we pull into a car park outside a Starbucks.

The sudden silence makes my ears ring. As the automatic side door slides open, the heat hits me, too. While I'm zipping my phone back into my bag, Lana comes up from the back, followed by Alli. She pauses by me.

"Jared insisted on doing the essential shopping on the way up. He has a fondness for this horrible instant coffee. I would take this opportunity to get something."

"Yeah, and it's not far now," Alli says brightly. Her hand's resting on the top of my seat and I notice she's wearing an unusual bracelet. It's of plaited white leather, with a lemon yellow feather and two wooden beads, one red and one yellow. "We won't be stopping again."

I step down after them into burning sunshine. Yunoo and Rav are waiting. Yunoo beams at me. "Mia, for the next few days, sleep will be irregular and insufficient. Coffee will

184

be your best friend. Take my advice: embrace the bean at any and all times."

Behind him, Rav is stretching out his back. "Take *my* advice," he calls to me, smiling. "Always take Yunoo's advice."

Yunoo grins. It's a broad, kiddish grin, even for him.

"It was Yunoo who advised me to risk breaking my neck and getting arrested by climbing a locked gate at the naval yard," I point out.

"And now look!" Yunoo says. "Here you are, with us!"

Yeah, I think, with a twinge of apprehension. *Here I am.*

As soon as we're inside, Lana and Alli disappear off to the bathroom. Yunoo goes to place the order and I try not to be too obvious about taking in the other customers. A lot appear to be tourists but there are also little groups of women in leisurewear, and a couple of older guys in baseball caps chatting over their coffees. Everything is so normal. And that twinge of apprehension deepens. This is the last stop before Halcyon House.

As soon as the coffees are ready, we head back to the minibus and take the same seats. The ice cubes in my iced latte knock together as we pull on to the road.

Rav changes the music to something with rapid, not quite rhythmically regular, plucked strings. Crashing cymbals. Insistent riffs. The song whips itself into a thrashing tornado of sound. Shrivener? It has to be. No one complains. Not even Lana.

When I've drunk about half my coffee, the highway

ends. The road dips, and ahead of us is what looks like a frozen tidal wave of pine trees. But we don't quite reach it. Instead, we turn off, on to a street with huge, expensive-looking homes with picket fences. Rocking chairs on the porches. Perfect lawns. Fibreglass hulls of boats gleaming on trailers on the drives.

We stop at a set of lights. Two tanned, barefoot girls going the other way on their bikes stare up at us; maybe they can hear the music.

Then we take a right – and the ocean is directly ahead. Almost the entire span of the horizon is blue. As we get closer, it brightens. The glittering patterns in the water keep shifting, so I have to keep looking. When there's nothing in front of us but a sand dune and that sapphire ocean, we angle hard left, on to a drive. It's curved, and densely planted with pines, so it's impossible to see from here what lies at the end.

The bus jolts along, Yunoo doing his best to avoid all the potholes.

By the time we finally come to a stop, we're shrouded by a cloud of sand and dust. I hadn't realized that the house would be right on the beach. There's sand everywhere. I haven't been this close to it since Holly died. Even at Coney Island, Tamara and I stayed back, off the beach.

I feel panic start to rise, and I do my best to swallow it down.

Yunoo cuts the engine. I hear Lana and Alli shifting in their seats, trying to get a better view.

18

After the door slides open, I step unsteadily out. I'm expecting an ocean breeze. There's none. Even the paper-thin leaves of a towering plane tree beside us are motionless. On the other side of the bus is some kind of sports car that's probably bright red, but its paintwork has been dulled with dust. Jared's car, I guess.

I look down, at the sand in among the weeds, and my toes curl. From the flat, low, glaring sky comes the empty call of a seagull circling. I smell a salty dry-rot stench of vegetation growing on the dune. A *whush-whush* fills my ears. It's the sound of my own blood, and waves crashing on the invisible beach. What with the sand, the heat and that stench, along with my own soaring anxiety, I'm suddenly fighting a wave of nausea.

"What do you think?"

Rav's beside me. He's squinting in the direction of the

house. Wrapping my arms, like reinforcements, tightly round my queasy belly, I force myself to follow his gaze.

Imposing. That's what Jared's report said.

Once it might have been. Now it sits squat in its overgrown landscape. Its roughly rectangular, three-storey brick body has been stripped of much of its white-paint skin. We're standing side-on to it. Protruding from the ground floor at this end is a broad bay window. The panes look to be all cracked or murky with dirt, or scratched by sea salt carried in the wind. Around to the left, to the front of the house, a short flight of rickety-looking wooden steps leads up to a covered wooden verandah.

Who builds a house that faces away from the sea, into trees, I wonder? Though I guess if it had been oriented the other way, the lower windows at the front would have faced into the dune.

To the front and side of the house, tall dark green pines grow thickly. Running along the treeline, I can make out what obviously used to be a longer drive, going on past the far end of the house, but it's overgrown now with more of the purple-headed weeds and long grass.

It must be years since anyone took any care of the house or the grounds.

Lana and Alli are already heading towards the front of the property. Rav and Yunoo go after them, and I make myself follow. The grasses scratch at my ankles and my calves, reminding me of the naval yard, and the insects, which only makes my heart race faster. But, if I'm stepping on grass, at least I'm not walking in sand.

Steeling myself, I face the weather-beaten steps, and look up.

The verandah's in a bad state. The dirty boards are warped and uneven, and there are jagged gaps in the roof. Either side of the door are two long windows. They're screened with moss-green louvred shutters, the dusty slats folded shut.

Up on the first floor are four square windows, also with shutters, though not all are closed. One of these has to have been Hanna's window.

Releasing my breath, I drag my gaze up, to the next storey. It's lower than the others – maybe only two-thirds of their height – and it doesn't span the full length of the house. Six very small square windows run in a line. Then there's what looks to be a roof terrace, which must give a view over the dune, to the ocean.

Alli and Lana whisper something to each other. Lana starts up the steps, making the planks creak.

Rav's walking with Yunoo along the overgrown drive, around to the far side, and I hurry to stay with them. We come to a single detached garage, with a rusty roller door, set back in among a stand of pines. From the grounds, I realize, you can't see any other properties, just Halcyon House. And trees, and the high sand dune, and the sky.

"I looked it up," Yunoo says by my ear, making me jump.

"It was built by a whaler in 1836. A man called Nathaniel Brown."

"A whaler?" I say, surprised.

Alli leans over the side fence of the verandah. "There were a lot around here," she says. "Southampton. Sag Harbor… They were big whaling centres back then. When the industry collapsed, some of them sailed their boats on to California, hoping to cash in on the Gold Rush."

"I read that a lot never came back," Yunoo says.

"They settled out there?" I ask.

Yunoo's expression tells me that's not what he meant.

"The journey could be treacherous," Alli says, by way of explanation. "I'm heading in. You coming?"

"We'll be right there," Yunoo says. He looks to Rav, who nods.

Together we walk back round to the front of the house. I steel myself to peer up again at the first-floor windows. *Which* was Hanna's? I wonder. I also find myself wondering how Franca Ambler could have carried on living here, in the place where her daughter died.

Unless, perhaps, in a sense, Hanna *is* still here.

A sharp creak makes me tense. Yunoo on the verandah. As he goes to the front door, it opens inwards and Jared Robertson appears. I can't help noticing that he's wearing that Ghostbusters belt buckle.

"Jared!" Yunoo booms.

"Hey," he answers.

"I hope we haven't missed anything," Yunoo says, with a smile.

"Not as yet. But I've only been here half an hour." He steps out on to the verandah, and a woman in a navy blue wrap dress comes out from behind him. Her long dark hair is tied back in a sleek ponytail. Huge glasses cover half of her face. I smell sweet, musky perfume. The only giveaway that she's middle-aged is the faint wrinkling of the skin on her neck and arms.

Glancing at her, Jared says, "Yunoo, Rav, Mia, let me introduce you to Amy Ambler."

Looking a little surprised, Yunoo thrusts out his hand. "Ms Ambler, it's wonderful to meet you."

She shakes his hand. Then, after Rav and I climb up the steps, she shakes Rav's, too. She stands right in front of me. "Mia," she says, her low voice seeming to waver. It's disconcerting, not being able to see her eyes. I'm not sure what to say, so I don't say anything, waiting instead for her to speak again.

But she turns to Jared. She opens her right hand, revealing a set of brass keys, which she hands to him. "You have temporary guardianship of Halcyon House," she says, with feeling. "I trust you all to do everything you can to document what's been happening here. I *need* to know, you see."

Jared nods sombrely. "I can promise you that your home is in the best possible hands."

She glances up – I'm not quite sure at what. Then she nods and steps past me to walk down to the grass.

"You're sure we can't give you a lift back to your car?" Jared calls.

Looking back, she shakes her head. "It's only a short walk away." She hesitates, seeming to take in the view of the house. "I'll be back in Manhattan, waiting to hear your findings. You will come in person when you have them?"

"As soon as we've concluded here, I'll head straight to your apartment," he says.

She gives him a tight smile. Her ponytail swinging, she walks quickly away, in the direction not of the driveway, but the dune.

"She couldn't have given you the keys back in New York?" Rav asks quietly.

"She wanted to show me around in person," Jared says. "And to see us safely in."

"Why didn't she drive her car up to the house?" I ask him.

"That's what I'm wondering," Yunoo says. "She's *worried* about bringing even her car to this house? *Why?*"

Jared smiles faintly. "If I owned a Mercedes Roadster, I wouldn't bring it over that driveway, either. She says she left it on a road further down."

"Oh," Yunoo says.

"Better recalibrate yourself, or you'll be jumping at shadows," Jared says, not unkindly. "Come on – have a quick look around then we'll get unpacked." He goes back inside the house.

Yunoo looks faintly unhappy.

"Don't be too hard on yourself," Rav says. "The one case Jared can't be sure of… I'll be jumping at every shadow."

With a sigh, Yunoo follows Jared.

"Ready?" Rav says to me.

I wonder how to respond to that. I'm at a property reportedly occupied by a poltergeist and the ghost of a child. And Amy Ambler clearly believes that something's been happening here. I'm so tense, my body's so stiff, I don't feel like my legs can move.

But I have no real choice other than to follow Rav – to step on to the last creaking plank of the verandah, and over the threshold – into Halcyon House.

19

We're in the entrance hall. The walls are panelled in wood that has been painted black. Above us, a candelabra of pale antler horn hangs from a steel chain. It's dark in here, and so much cooler than outside.

Ahead of us is a steep, narrow staircase with a once-black carpet and a dark wood banister. To our left is a black door with a tarnished brass handle. It's closed. To our right, an identical door is ajar. I guess Jared and Yunoo went that way.

I'm nervous. Of course. My heart is racing and the temperature drop is making my sweaty skin shiver. But so far, anyway, I don't feel anything definitively odd. No tickling on my legs. No shadows over my shoulder.

I peer down at my feet. Grains of sand are clinging to my toes and I'm desperate to brush them off, but I don't want to touch them. So I lift my feet, one at a time, to rub them against the back of my trousers, hoping it will all fall to the floor.

The candelabra suddenly trembles, making me jump. There's a *creak-creak* of someone walking overhead, then Alli's voice from upstairs: "This one?"

Rav goes to peer up the staircase.

"You think it was like this when Hanna lived here?" I ask him. "All black?"

Running his fingers over a dusty wall panel, he says, "Knowing about the house's reputation, maybe your brain is jumping to *dark, occult, danger, black magic.* But she might've thought it was cosy. Like living in a cave."

"A *cave*?"

He turns, catches my eye. "A well-appointed cave with the very latest in animal-horn light fittings."

But there's nothing anyone could say right now that could possibly make me smile.

Going to the open door, he pushes it wide. "And antique sofas…"

Wiping my palms on my trousers, I follow Rav into a long, crescent-shaped room. A sharp smell of dog makes my nose wrinkle, and I cough. The wall on the right is almost all window: one long swerve of glass, its black louvre shutters folded back so that dusty light floods in. On the other long wall, which is painted dark grey, is a fireplace with a heavy black stone surround. Beside it is a low-backed midnight-blue velvet sofa. Gold trim around the arms is coming away. The velvet's scattered with white animal hair. The source of the smell, I guess.

Yunoo and Jared are over by the window, talking about the room.

"No other furniture…" Yunoo says. "Why do you think they left the sofa?"

But Jared doesn't respond because he's saying to us now: "There are seven bedrooms upstairs but we'll sleep in pairs. Lana and Alli will no doubt go in together. I think they went to pick one out. Mia – you OK with Rav?"

I nod. I've just stepped over to the fireplace. It's so much colder in this room than even the entrance hall. Could there be some kind of draught coming from the grate? Then I notice a brass grille set into the dark floorboards right by the fireplace surround. When I hold my hand against it, I feel a chill.

"Yeah," Jared says. "The AC is a problem. I haven't located the controls yet."

"I'll see if I can find them," Rav offers.

"Actually, when the gear's been unloaded, I could do with you in the kitchen to help me with something – if you don't mind."

It doesn't really sound like a question.

To Yunoo, Jared says, "Can you, Lana and Alli check out the AC and set up? I'll give you all a full briefing when that's done."

"Sure," Yunoo says.

Aren't Rav or Yunoo going to ask, I wonder, or do they already know? I do my best to clear my throat. It's not easy. I have to swallow hard. "The reports about the poltergeist activity – where did it happen?"

"Various parts of the house," Jared says vaguely. "Look, I know you have questions. I'll take you through some more of what I know a little later. But for now would you mind pitching in with the unloading first? Then maybe you can help with setting up some of the equipment? Yunoo will let you know what has to be done. But there's one really important rule: don't go anywhere alone. It holds for all of us." His gaze takes in Rav and Yunoo, too. "The only place you go by yourself is the bathroom. And then for the shortest possible time."

"You really think there's a risk to us?" My voice sounded so quiet I wouldn't be surprised if no one heard.

But Jared replies at once. "My primary concern will always be our safety. However, the biggest risk is that, if anything unexpected does happen, there *cannot* be only one eyewitness. What I need from this investigation is corroboration, corroboration, corroboration."

Yunoo's forehead creases. He holds up a hand. "Listen."

There's a cranking sound. I experience the increasingly familiar sense of fear spreading through my veins. Then a *thunk* echoes through the floorboards and a noise I'd barely been aware of stops.

*

We all go back through to the entrance hall, where we find Lana and Alli coming out of the opposite door.

"Did you just do something with the AC?" Rav asks.

Lana gives him an arch look. "Find it and sort it, you mean? If so, yes."

"Why do we need the AC off?" I say.

"We need to create a temperature map of the house," Alli explains. "AC would interfere."

"My *uncanny* ability to open cupboard doors must be why I get paid the big bucks." Lana gives Rav a smile I can't quite read.

I'm not sure what's going on here. Is she being rude to him? Or just joking but without the usual signposting?

"So, division of labour," Jared says, clapping his hands. "Rav's gonna help me out with something when we've unloaded. Can the rest of you set up?"

Lana glances at Rav, wondering, I guess, what Jared wants him for. Then she says to Alli: "We could handle the cameras?"

Alli nods. "Maybe I could do the infrasound map while you fix them up."

"I'll take the temperature sensors," Yunoo says. "Mia, you OK coming round with me?"

I nod. I don't think I really have much choice. But, even if I had one, I'm not sure what I'd opt to do, anyway.

We head back to the minibus and start to unload. Apart from a couple of crates of kitchenware and food, we stack everything in the other room off the entrance hall. It turns out to be the one with the broad bay window that I noticed when we first arrived. It, too, is empty of furniture, and panelled in wood, painted black. A single painting hangs on the wall. It's of an old wooden ship, straining in a storm.

At all times, I'm careful to stay with someone else, so I'm never inside on my own. At one point, Yunoo goes over to the painting. "The sofa, this painting... Just a few things have been left," he says, frowning. "I wonder why."

"I guess Amy Ambler didn't want them."

"I guess not, and I don't think I totally blame her... If at any point—" He hesitates. "I'm sure Jared will run through what he expects of us all, but, if at any point you feel anything like you did in the lab or in the hospital, you will tell someone?"

A slight shudder passes through me. I nod.

But after moving in and out of the sunshine, working with the others, I feel a little more relaxed. Or rather I feel less intensely anxious – less afraid that something could happen at any moment. After everything's in, though, and Jared and Rav disappear in the direction of the kitchen, and Alli and Lana trudge upstairs with a folding stepladder, a black backpack and two of the crates, leaving Yunoo and me alone, my apprehension about being here starts to flood right back.

Yunoo pulls a polythene bag filled with doorbell-sized black objects and a bag of wipes from a crate. Together we head into the crescent-shaped room, which might have been the living room, I think. The plan is to start distributing the sensors in here.

The process is extremely simple, Yunoo explains. I have to use an alcohol-based wipe to clean a surface, peel the backing from the sticky strip, then press the sensor into place. He's given me five, and taken five for himself.

I crouch to stick a sensor to the skirting board, near the fireplace. The grate is cast iron. Old. Thick with dust. I find myself remembering what Jared said in his talk about part of a fireplace in the Enfield house being thrown around, and I shiver. Part of me doesn't want to hear what poltergeist activity has been reported in the house. But, if I don't know, I won't have any idea what to potentially guard against. Quickly I move to the brass grille in the floor. "Why so many sensors?"

Yunoo gets up from down near the sofa. "You can get really small temperature fluctuations in a room. This is an old house. There'll be gaps around the windows, maybe even cracks in the walls. And we could still get draughts of air up through the air-con vents. You've watched ghost-hunting shows on TV, right?"

I finish attaching another sensor to the wall. "Not really."

"Oh. Well, they all do it: a fall in temperature signals the arrival of a ghost, right? Or that's what they say, so now everyone takes it as established fact." While I move along the wall, he goes to the windows. "Actually humans are very sensitive to small changes in temperature. But we're poor at knowing how big they actually are. Reduce the temperature in a room by just one degree, and you can get people saying, 'It's *freezing*.' Having a real-time temperature map of a property under investigation is important."

"So, if one of us feels something but your map shows we've just moved into a cool spot…?"

"Yeah, it wouldn't prove there wasn't a ghost. But it would help build a case for there being a natural explanation." He drops his little handful of backing papers into the bag. "I think we're done?"

We move on, through the far door, into what turns out to be the kitchen.

The room is huge, at least compared with the others. Jared and Rav are at an eight-seater black-lacquered table, which takes up only about a quarter of the space. A copper pendant light suspended just above their head level shines a soft light over their open laptops. The one Rav's using has a Ghostbusters sticker on the lid.

"Hey," Rav says, and smiles. Jared doesn't look up from his screen. Yunoo gives Rav a thumbs up.

The table is long-side-on to a picture window with a view of tall grass and weeds, and a dark mass of pine trees beyond. At this end of the kitchen, black-lacquered units, a black sink and a stainless-steel double fridge are arranged over three sides of a rectangle.

After wiping my palms again, I take five more sensors from the bag. I stick one near the sink, above which is a square window with a view right into the dune – which I try not to look at – and space the others round the units.

Yunoo takes the area around Rav and Jared. Then he grabs the bag, and nods towards another internal door, to the right of the table. I follow him into a utility room.

It's narrow and very warm and stuffy. Sunlight is pouring in through a dirty window above a ceramic trough sink at the far end. Beside the sink is an external door, with a large flap. Too big, surely, for a cat. Then I think of the dog hair.

Along almost the full length of the side walls are black granite worktops. There's nothing else in here, apart from an old top-loading washing machine and a faded green plastic laundry basket, which is empty. There's a faint whiff of mould but I can't see any on the walls.

Yunoo's trainers squeak on the dark grey floor tiles. "Here." After taking out a handful of sensors, he passes me the bag. "A few over there, thank you."

It doesn't take long to kit out the utility room. Now the only room left on the ground floor is our storeroom. We stick four round the window, three on each of the long walls, two by the door – and we're done.

I haven't actively been trying to feel anything while we've been working our way through the ground floor. But so far I haven't been aware of any unusual sensations. Everything that I'm feeling – the tightness in my throat and chest, the dampness of my palms, my jumpiness – has a very obvious explanation.

I follow Yunoo into the entrance hall. He stares up at the narrow staircase.

"Is it me?" He tilts his head to one side.

"No," I answer. "They are definitely sloping."

He takes the first step, which creaks, then the next. I follow him. My eyes and my inner ears are telling me that the stairs are clearly all slanting slightly to the right, but my brain seems to be having a hard time adjusting. I have to reach for the banister to steady myself.

We come out on to a wide landing with a deeply recessed window fitted with a seat upholstered in faded dark blue velvet. A bare bulb dangles from the ceiling. It's off but light is coming through the open shutters, reflecting dully off the stone grey walls. It's even stuffier than in the utility room. Sweat prickles on my arms, and along my back. The still air smells of clothes that have been stored away for months.

To the left of the bench seat is a narrow white door. Past that is a short corridor with two doors off to one side, and one to the other. Leading from the other end of the landing is a longer narrow corridor with four yellowing doors in a row to the left. Like the stairs, the bare floorboards of the corridor seem to be slanting.

As I look uneasily around, my gaze snags on scratches in the floorboards, cracks in the plaster, brownish stains on the once-white doors.

A low, muffled voice makes me stiffen.

It's only Lana, I realize. In one of the rooms off the longer corridor. Only Lana talking to Alli.

"Let's start down here," Yunoo says. He heads briskly towards the door on its own in the short corridor and reaches for the handle. It opens, showing darkness.

As I go to stand beside Yunoo, I hear the flick of the light switch. Nothing happens. He flicks it back. Then he unzips a pocket in his shorts and pulls out a silver torch. The beam picks out a sash window, with external green shutters, which are closed. A plain iron double-bed frame with a bare yellowed mattress. A chest of drawers veneered in the same kind of black lacquer as the kitchen cabinets. Slate-grey walls. I'm trembling, my breathing coming fast and shallow.

"Back at the institute, Jared showed us a plan of the house," Yunoo murmurs. "Just so you know, this was definitely not Hanna's bedroom. This was a guest room."

But my pulse doesn't slow down at this news.

"Can you hold this?" Yunoo asks. "Keep it on me if you can."

Doing my best to control the shaking in my hands, I grip the torch, and Yunoo takes his bag of sensors over to the mattress. Unsteadily, I hold the torch as he sticks one sensor, then another, round the chest.

"Please. Over here." He points to the window.

When I re-angle the beam, my trembling gets worse.

Fixed to the bottom frame is a dirty little while plastic case. A discoloured white cable connects it to a panel that's screwed into the wall.

Yunoo curls his index fingers under two brass metal hooks in the lower frame. He pulls. The window jerks up a few centimetres. He shakes it, making me flinch, but it doesn't look like it'll go any higher. Pushing it back down, apparently satisfied, he grabs a few more sensors and sticks them round the frame.

"If Hanna's window is like this one, it's hard to see how she could have opened it," I whisper, and only realize after I've spoken that it was out loud, not in my own head.

"It is hard," Yunoo agrees.

I take a deep breath. A question tumbles out before I can even think about trying to stop it. "Do you think something supernatural might have been involved in her death?"

Yunoo turns to fix a cautious gaze on me. "As a famous parapsychologist once said, there's no such thing as *super*natural. If anything happens, it's natural – we just don't understand it yet."

"I don't think that counts as answering the question."

He shrugs. "It's the best answer that I have." He goes back to the bag and pulls out two more sensors.

"Does Lana believe there are, I don't know, entities that can interact with us but that we don't understand?" I whisper.

"I'm not sure," he says quietly as he bends down near the bed. "Alli is certainly more open to the idea of ghosts."

"Why?"

He attaches the second of the sensors and gets up. "You should ask her. But her father runs psychedelic experience weekends out in a cabin in a state park. Magic mushrooms, ayahuasca ceremonies. All for city types who want to feel more connected to others and to the universe." He steps back to the window. Again he starts fiddling with the catch. "He's a spiritual person. Maybe Alli also feels that there's more to existence than what we know. *Ah*."

By pinching the plastic case cover hard between this thumb and forefinger, and twisting, he's managed to remove it.

Inside there's a keyhole. No key.

He exhales hard. "Even if she could have got the casing off, she'd have needed the key..." He gets up. "Now the en-suite."

Yunoo goes in first but I'm right behind. It's a tiny bathroom with a corner shower and black stone tiles flecked with grey.

Yunoo fixes a sensor by the shower and another to a dusty glass shelf on the opposite wall. Then he moves to the basin. I'm doing my best to train the beam on to his hands, but some of the light reflects off the mirror above. His head is suddenly surrounded by a glare so intense, it's almost buzzing. He looks up, and his face is completely blank.

Panic hits me.

"Mia?"

I take a few stumbling steps backwards.

"*Mia?*"

His features reappear.

"What's wrong?" He's looking concerned.

I swallow and I blink at him. Everything's there. Where it should be. I glance back at the mirror. "Nothing," I manage to say at last. "It was just the light."

"Are you sure?"

Yunoo is no ghost. Whatever I saw, it was in my own mind. I nod.

"Like I said, you must tell me if you feel something. But – I know from personal experience – it's also really easy just to get spooked in a place like this." He gives me what I think is meant to be a reassuring smile. But his eyes don't seem convinced, and my heart is still racing. When I blink, I see the blank almost-circle of white where his face should have been—

"Anything else?" he asks. "Any feeling of presence?"

I let my breath out slowly. Shake my head. "Only yours."

*

We move on to distribute temperature sensors in the two other rooms off this little corridor. They also turn out to be guest rooms, with almost identical, tiny, windowless en-suites.

As we step back on to the landing, a thought occurs to me: "Where did Franca die?"

Yunoo is creaking his way over to the first of the doors off the longer corridor. "Honestly I don't know. But I would think the hospital." Stepping inside, he says, "Ah. I will nickname this the Blue Room."

As I come in behind him, the first thing that strikes me about this room, apart from the fact that it's painted a rich royal blue, is that it's at least twice the size of the ones we've seen so far. Also the shutters on both the sash windows are open. The dusty sunshine shows a scattering of faded patches on the walls, a stripped king-sized bed and a cast-iron fireplace, moulded anchors and cherubs decorating the grate.

Yunoo drops the bag and the torch on the mattress, then collects a handful of sensors. "I think we should go crazy, mix things up… Bathroom first this time." He smiles faintly.

He leaves the door to the en-suite open behind him, and I'm about to follow him in when there's a very soft swish from behind me. And a cool draught on my neck, which makes the hairs rise.

I spin – and I see Lana in the doorway just a fraction of a second before I hear her voice: "Mia!"

She looks surprised and annoyed. But almost immediately the annoyance vanishes.

"Sorry," she says, and shrugs the strap of the backpack over her shoulder again. "I didn't know anyone was in here."

Alli arrives, carrying the stepladder, just as Yunoo appears from the bathroom.

"Unfortunately there seems to be no electricity on this floor," he comments.

"Yeah," Lana says. "I'll check it out when we've set up the cameras."

"I could investigate—" he starts.

She shakes her head briskly. "I think I'll be perfectly capable, Yunoo."

He flashes me a look, one eyebrow raised, but I don't return it. I must be starting to like Lana.

After we distribute our sensors in here, Yunoo and I go into the next bedroom.

"The Pink Room?" I say.

"Yes… Unexpectedly the Pink Room."

There's no trace of black anywhere in here. Mix candyfloss with cloud and add a patina of dirt, and that's the colour of the walls.

The king-size bed has also been stripped. There's a wardrobe. Plain white. Empty but not thick with dust. A marble-topped table with wrought-iron legs stands by the head of the bed. On impulse, I tug open its little drawer, and at once I'm hit with a familiar scent. It's light, floral. There's a hint of juniper. Memories come rushing back. Because if this isn't the perfume that Holly's mum used to wear, it's incredibly close – and suddenly, I'm in Holly's living room, hugging her chocolate cocker spaniel, Teddy, inhaling the scent of that perfume from his fur.

"I guess this was Franca's room," Yunoo says.

But I'm still too far back in the past to respond. Holly loved that dog so much. When Patrick moved in, he wanted to get rid of it. He didn't like dogs. Dad agreed that we'd take him. But Holly was so upset Patrick was forced to relent. After Holly died, her mum told me that Teddy had gone to live with Lauren, Holly's sister. I have no reason to doubt it, but I still sometimes wake up in the middle of the night, desperately hoping that it's true.

"Mia?"

This time, Yunoo's voice startles me back to the present. Shoving the drawer shut against that scent, I manage to say, "She liked colour, at least."

As I follow Yunoo into the spacious en-suite, we discover yet more colour: a Moroccan-themed interior of ochre, salmon pink and olive green. A free-standing copper bath almost gives off its own light. Through the little window, I can at last glimpse the dazzlingly blue ocean beyond the dune. It makes me realize how trapped the house feels, with the ocean so close but hidden by the dune and the pines.

Yunoo sticks sensors round the sink and shower. Then I help him fit out the bedroom. And we move on.

The third room – "The Green Room!" – might once have been an emerald shade. It's a little smaller than Franca's. There's no bed. On the wall above the window, someone has painted fluffy clouds.

My throat tightens. "Was this—"

But Yunoo's already shaking his head. "Hanna's room

210

is the next one." He sticks a sensor near the window and follows my gaze. "Sheep?" he says. "For counting?"

"…Don't you think they're clouds?"

He smiles slightly. "And here's a problem with eyewitness testimony. Even when two people are looking at exactly the same object, they see different things."

"Except they *are* clouds."

His smile broadens. He resumes applying sensors. "This must have been the baby's room," he says.

I frown. "You mean when Hanna was a baby?"

"No, there was also a baby. When Hanna died. Four or five months old, I think." He sticks another sensor on the skirting board.

"But what happened to it? After Hanna died and Jon James died?"

"I read a few stories when I was doing my research. We know Franca struggled after Hanna's death. After Jon James died, the baby went to live with a brother of Jon's and his wife in a ski-resort town in Canada. The baby had a happy escape into the home of loving relatives."

"So Franca lost one child, and then she just let the other one go?" I realize I sound incredulous but I'm having a hard time absorbing what he's telling me.

"She wasn't well, remember. It's hardly surprising that her decisions don't seem rational to other people. They must have made a kind of sense to her."

A sudden heat burns in my chest. I'm thinking of my

own mother, and some of her decisions.

"I think we're done," he says, straightening his back.

As we head for the door, a flashing red light above the top right corner of the door frame catches my eye. It's pulsing from a black unit that's only slightly bigger than a temperature sensor.

"One of our cameras," Yunoo says, following my gaze.

We step back out in the corridor and head for the final door. There's a hard, dense weight in my stomach.

His hand resting on the handle, Yunoo turns to me. "If you don't want to go in now, you really don't have to. I'll need you to watch me but it can be from the doorway."

I feel every sharp contraction of my heart. "I should probably go in," I whisper.

"There's no *should*. Not now. At this point, we're only setting up. Really, Mia."

He presses down on the handle. The door creaks on its hinges as it opens inwards.

I manage to make it to the doorway. But, even if I wanted to step through, I don't think I could. Only my eyes seem capable of moving. They scan the room in quick jerks – like if they don't rest in any spot for long, I can't get burned.

I see canary-yellow walls. A child's bed. It's oval-shaped, with a faded red duvet with white spots and a black headboard cut to look like the head of a ladybird. On a white chest of drawers, I see a dusty globe lamp.

Tacked to the wall beside the bed are three photos with

curling edges. Above these are white shelves packed with stuffed toys, their lifeless eyes staring.

On a little circular green rug by the bed is a plastic castle, its dusty drawbridge down. Two plastic knights look like they've just tumbled from a turret. And there's a single purple sandal on its side beside them. Heart-shaped holes puncture the leather. The strap is crinkled from use, unbuckled.

Everything inside me tightens, like I'm being compressed by my own flesh and skin.

The room hasn't been cleared. *Why* hasn't it?

The window is closed. I can't help wondering who closed it.

I stare at Hanna's things … and, when I catch sight of a Barbie doll near the bed, I'm thrown back again into the past, into Holly's room, when we were six or seven.

In my mind, I see Holly lying on her front on the threadbare pink carpet, skinny ankles crossed, playing with a Barbie whose hair we'd streaked black using an old mascara of Lauren's. She was happy. We were both happy.

Then it strikes me… This doll. The scent in Franca's bedroom. A dead girl. Reports of a haunting. My mind feels like it's rocking, like I'm that whaling ship in the oil painting, struggling in a sudden storm. Did Holly somehow *bring* me here?

Could she have?

No. *No.*

"Mia?" Yunoo's returning to the door with the bag. "OK?" he says. "Ready to move upstairs?"

I stare at him, uncomprehending. I press my hands to my eyes.

"Mia?" He sounds concerned.

"Just memories," I manage to whisper, and I let my hands drop. "I was thinking of a friend."

He nods slowly. "Well, I'm done in there, so we can leave this part of the house now. If you're ready?"

I take a deep breath. "OK."

"The door by that window seat…" He's looking along the corridor to the landing. "You get up through there."

The purple sandal with the heart perforations is suddenly vivid in my mind. "Why hasn't her room been cleared?" I ask him, my voice strained.

"I don't know," he says softly. "Maybe Amy Ambler wants to do it herself. Only she hasn't been able to bring herself to attempt it yet."

"But Franca—"

"Hanna was gone, and she couldn't accept it? Or Hanna was gone, and she couldn't bear for anything in that room to be touched. I can imagine either scenario being true." He starts off towards the landing.

"So we go up through this little door," Yunoo says. He's standing at the far end of the window seat.

My legs shaky, I go to join him. "What's upstairs?"

"I'm not sure," he says. "I just know from the plan that

we get up this way." I must be looking apprehensive, because he says: "What's the worst thing we'll find up there? I'll tell you: spiders. Bugs. You're not afraid of those?"

I feel a strong impulse to press a hand over my belly button. I force myself to resist it. "No," I tell him.

He smiles but it seems half-hearted. I get the distinct feeling he's also trying to reassure himself. "Then there's nothing whatsoever to worry about," he says firmly. "As we will now see…"

20

We're loud. Overloud, in what feels to me a forced kind of way – like, if we *act* like everything's totally fine, we can convince ourselves that it is.

We're all sitting round the kitchen table, Yunoo to my left, Rav opposite him, Alli across from me, Lana and Jared at each end. Rav and Jared have prepared dinner. Roast chicken for them, Yunoo and Lana. Baked aubergines with garlic and feta for Alli and me. New potatoes and a herb salad. Water and a bottle of Coke.

"Alcohol is a no-no in any investigation," Yunoo says to me as he passes me the water jug.

"No drugs of any kind," Alli says, and I can't help thinking of what Yunoo told me about her father.

"Except caffeine," Yunoo adds, smiling, as he reaches for the Coke.

I spoon potatoes, shiny with butter, beside my aubergine

and hand the potato bowl to Alli.

"Rav, this is a feast!" she says happily.

"Hey," Jared says, waving his finger, "I claim at least five or six per cent of the credit."

"You did boil the water for the potatoes," Rav concedes.

"And prepared all the garlic!"

"And put the garlic through the crusher. No one can take that away from you." Rav smiles.

"So," I ask, "is Amy Ambler thinking of living here? Is that why she wants a survey done?"

Though Yunoo's sensors wouldn't reflect it, it feels like the temperature drops five degrees.

"I don't know," Jared says, his expression totally serious again. He takes a sip of water. "I didn't ask her."

"There are various reasons people want parapsychological surveys," Rav says, mostly to me, I think.

"All kinds of reasons," Alli agrees. "But it's often because they're scared. Or they want someone official to validate their experiences. Tell them they're not imagining it all."

"Often both," Jared says.

Rav nods. I force myself to cut a potato in half and eat a piece.

Rav starts talking about one of Franca Ambler's movies, but I tune out. I still can't help wondering if Holly somehow brought me here to this house, and if so, why. And I'm thinking about what Yunoo and I found upstairs in the attic room.

It runs half the length of the house, and it was stifling, the ceiling too low for Yunoo to stand up straight. At the far end, there was a half-sized door, which must give access to the roof terrace, but it was padlocked. I tried to open the clasp but it wouldn't budge.

Yunoo was right – there was nothing up there but dust, cobwebs and desiccated insects. The only other thing was a plastic knight with a cracked green shield, which I found wedged into a gap between the rough floorboards. I realized Hanna must have played up there, in that claustrophobic attic. A kind of hot chill ran through me.

"It's true!"

The exclamation snaps my focus back to the dinner table. Alli's talking, waving her fork.

"The smell of rain coming," she's saying. "It's got a name I can't remember. But there's this guy I heard about with Parkinson's disease. His olfactory nerves have been damaged, so his sense of smell is poor. He was on holiday, and he smelled burning leaves. Then oniony gas. Then burnt wood. It stopped. A few weeks later, when he was back home having breakfast, it happened again. By the time he got into his car to go to work, a storm had hit. After a while, he realized that he gets these smell hallucinations a few hours before a storm. Even up to ten hours before."

"What's he detecting?" Rav asks.

Jared looks up from his plate. "I imagine it's to do with the fall in air pressure."

Yunoo nods in Jared's direction. "Right. With reduced air pressure, like you get before a storm, our sense of smell actually gets worse. And when it's already impaired—"

"The likelihood of hallucinations increases," Alli finishes.

"Smell hallucinations?" I ask.

"I think you can have hallucinations in all of the senses," Lana says.

"Some people with impaired hearing hear tunes," Alli says. "Some people who are visually impaired hallucinate colours, faces, patterns, even complex scenes."

Rav nods. "I once read about this woman with that syndrome, and I remember what she said because it was so specific. She sees the faces of unfamiliar, well-groomed men."

Lana pulls a face. "That is too horrible."

"For some people with impaired vision, their visual cortex becomes overactive," Jared says. "Visual stimulation can then start to do strange things. Especially in dim light."

I look up sharply. "Maybe some ghost reports…"

Everyone turns to look at me, making me flush.

"Are hallucinations?" Jared finishes, and nods. "In the dark, late at night, heart pumping from anxiety and caffeine, brain primed with stories of apparitions and expectations… Yeah. I could imagine how someone could actually see a ghost."

"Actually *see* one?" I say.

Lana pushes away her plate. "Vision happens in the brain, not the eyes, right? Your brain takes in data from your eyes and all your other senses, but it also uses expectations and predictions based on previous experience to generate perceptions. What you perceive or I perceive is never a perfect reflection of some objective reality."

"Look at the dress," Yunoo says.

I'm feeling really confused now. "What dress?"

"*The* dress," he says. "You know, it practically broke the internet. Was it blue and black or white and gold?"

I realize that I do know what he's talking about. I remember seeing a picture on Freja's phone.

"Some people saw it as one combination, but some as the other," Jared says. "And everyone was totally sure they were right. How could there be such disagreement? Because it all depended on how their brains were controlling the type of light. If you assumed, unconsciously, that the dress was in daylight, it looked different to how it did if you assumed it was indoors, in artificial light. For those groups of people, their realities – what they actually *saw* – were different."

Yunoo says, "All kinds of things influence perceptions. But I cannot work without coffee. So I will have to try to consciously control for the effects of caffeine at night."

My head is still buzzing from what Jared just said about realities being different. Of course, I'm thinking about Mum. But I also wonder what Yunoo's saying. "You're not going to stay up to monitor the temperatures?"

"There's no need. It's all recorded. But, if we are going to try to understand some of the reports of events in this house, we'll have to attempt to recreate the circumstances – the timings, the locations – as accurately as we can. As I gather many of these reports happened at night, I think, that's when we'll have to be active? At least for some of the night. Right?" He's looking at Jared, who nods.

"But the cameras are recording everything?" I say.

"We cannot expect our video to function as stand-alone evidence," Jared says. "Video can always be manipulated."

I try to get my head round what he's saying. "So, even if we record something that we can't explain, it won't definitely convince anyone else?"

"We have different procedures now compared with Enfield, say, and video images would definitely help to build a case," Alli says. "Also, of course, Jared has his reputation. Other parapsychologists might want to reserve judgement. But they wouldn't assume he'd manufactured evidence."

"Well, I'd certainly hope not," Jared says a little archly.

Alli looks a little uncomfortable. "I meant—"

He waves a hand. "No. No, you're right. It's tough. It's possible that no study will ever convince everyone. And I suspect that nothing we gather or do could be sufficient to persuade a hardline sceptic. But, in this case, if I'm satisfied, if *we* are convinced, that will be enough for me. And I think it'll be enough for Amy Ambler, too."

There's a silence. The only sound is of Yunoo's fork stabbing a piece of potato.

Then Jared says, "Did we get anywhere with getting the electricity back on upstairs?"

"I've checked the fuse box," Lana says. "There's nothing obvious. I think either we have to get an electrician in, or we have to work without it."

I'm thinking about what it'll be like to work upstairs in the dark with only torches, and I don't sense Alli's eyes on me until she says: "Mia, can I ask, have you always known you can sense things that other people can't?"

I look round at her. The expression in her deep brown eyes is warm. She gives me a slight, encouraging smile.

How do I even begin to reply to that? But maybe there is a way I can answer her without talking about Holly. "There are places I really don't like being." This is true. "That would make me feel weird. When I was younger. Dad would tell me not to be silly, that there was nothing to be scared of."

"What kind of places?" she asks.

"The library at home, in Sheffield. The staircase down to the children's library... The top landing of a friend's house."

It seems odd to be saying these things out loud.

It's not unusual for a kid to be scared of dark staircases or little-used rooms. But the feelings I had in those places were more intense than a general sense of anxiety, I think.

"That top landing, then. Did you feel anything specific up there?" Lana asks.

"I don't think so. I just felt … odd."

"An energy?" Alli asks, leaning towards me.

"…Maybe. A presence of some kind."

I realize Rav hasn't made any comment. My gaze jerks to him. He's watching Jared's face.

"Something you might call a *ghost*?" Jared asks me now.

I shake my head vaguely. "I'm not really sure what I felt in those places. Infrasound, maybe. A magnetic field?"

Jared slides his knife and fork together. The gentle scraping catches at the back of my neck, making the hairs rise. "But when you didn't know about those kinds of influences? It would not have been unreasonable for very strange feelings in relatively unfamiliar places to make you feel that a spirit was there."

"We jump to conclusions all the time," Yunoo puts in. "We have to. And so often we have to make judgements based on partial information."

"Some of us are *actually* more rational than others," Lana says, looking at Rav.

"When our data has gaps, we are of course more prone to drawing mistaken conclusions," Jared says, ignoring her. "We connect a to x and c to y and we're *sure* there's a meaningful link, even when there's none."

"That's what ghosts might be?" I find myself asking. "A to x and c to y?"

The room's suddenly so quiet, I can hear even Lana, at the end of the table, breathing.

"I guess this is what this house may show the world," Alli says. "That it's more than that."

"Perhaps you should ask Jared again in the morning," Lana adds softly, to me.

Suddenly Yunoo scrapes back his chair, making me flinch. "Rav, you've set the bar too high!" he exclaims as he collects Rav's plate and noisily places it on top of his. "When I serve beans on my cooking duty, you can't say I haven't warned you."

"No beans," Jared says. "Or I can't in all conscience enforce bedroom sharing."

Yunoo laughs.

"That is disgusting," Lana says but she can't quite suppress a smile. Maybe she's glad of the change in atmosphere, too.

Alli still looks thoughtful. Like she's not quite ready to move on from the discussion.

"So, Rav, what's for pudding?" Lana says. She takes Alli's plate and scrapes an edge of aubergine skin on to her own.

"Cookies," Rav says.

Yunoo grins. "All the best meals end in cookies."

"…Is not actually true or a saying, even if you try to make it sound like one," Lana says but there's still a faint light of a smile in her olive eyes.

I get up and carry my plate over to the worktop by the sink. And I find it impossible not to look out through the window. How many times, I wonder, must Franca Ambler have stood in this exact spot, after Hanna and Jon were dead? That thought alone makes me feel uneasy. Then there's the dune. Moonbeams breaking through the dying twilight are colouring it a silvery grey. All that sand, massed just out there.

The doll. The scent in Franca's room. A dead girl. All that sand… Coincidence? I just don't know.

I take a ragged breath in. And then out.

"If I can have you all back in your seats," Jared calls. "Before we do properly get to work, there are some details about this case that I would like to share."

21

It's 8.57 p.m. and the heat of the day has settled. I even feel a cool draught coming in from round the door to the utility room.

We're all sitting back at the table. Rav opens a plastic tray of chocolate chip cookies and Jared drags over the laptop with the Ghostbusters sticker on the lid.

"First I'm going to read you something," he says. "It's the transcript of an interview I conducted with Jetta Amos, then aged forty-two, housekeeper to Franca Ambler and Jon James."

His gaze taking in each of us in turn, he goes on: "Jetta Amos was one of the first members of staff taken on by Mr James and Ms Ambler. She lived in her own home but worked five days a week here at the house. This interview took place a week after Hanna's death. Franca Ambler was staying with relatives. I'd assumed that I had her permission to be here. When I realized I did not, I decided to keep the few interviews that I'd conducted confidential. No one else has ever read or heard this."

His voice is sombre but there's a definite charged tone to it. I guess finally being able to share something he's had to keep secret for so long must be a big moment for him.

Jared focuses on the screen. "I ask Jetta if she's ever experienced anything unusual in the house. She says: 'So many times.'

"I say, 'Can you describe those experiences?'

"'It watched me. In the hall outside the bedrooms, one time, I saw it.'

"'Saw what?'

"'Like a ... light. A figure of light.'"

I feel a prickling of tension rise up my neck.

"'What did you think it was?'

"'It was a spirit.'

"'Can you describe anything else about the figure?'

"'It was male.'"

In the glow of the pendant light, and in his black T-shirt, Jared looks like he might be an actor in a one-man show. But he's keeping the emotion that Jetta Amos must have been feeling out of his voice.

"I ask: 'A man or a boy?'

"'A man.'

"'Did it do anything?'

"'It just was … there.'

"'Were you afraid?'

"'Not then.'

"'Even though you believed you were seeing a spirit?'

"She doesn't reply.

"'As far as you know, has anyone else seen this spirit?'

"'Mr Jon and Ms Amy. She saw it first.'

"'And they told you about those experiences?'

"'Mr Jon told me.'

"'In the same spot or somewhere else?'

"'That exact same place.'"

Jared looks up again from the screen. "So, Jon James has told her that he and Amy Ambler have seen a ghostly figure in the hall. The expectation of it has been seeded in her mind."

"But I don't get it," Alli says. "If Amy Ambler's already sure she's seen a spirit in the house, why's she called us in?"

"I think the reported sightings of Hanna in her bedroom after her death, and the idea that perhaps a spirit or poltergeist was connected with her death, concern her more than this," Jared says.

Lana's frowning. "You didn't video the interview?"

"That first time, she asked me not to," Jared says. "She agreed that I could use a dictaphone. But she didn't want to be videoed."

"She say why?" Rav asks.

"She was very upset. This is a week after the little girl died, remember."

"She said she wasn't afraid *then*," I say.

Jared jabs a finger in my direction, like he's spiking my thought. "Right. At this point, I had to stop the interview because she started crying. I went back the next day. This time she allowed me to video her."

His finger taps on the touchpad, then he spins the laptop round. "This is eight days after Hanna's death."

Lana and Rav drag their chairs round behind Yunoo and Alli and me, so we can all see the screen.

A video has been paused. Slumped in a worn leather chair is a big woman in a black blouse. Her bobbed dark hair looks like it hasn't been washed for a while.

Jared taps the touchpad, and she comes to life. Her breathing is heavy.

We hear Jared's voice: "Mrs Amos, can I take you back to the house? We talked about you seeing the spirit in the hall outside the bedrooms. You said you weren't scared then."

Her bloodshot eyes flicker to gaze directly into the camera lens. She looks afraid. Exhausted.

"Can you give me an example of a different incident?"

"There were a lot of incidents, if that's what you're calling them."

"Maybe we can start with one example…?"

"Well, like the time I was in the utility room, sorting

the washing. I had it in two piles, all ready for ironing. The front door bell rang. It was a delivery man with something for Mr James. After I took in the package, I went straight back to the washing – and it was all over the place. Those clothes had been shaken out, thrown around."

"It could have been Hanna? Playing a game?"

"Hanna was a baby then. Asleep upstairs in her cot."

"Who else was in the house?"

"Just me and Hanna and—" Her eyes fill with tears. She presses a crumpled tissue to her face.

"You and Hanna and…?"

"That spirit," she whispers.

"Did you tell Ms Ambler or Mr James what had happened?"

Wiping her eyes, she nods.

"What did they say?"

"Ms Franca said I had to be mistaken. Mr Jon said he suspected as much."

"What did you think he meant by that?"

"He said he'd heard furniture being dragged about. And banging, upstairs, when he was the only one home. He knew there was a spirit in the house." She falls silent. The cold focus of the camera on her face feels brutal. I think of standing at the foot of the stairs at home, hearing things moving in my room.

"Someone else might have handed in their notice.

Never gone back to Halcyon House," Jared suggests.

She sighs. "I did think about it but it was good money. And they were good people. And Hanna was the sweetest baby. Hardly ever cried." She presses a fresh tissue to her eyes.

"Were you afraid to be on your own in the house?" Jared asks.

She lowers the tissue. There's a look of real pain in her eyes. "At first. Then I thought, if the worst you can do is move furniture and throw clothes around, well, I can live with that. That's what I thought. The worst…" She shakes her head.

"Did Hanna James ever mention to you about seeing or hearing furniture or anything else moving around in the house?"

She shakes her head.

"Was she scared to be in the house?"

Again Jetta Amos shakes her head. "She was such a happy little thing."

"Apart from that incident with the laundry, did you personally have any other experiences suggestive to you of poltergeist activity?"

"Doors banging. I got used to the doors."

"Did you ever see a door bang open or shut?"

She nods.

"And did it happen in one room or many?"

"It was the dining room most often. I'd be in the kitchen,

unpacking groceries or washing pots, and I'd hear it going, like a storm was blowing."

"Did you ever go to investigate?"

Her dark eyes flicker shut. Then she opens them. Almost angrily, she says, "What I *thought* was: let it get on with it. Live and let live… Live and let be. I thought we could exist side by side." The anger fades from her eyes. She seems to be thinking about something. Very quietly, she says, "Can they see us – when we see them?"

After a moment, Jared says, "I don't know."

There's a longer silence. Then Jared asks, "Was Hanna ever with you when you heard or saw these things?"

Jetta Amos presses the ball of her right palm to each eye in turn. "She must've been."

"But Franca Ambler denied that any of this was happening?"

Jetta purses her lips. "She said she'd never experienced anything like that herself and Hanna wasn't to be frightened. That's what she said."

"Did anyone else apart from Mr James and yourself witness any similar events? You mentioned Amy Ambler?"

"Ms Amy heard the doors go. She might even have been the first to hear them. When she was upstairs, getting ready in a guest room. I remember her coming down and asking me if I'd heard them."

"Was Hanna with her?"

"…I don't know."

"Do you think the spirit that you saw in the hall was responsible for the poltergeist activity?"

"Well, I don't know."

Another silence.

Jared clears his throat. "I have to ask you a more difficult question. I don't want to upset you. But do you believe that a malevolent spirit played a role in Hanna's death?"

Jetta lets her breath go in one long exhalation. Fresh tears roll down her cheeks. "I cannot doubt it," she says.

*

Jared closes his laptop. For a few moments, no one moves. The room is silent.

"So there you have it," he says. "The first of four interviews with people who spent substantial time in or around the house and who all reported at least some of the same experiences."

"She seemed to believe what she was telling you," Yunoo says.

"I cannot doubt it," Jared says, echoing the final words of the video. "I also interviewed Amy Ambler at the time. She was very upset, mostly by the idea that, if the spirit could slam doors and move furniture, perhaps it could tamper with the window lock in Hanna's bedroom. And I gathered testimony from Jon James, who told me about banging doors and hearing furniture being moved."

"Did any of them report finding that furniture actually had moved to a different place?" Lana asks.

"Amy Ambler used to sleep in the main guest bedroom to the right of the landing. Your Blue Room, Yunoo. She said that sometimes she'd find the bed moved away from the wall. Jon James said that every time he went into one of the smaller guest rooms, he'd find the chest of drawers in a different position."

"Who's the other witness?" Alli asks.

"The gardener," Jared says. "He saw, rather than heard, things he couldn't explain. Before Hanna's death, he said he saw movement in bedroom windows when everyone was out. Lights flashing from the windows in the attic. Then, after she died, he saw her face at her bedroom window. I also interviewed a neighbour who brought a basket of food to the house a few days after Hanna died, and she said she saw lights flashing up in the attic and heard a child laughing. When she rang the bell, no one answered. Jon James later confirmed that the house had been empty. He'd taken Franca with the baby to see a grief counsellor. There were a few other isolated reports: a cleaner said that two days after Hanna died she saw her sitting on that velvet sofa – the one through in the other room. A delivery driver said he heard a girl in the garden, laughing."

"It could have been a girl on the beach," Rav says.

Jared nods. "It could."

"The gardener's stories definitely couldn't be explained by Hanna playing in the house?" Yunoo asks.

"He insists that he saw lights flashing even when everyone in the house said they were away," Jared says. "But, after he saw her face at her window, he didn't see the lights again."

"He's the only one who saw this?" Alli asks. "Hanna at the window after she'd died?"

"Memories…?" Lana says. "Expectations. Hallucinations. High emotions. He was upset."

Jared nods. "It's possible… The witnesses did talk of other things, too. But, as you'll understand, I cannot share all of their reports with you. I can't fill your heads with expectations."

I've been silent all this time. I take a sip of water. Try to gather my thoughts. "Did the reports of this poltergeist spirit or people seeing or hearing Hanna stop at any particular point?"

"Good question," Jared says. "It's hard to say. After Jon James moved out with the baby, I gather Franca gave all the household employees their notice. She stayed here without help, and with only very occasional visitors, as far as I know. Franca didn't mention any further incidences to anybody else. Of course, that doesn't necessarily mean that nothing happened here during those years."

"Going back," Rav says, "did anyone see or hear anything unusual in Hanna's room around the time she died?"

Jared shakes his head. "When she fell, Franca was downstairs, in the kitchen. Jetta had gone home. Jon James was driving a friend who'd been staying with them for a weekend party back to Manhattan."

"And Amy?" Lana says.

"Amy didn't live here. She was a frequent visitor but she was home in New York."

"So Franca found Hanna?" I ask.

Jared nods. I don't know if he has kids – I only know he has an ex – but he looks suddenly very tired. The lines in his forehead darken. And I feel tears in my own eyes and my memories starting to open again – memories of Holly the day she died – but I *have* to keep them inside for now. I just have to.

Lana leans forwards across the table. "What do you want us to do tonight?"

Pulling the laptop back towards him, Jared says, "I suggest that for the next two hours we all spend some time, in pairs, in different rooms. We can rotate. Mia, if environmental factors are implicated in some of the experiences reported in the house, you're the one who's most likely to feel something unusual. If you do, speak up. Right away. If nothing interesting has happened by –" he checks his watch – "eleven, eleven thirty, we can probably get some sleep and check for camera or temperature alerts in the morning. Unless any of you actively *want* to stay up."

"Alerts?" I ask.

"The software report will highlight any atypical recordings for motion and sound and temperature," Lana explains.

"So, Rav and Mia, you're together?" Jared says. "Yunoo, you're with me. And now for the million-dollar question: who wants to start where?"

22

Jared and Yunoo opt for a guest room and Lana suggests to Alli they start in the attic. I'm relieved because I don't much want to be up there. But then I'm worried in case Rav suggests Hanna's room.

"Franca Ambler's bedroom?" Rav says, half to me, half to Jared.

Jared nods. "Right now, one room is pretty much as good as any other."

After fetching more torches from a crate in the dining room, we go upstairs in pairs. Rav and I are the last to head up. While I'm still on the staircase, there's a sudden creak through the ceiling, making my head jerk up. It has to be Alli, I tell myself, or Lana, up in the attic.

The moon is fully out now. Its cool light drifts in through the recessed landing window, bleaching everything of colour. Even our skin. I take a deep breath.

Very slowly I let it out.

As we head into the longer corridor, I realize that it must have been somewhere around here that Jetta Amos and Jon James saw the figure of light. Rav is shining his torch along it, sending shadows skittering. Gripping my own torch tightly, I stop, to see if maybe I'll feel anything… Yes, I'm scared, even though I'm telling myself not to be. But I'm meant to be here to feel, and Rav is with me.

I try to move my conscious attention around my body, in the way that Mum once taught me to do, as a form of meditation.

My pulse throbs in my neck, and in the backs of my knees.

Pins and needles prick the instep of my right foot.

High up in my nose, I can smell something musty.

I can hear – I *can* hear – the ocean. A gentle crash, then a lull, then a crash. Another sudden creak overhead makes my body jolt. From the guest room back behind us comes the deep tone of Yunoo's voice. I can't make out what he's saying but it's a comfort to hear.

"Mia?" Rav says, his voice close.

I shake my head. "I can't feel anything."

"OK," he says. "That's OK." Shining his torch on along the corridor, he walks to Franca's bedroom door, and he beckons to me.

Inside the room, the moonlight is bright. We don't really need the torches. Rav's already by the bed, peering up at the ceiling rose. Trying to avoid even glancing at the bedside table, I shut the door behind me.

"What're you looking at?" I ask him.

"I felt something on my arm... Probably just a flake of paint."

Leaving my torch on the bed, I go to the window. I rest my hands on the cool sill. Directly below is a dark stretch of overgrown lawn. The crashing of waves is louder in here. And I can just about make out the ocean – a blacker layer beyond the dune.

I know Rav is here but even so I'm right on edge, trying hard to keep a lid on what I know would instantly become terror if I saw something, felt something. How could Franca stand to live here by herself? Did she used to go into Hanna's room, I wonder, and sit among her things?

I know that Holly's bedroom was cleared. At the funeral, after the service, in a hideous hotel function room in which a screen was displaying photos of Holly on a loop, her mum offered me whatever I wanted from it. A keepsake.

I remember staring at the screen as the photo changed to one of Holly and me in plastic tiaras, Holly blowing out the seven candles on her fairytale palace cake. I couldn't speak. I could only shake my head. Holly's mum said she understood, but she looked sad. I wish I could go back in time, and take something for her.

I also wish I could feel something in this house that might help Hanna's aunt. Taking a deep breath, I let my gaze run over the window, down to the little plastic casings. "In all the haunting reports you've heard about, have there ever been reports about poltergeists opening windows?"

Rav doesn't answer right away. "I don't think so," he says at last. "At least I don't remember any. But Jared would have a better idea about that." He sits down on the bed. "Your friend Holly," he says quietly. "What happened to her?"

I stiffen.

"Was she sick?"

I shake my head.

"An accident?"

I don't answer.

"You don't have to tell me. Obviously. But, Mia, this thing with her – I'd like to help. That's the reason *you're* here, right? To get help, or help yourself, one way or another? Hopefully to find some kind of resolution? Maybe I'd be able to help more if I knew what happened."

I wrap my arms round my chest, and just about manage to say, "How?"

"I'm aware of all kinds of reports of circumstances around possible hauntings. I don't have anything like Jared's level of knowledge but I do have experience."

I look down at the floorboards. The crashing of the waves from behind seems to get louder, like the blood in my ears. I can feel it rushing in my skull. "I'm meant to be concentrating on this house."

"But are you feeling anything in here? Tingling? Sudden discomfort? Any sense of presence?"

I shake my head.

The bedsprings creak as he changes position. "You talked about sand. Were you on holiday when it happened?"

I shake my head quickly and turn away. I rest my forehead against the window, feel the cool, solid press of the glass.

"But it was summer?"

I squeeze my eyes shut. "…Yes," I whisper.

"You were at some kind of playground?"

I feel sick. Like something's being pulled up out of me, and it's dredging my stomach. "Sheffield by the Sea."

"Sheffield's by the sea?"

"It's *nowhere* near the sea." I press my head harder against the window. "That's what they call it. In summer, they bring sand into a big square in town. Make a beach, with deckchairs, and buckets and spades, and stalls set up around. The fountains are meant to be like the sea."

"What kind of stalls?" he says in a low voice. "Ice cream? Target shooting?"

"…Candyfloss." I clench my fists even tighter. But it's like I can feel the sticky residue on my fingers. "Swingboats. Hook-a-duck."

"You used to go with Holly?"

"Every year," I whisper. "Since we were four."

In my mind, I can see a rainbow in the coarse spray from

the fountains. I hear plastic spades scrape on the flagstones beneath the shallow layer of sand. Kids are shouting. There's a sploshing from the hook-a-duck stand.

"That day you ate candyfloss? You went on the swingboats?"

"We'd got too old. You had to be twelve or under but they let us on."

"What did you do after the swingboats?"

"…We got chips." My body's so still, it feels like it's only my lungs and my heart that are moving. "All the benches by the beach were full. We went up the steps, to a bench by the road. We were talking about her sister, Lauren, and her boyfriend. They'd just bought a flat…" My voice dries up.

"Was it just the two of you?"

I nod.

"What happened?" he asks.

I hold my breath. I can smell the sharp tang of vinegar from Holly's chips. She used to pour it on till it puddled. Somewhere in my mind, I hear a faint creaking. But I can't tell if it's here, in Sheffield, or back in the house.

"She saw him first."

"Who?"

"…Her stepdad. He just appeared out of the crowds. He was walking past."

There's a pause before Rav speaks again. "And he saw you on the bench?"

I snatch a sharp breath. "He was swaying. He must have been drinking in a pub in town. He might have been looking for a taxi, or a bus. He saw us and came by the bench. She told him to go away – he stank of beer – and he got angry, and grabbed her shoulder. I shouted at him to leave her. I was shouting and people were looking. She tore herself free and she ran."

I can see Holly's wide eyes. I feel sick with fear and the stench of chlorine from the fountains, like it's happening again. I smell the alcohol on his breath, and I watch her twisting, yelling at him to get off, dragging herself from his grip. She sprints blindly away from the bench, stumbling into the road.

"There was a bus. It couldn't stop in time…"

I hang my head. Hot tears flood my eyes. I don't want to cry. I make myself turn round to face Rav.

"The first time she appeared to me, after she died, I thought she was just sad. But actually she hates me."

Silence. Then he says, "But you know it wasn't your fault, right? You tried to help. There was nothing you could have done. It was an accident."

"So you say."

"Like I'm sure your mom said," he says quickly. "And your dad. You were her best friend. Why would she hate you?" He pauses for a moment. "Did you see anyone – after she died? A counsellor?"

I wipe my eyes. "There was one who came to school

but..." I stop. Nothing the counsellor said made me feel any better.

I stand there, trembling, my heart shaky, my breathing rough.

"Mia—" Rav starts again but he doesn't finish his sentence because a startled yell suddenly comes through the ceiling.

He looks up. Then he snatches our torches from the bed and hands one to me. Eyes fixed on mine, he says, "We'll talk more later. All right?"

I nod, and together we hurry out into the corridor.

For a few moments, we're motionless, listening. All I can hear is our breathing. I try to get mine back under control – enough to deal with whatever's happening, at least. My head is still full of Holly. But whoever just shouted, it wasn't in anger, but alarm.

"Lana?" Rav calls. "*Alli?*"

I couldn't tell which of them called out. But it was definitely a woman's voice.

Rav hurries to the narrow door by the bench seat – the door up to the attic.

"Why aren't Jared and Yunoo out here?" I whisper as I join him. "They must've heard that shout from the guest room?"

Rav shrugs and yanks opens the door to the attic. Into blackness, he shouts, "Alli? *Lana...* You OK?"

My heart thumping, I knock on the door to the guest

room. No answer. Quickly I jerk the handle and shove the door open. It's dark. Staying in the doorway, I sweep the room with a shaky beam – just enough to make sure that it's empty.

"Mia?" says Rav.

I step back on to the landing, my legs weak. "They're not in there."

"What? You *sure*?" He turns and peers up the dark staircase. "They might've already gone up. Jared?" he shouts, in no particular direction. "*Yunoo?*"

When there's no response, he aims his torch up the bare wood steps and starts to climb. I follow right behind him, Holly's scared face still raw in my mind.

Who was it who shouted? I wonder again. Where are they all?

"Lana?" Rav calls but more cautiously than before. It's almost as though he's afraid of his own voice. Or of what might hear it. "Alli?"

As he reaches the top of the stairs, there's a thunk, and he mutters something under his breath. I guess he just banged his head on the low ceiling.

"You see them?" I ask.

They'd have heard us, surely. As Rav moves into the attic, I go to stand beside him and we sweep the space with the powerful torch beams. They easily reach all the way to the little door at the end.

"They've gone," Rav says. "But the shout was from up

here, right? We came straight out. They couldn't have got down and gone off somewhere without us seeing them."

"That door must lead to the terrace," I say, pointing to the other end of the attic. "But it's padlocked."

Hunched over, because of the low headroom, Rav starts towards it. My legs feel so heavy but I stay with him. At the far end, he focuses his beam on the metal handle. The padlock that I saw when I was up here earlier with Yunoo has gone.

"It was locked," I whisper hoarsely. "With a *padlock*. There was no key."

"Then they must have broken it."

He pushes the door, and it swings back. A warm breeze sends a wave of goosebumps rolling over my skin.

I smell seaweed. Rot. Salt. We walk out on to a flat concrete roof. Just like at Sadie's place, there's no fence around the perimeter – nothing to stop you from falling to the ground. Which is why the door was locked, I guess. To keep Hanna safe.

"Lana?" Rav calls, waving his torch.

"*Rav?*"

We both spin to the left. *Alli*. She's standing, knees bent a little. She's almost right at the edge.

He hurries over to her. "What're you doing? Where's Lana?"

The breeze whips Alli's hair over her face. She pulls it back with both hands. "She saw something."

I spin my torch beam all around. There's no one else up here. "But where is she?" I ask.

Alli points off the edge of the roof.

"How'd she get down?" Rav demands.

I step as close to the edge as I dare. My heart's thumping so hard, my torch beam's twitching in time with my pulse. It's picking out nothing but branches and grass.

Alli shakes her head. "I don't know. By the time I realized she wasn't with me, she was already down."

Rav walks round the roof, scanning the grass and the dune with his beam. As he reaches into his shorts pocket for his phone, he calls to Alli: "We heard you shout – or Lana. What happened?"

"That was me," Alli says, and there's a quiver in her voice. "Something touched me."

"In the attic?" he asks, bringing his phone to his ear. I guess he's calling Lana.

"What kind of touch?" I ask, trying hard to keep my own voice steady.

"Something very soft. Brushing my cheek."

"It was Lana?" Rav says, phone pressed to his ear, still scanning the garden. "Her hair, or her clothes?"

"She was too far ahead."

"Then it was a spiderweb?" he says. "Or an insect?"

"I don't know," Alli says quietly. "We came out here and she saw something in the trees."

I feel another wave of panic start to build. Then, out

of the corner of my eye, I see a figure. Lean. Long hair. Over by the pines at the far side of the garden.

I take a few steps closer to the edge. "Lana!"

Rav's beside me in a second. I point.

"*Lana!*" he yells.

She doesn't move.

"*LANA!*"

The breeze is rustling the leaves of the plane trees, and the waves are crashing louder than before. Perhaps the tide has turned. Still, surely she can hear us.

"*Lana!*"

Alli's voice was so loud and close to my ear that I flinch. At last Lana turns.

"What're you doing?" Rav yells. "How'd you get down there?"

She just points to the side of the building.

"What are you *doing*?" he repeats.

I'm not sure she's heard him. But then she cups a hand to the side of her mouth. "Looking for Jared and Yunoo!"

Rav quickly turns. Hunching his shoulders, he hurries back into the attic. Alli and I follow – down the narrow steps, then the main slanting staircase, through to the kitchen, and the utility room exit to the garden.

At ground level, it's harder to locate Lana.

"There!" Rav says.

We run towards her. I try not to think about the sand in the grass, and I glance over my shoulder at the house.

Something's dangling from the roof terrace. My torch beam picks out a rope ladder. A fire escape, I guess. So that's how Lana got down.

Alli reaches her first. I hear Lana whisper, "Sorry," just as Rav and I catch up.

"You saw Jared and Yunoo out *here*?" he asks. "So where are they?"

Lana exhales hard. "I was also trying to stay with Alli. I shouted but they didn't stop. I lost them."

"What were they doing?" I ask her.

"They were just over here, talking! They did not look happy."

"We're meant to stay in *pairs*," Rav says.

I expect an angry response but Lana deflates. She shakes her head, like she's frustrated with herself. To Alli, she says, "I'm sorry. I thought you'd be OK, and I felt like Yunoo and Jared needed help. But then, when I got down here, I couldn't see them."

"So you should have gone back to Alli," Rav says.

"I was just trying to find them! They'd vanished."

"Why would they be out here?" I ask.

"They must have seen something," Alli says. "From the window in the guest room?"

Rav aims his torch past Lana, sweeping gnarled trunks and dense branches.

"How did you get out on to the roof?" I ask Lana.

She looks at me like it's a particularly dumb question.

I force my voice to stay level. "When I went up there with Yunoo this afternoon, that door was padlocked. Where did you find the key?"

She shakes her head. "There was no padlock."

I stare at her. "A big steel padlock! I even tried it."

"Was that before or after the cameras were set up?" Rav asks.

"It must have been after!" I exclaim.

"You didn't see the padlock when you went up the first time?" he asks Lana.

She shrugs. "We didn't go near that door. I fixed up a wide-angle full-spectrum near the entrance. It covers the room space."

"It *was* locked," I repeat.

"Then I don't know what to say," Lana says impatiently. "Someone got rid of the padlock."

"How? Where was the key?"

Alli says, "It'll be on the video. If someone unlocked it."

Rav shakes his head. "We really shouldn't need video evidence to corroborate our own statements."

"Well, it seems like we do," Lana says.

He frowns into the woods. "You've tried phoning them?" he asks her.

She rolls her eyes. "It goes to voicemail. For both."

"So now what?" I ask.

"I think we go back," Alli says. "We have no idea where they've gone, or why."

Rav says, "I agree."

Lana sighs hard. "I suppose I agree." She starts to stride away through the grass, back towards the house.

"I agree, too," I call, surprising myself. But I guess my emotions are running high.

Rav looks at me. "No point," he says in a low voice. "She really doesn't care."

"She does," Alli says, making us both turn to her. "She *does* care. Ask yourself: if you're smarter than everyone around you, only you're just the hired help, how would you feel?"

"She isn't smarter than everyone else," Rav says irritably.

"I'm not gonna argue with you," Alli says, "but you know it's true."

Then she strides after Lana, who's already at the utility-room door.

I glance up at the terrace. From here, I can't see the door to the attic. But I know we left it open. "We should go and shut that door?" I say to Rav.

"Yeah," he says, his eyes still on Alli.

"Through the house or up the ladder?" I ask him, picking out the ladder with my torch.

"Ladder would definitely be quicker," he says.

We jog back through the weeds to the wall. I reach as high as I can and grab each side of a wobbling rung with both hands.

When I'm about six rungs up, Rav calls, "Wait. Or I won't be able to see you at the top."

The ladder judders as he steps on to it. But, after the initial swaying, his weight makes it hang straighter, so it's easier to climb.

At the top, I haul myself on to the roof, and wriggle forwards on my stomach. Cautiously I stand up and glance behind me. The ends of the twin ropes are tied to metal anchor points. The rope is still trembling, which means Rav's still climbing.

I look back across the cracked concrete. The attic door is open, just as we left it. But then a strong gust of breeze comes in from the ocean. It blows my hair over my face, and I'm still pulling it from my eyes when I hear a slam. That door, banging shut.

Pulses of electricity spark through my body.

The wind, I say to myself. *The wind.*

But a blast from the direction of the ocean would have pushed it back against the wall. Surely.

A scuffling makes me turn. Rav's hands are gripping the top rung. Then I hear a voice from inside the house. *Lana's?*

"*Where've you been?*"

Can that be Lana? How am I able to hear the words so clearly?

"*Where've you been?*"

My legs feel like they're going to give way. I know that voice. It's not Lana's. Or Alli's.

It's *Holly's.*

23

"Where've you been?"

This *is* Lana speaking.

We're in the kitchen. All of us, round the kitchen table, but standing because we're too on edge to sit. Jared and Yunoo are sweaty, their clothes speckled with grass seeds.

I'm watching them, and listening, and I'm not sure what's happening. Time doesn't shift direction. A reverse-echo is impossible. But, just before Rav appeared beside me on the roof, I heard a voice from somewhere inside the house saying these exact words. Only I know it wasn't Lana's.

"Yunoo saw someone from the window," Jared's saying.

"We tried to follow," Yunoo says, rubbing a hand across his face. "We lost him. Or her."

"What exactly did you see?" Rav asks.

Another sheen of sweat has already formed on Yunoo's

forehead and he wipes it away. "It was hot. I managed to get the window open enough so that I could push the shutters back. As soon as I did, I heard something outside. When I looked out, I glimpsed someone. Over by the pine wood."

"Doing what?" Alli asks.

"Just standing there," he says.

I lick my dry lips. "Watching the house?"

"I don't know." Yunoo shrugs. "They were in the shadows. I just saw a silhouette."

"I saw them, too," Jared puts in. "And, by the time we got out round the side of the house, they were on the move."

"Maybe it was someone from town?" I suggest. "They saw your car and the minibus and they came to check us out."

"That is a probable explanation," Jared says.

Rav says, "How far did you go?"

"All the way to a path," Yunoo says. "A boardwalk. It looked like it goes up to a road and down to the beach."

"You're sure it was just one person?" Rav asks.

"We only saw one," Yunoo says. He rubs his hands through his short hair, sending brown pine needles falling to the ground. "Maybe we shouldn't have gone."

"Well, *I'd* like to know if locals are checking us out," Lana says. "I have motion-sensitive video set up in the garden. It could create all kinds of false alerts that I'll have to review."

"Birds and squirrels are gonna give you a bunch more

false positives than curious locals," Rav says.

"And so?" she says hotly. "I just don't bother with video outside?"

"Look," Jared says firmly, "it's late. Unfortunately, we can't draw any conclusions from this particular observation. Does anyone have anything else from the evening that they want to share?"

"I think you should have told someone," Alli says. "We were worried. Lana went off looking for you. You didn't answer your phones."

Jared nods. "Noted, and fair. We had to move quickly but we should have informed you. Our phones were on silent. I guess we didn't hear them. But I can't think of an investigation-critical reason for phones to be on silent, so I suggest we all keep our ringers activated. We need to make it as easy as possible to stay in contact. Anything else to report?"

He looks from Alli to Lana to Rav. They all shake their heads.

I take a deep breath. "When I went up into the attic with Yunoo this afternoon, the door out to the roof was padlocked. When Lana and Alli were there tonight, the padlock was gone."

He looks at Lana, who shrugs and nods. Then he turns to Yunoo.

"The fact is I didn't see," Yunoo says. "Mia, it's *not* that I don't believe you. I was focusing on where to put the temperature sensors. I just didn't look closely at that door."

"So who removed the padlock?" Jared asks.

Silence.

I have to wrap my arms round myself to try to stop my body from shaking.

"In that case," Jared says quietly, "Lana, I want you to review the footage from the attic, from the minute the camera went up. Anything else?"

I think about the attic door slamming shut. But maybe I was wrong about the direction of the wind. Holly's voice… I still don't know what to think about that.

"Then I may stay up a while but I'll be setting my alarm for seven," Jared says. "Let's plan to meet down here for breakfast at seven thirty."

*

In the dining room, we find our gear and help ourselves to the sleeping bags and pillows, floor mats and towels, and camping lanterns.

Jared and Yunoo return to the guest room. Lana and Alli carry their bedding and bags into Franca's bedroom. Rav and I head for the room with the sheep/clouds.

While he uses the en-suite bathroom, I try to focus not on the fact that I'm going to be spending the night in this house, but on finding my toiletries and a pair of shorts to sleep in, and rolling out my mat along one wall. It takes a while because my hands are trembling – from telling Rav

257

about Holly, from hearing her voice, from seeing that door slam shut, because the padlock is missing.

I also check my phone and send upbeat replies to messages from Dad and Mum and Sadie. To Tamara, who has simply sent:

OK??

I send back:

So far xx

Rav pads out of the bathroom and unfurls his mat by the opposite wall. By torchlight, and avoiding the mirror, I do what I need to do in the bathroom as quickly as I can.

I come out to find Rav already lying down on his side. He's taken off his T-shirt and pushed the sleeping bag to his waist. The lantern's on the floor by his mat, shining its steady white LED light.

I slip into my sleeping bag and pull it right up to my neck even though it's hot.

"Lantern on or off to sleep?" he asks.

"On," I answer. Then I snatch a breath. "When I was on the roof, while you were still climbing up, I heard Holly's voice. She said, '*Where've you been?*'"

He's silent for what feels like a long time. "That was Lana. In the kitchen."

"Earlier. On the roof. It was Holly's voice."

He props himself up on one elbow. "It wasn't her. It was your memory messing with you. You'd been talking about her to me. You feel guilt about what happened, even though it wasn't your fault. It was in your mind."

"I *heard* her. I don't know—" I pause. I was going to say, I don't know if maybe she's brought me here for a reason. As punishment, even. But right at this moment, something else is weighing even heavier on my mind. "And I saw that padlock."

"Are you sure?" he says quietly. "Completely, one hundred per cent sure about the padlock?"

I force all the air out of my lungs. And I twist on to my back, to stare up at the sheep/clouds. "I even touched it," I tell him.

"…Then I don't know," he says at last. Because he doesn't want to argue with me, I think.

Apart from the sound of our tense breathing, the room is silent now. Outside the glow of the lantern, the darkness seems to hang all around us. I shift a little, so I can see him. "Except for when you thought you felt your grandmother stroking your arm, have you ever felt anything else like that? That you couldn't explain?"

Eventually, he says, "There was one thing but it'll sound stupid."

"I really promise not to laugh."

He turns to face me. "I'm gonna preface it by saying

that at the time I thought it was a paranormal event. Now I realize it wasn't."

"OK," I say.

"So, when I was eight, I had a pet hamster. I kept him in a cage in my bedroom. He used to run in his wheel at night, and I'd go to sleep listening to that sound. Now it would keep me up. But kids sleep differently, right?"

I nod.

"I used to get him out sometimes. I had this plastic ball he could run in around my room. When I put him back one night, I didn't close the lid of the cage properly. When I woke up in the morning, he was gone. We looked everywhere. Under the beds, in the wardrobes. Everywhere. He was missing, presumed escaped outside. Presumed dead. Then, this was maybe a week later, I got into bed and turned off my bedside light. And I heard him, running in his wheel."

"He'd got back into his cage?"

"Mom had put the cage in the garage."

I frown. "So you heard…?"

"Him, running in his wheel. *Exactly* the same sounds that he used to make when he was alive and in it. This wasn't some fuzzy, distant echo. It's not like I was hearing the dishwasher or something and thinking it was the wheel. It was the *exact same sound*, the same volume, the same erratic scrabbling of his feet, the same clicking where two of the little metal bars were too close together."

"And you thought it was, what … your hamster's ghost?"

"I was eight. What else was I meant to think?"

"Did you tell your parents?"

"No."

"You think they wouldn't have believed you?"

"They would certainly have tried to talk me out of believing it. But I thought I knew what I was hearing. And it happened every night, every time I turned off the light, for about two weeks. As soon as I turned it on again, it would stop."

"So what are you saying it was?"

"Wait, I haven't told you *how* it came to stop. You see, I'd been blaming myself. I thought it was some kind of punishment for leaving the door open. But, after two weeks, I said to myself OK, but I didn't mean to leave the door open. It's not my fault he escaped… And after that I never heard the sounds again."

I feel suddenly cold, despite the cocoon of heat around me. My voice low, I say, "Are you comparing—"

"That to Holly? *No.* But I'm telling you something that's true and that I've only ever told one person before. Jared." He sits up straight. "The sounds stopped. So it was all in my brain, right? Memory isn't meant to work like that." He taps the side of his head. "It's not meant to work like a camera or a recording device. Only in this case it did. And my mind replayed the sound of him in his wheel until I let go of the guilt. But at the time I would have sworn to anyone that it *was* my hamster, in his wheel. Not a memory. Not a hallucination. That's how vivid it was. It was real to me. It was my reality."

"...But it was a hallucination?"

"Yeah. I see now that it was."

"What did Jared say when you told him?"

"He was interested, of course. But we can't go back in time and scan my brain, to see exactly what was happening when I was experiencing those memories – how they were replayed like that."

I try to work through a mess of questions that are suddenly popping up in my head. "When Mum hears her voices, do you think it could be something like this?"

"...I honestly couldn't tell you."

I feel stiff but I manage to flop again on to my back. I can't help feeling like I'm sinking deeper into uncertainty, rather than climbing my way out of it.

"Lots of kids hear voices," Rav goes on. "They have imaginary friends. Not everyone has them but it's more than you think. It's not unusual to hear people – even see people – that no one could say objectively are there. It's not a huge leap to think that some people have these experiences as adults."

"Isn't that scarier than believing they're spirits?" I say quietly. "At least ghosts aren't inside you."

"Scarier? I don't know. Once you accept that we all actually conjure up our own worlds, it's not scary. In any case, facing up to what's likely has to be better than making stuff up to cover what we don't understand."

I turn my head to look at him. "I'm not making Holly up."

"That's not exactly what I meant. But let me ask you – after she died, how did you feel? Like somehow, in some way, it was partly your fault, right?"

"I tried to help her."

"But you didn't succeed."

I'm so surprised at what he just said that my muscles suddenly seize up. Tears spring to my eyes.

"Mia, you were a kid. *Whatever* happened, it wasn't your fault. You have to let go of whatever deep-seated belief you're hanging on to that tells you it was."

"So you really are comparing me and Holly to you and your *hamster*."

"No! I'm just trying to work through what you were feeling."

"And how were you *feeling* around the time when your grandmother came to you?" The words come out a lot more bitterly than I'd intended.

"Lost," he says. "Scared. Sad. Ashamed. Alone. Sick every morning because I didn't want to go to school, but I had no choice. And, no matter what I did to try to make myself vanish in the corridors, it never worked. They always found me."

His words shatter a defensive barrier that's been

building up around me. They go in deep. I whisper, "You think because you were so upset she somehow found a way to you?"

He looks at me. "Either that, or I conjured her, as solace. Right? One or the other. And, while I'm not shutting out the possibility of the former, I am leaning towards the latter."

I hold his gaze. "What if we find things in this house that we can't explain?"

"Then we re-evaluate. Based on the new information."

"You really think I could be hallucinating seeing Holly, and hearing her – and things like the sand? Even the *padlock*?"

"I think only you can make that call. But I know that when I heard that wheel going it was totally real. And, like I said before, with your environmental sensitivities, no wonder you have strange experiences sometimes."

I lie there, trying to think. He said something similar outside the naval yard hospital, but I didn't accept it. Now I feel like maybe he's finally slow-punctured a belief that I've been holding on to for so long.

Maybe it *could* be in my head.

Holly hasn't *brought* me here.

Perhaps ghosts don't exist after all.

24

I wake to vibrant sunshine. Before my vision even clears properly, I realize that they *are* sheep on the walls. In this bright morning light, I can make out the faint outlines of faded heads. Not clouds, then.

"Morning," I say.

Rav sits up suddenly, his hair half over his face. Then he pats at the floor beside him and locates his phone. Squints at the screen. "Six forty-eight." He rubs his face and yawns. "How long've you been awake?"

"About a minute."

"How'd you sleep?"

"Surprisingly well."

He smiles. "Me too."

"If you'd told me yesterday the worst I could expect after a night in a haunted house was a sore back, I'd definitely have taken it."

He grins and wriggles out of his sleeping bag. "Hot shower should help. I'll be quick."

Ten minutes later, we're both showered and ready to face the day. I've put on blue cotton shorts and a loose T-shirt and a pair of trainers instead of my sandals. I grab my phone from beside my makeshift bed. "Ready?"

"I guess so," he says.

As we head into the corridor, a certain amount of unease returns. But I think it's just because I'm reconnecting with the house, and I can't help feeling apprehensive about what the day will hold.

As we reach the kitchen, I smell coffee, and something sweet.

"Hey!" Yunoo says brightly.

He's by the hob, plunging a silver-framed cafetière. His pink polo shirt and blue chino shorts make him look like he's off for a day at a country club or something. The incongruity makes me smile. "Hi," I say.

"Good morning, all," Rav says.

Turning, I see that Alli, Lana and Jared are already seated at the table. What look to be blueberry pancakes are piled on a white platter in the centre.

"I thought you said it'd be beans when it was your turn," I say to Yunoo.

"I wish I could take the credit for the pancakes," he says with a smile. "But I *have* managed to add boiling water to coffee!"

"It shouldn't actually be boiling," Lana murmurs, looking up from her phone.

"...So, Mia, what I have *actually* managed is to mess up even the coffee."

I smile. "I'm sure it's great."

"But, if the pancakes aren't, you'll have to blame me," Jared says. "Morning, Mia. Rav. Come, sit. Eat."

Yunoo pours coffee into white mugs, which I help carry to the table. Alli smiles at me. She twists her hair, which is still damp from the shower, back behind her shoulders. Lana glances up momentarily, and nods.

When we all have pancakes, cutlery and coffee, Jared says, "So, first, is there anything important to report from the night?"

We look at each other. No one offers anything.

I take a sip of the coffee. It might not be Roberto's but I'm very thankful for it. And for the pancakes. I'm starving, I realize.

There's a general clinking of forks on plates.

"Lana," Jared says, "have you had a chance to review any software alerts from last night?"

She puts down her mug. "There were a hundred and fifty-seven." She frowns hard at Yunoo. "You flinging yourself around accounts for a hundred and twenty-three of them."

He grins. "What can I say? I'm expressive even in my sleep."

"Try to express yourself a little less," she says. He gives her a mock salute.

"What about from the garden?" Jared asks.

"There *was* something," Lana says, and we all look at her. "But it's indistinct. A figure moving in the trees. Where you said. All we have is a rough silhouette. I can't even tell if it's a man or a woman."

I rest my fork down on my plate. "What about the padlock?" I ask.

She fixes her gaze on me. "Mia, at no point can I see any padlock."

My pulse picks up speed. "But—"

She raises a hand to stop me. "*But* the night-vision resolution at the end by the door is too poor to see detail. I can't say there wasn't ever a padlock. It's just not possible to see one in the video."

My eyes flick to Jared's face.

"There's no footage of anyone by the door?" he asks.

She shakes her head. "It shows Alli, from when I was fixing up the camera and she was doing an infrasound check. Then Yunoo and Mia doing the temperature sensors. Then, later, Alli and me going through to the roof, and then Rav and Mia when they came in search of us. That's all."

Jared nods. I guess there's nothing more to say about the lock right now. But I know what I saw and what I felt.

I focus on my own plate. The pancakes are fluffy and soft. Perfect.

When we're about finished, Jared says: "Jobs. Lana, I'd like you to help me survey outside and around the garage. I want to make sure the infrasound map is complete. Rav and Yunoo, can you measure up inside and out? This is an old house. If there are significant wall spaces or hidden passages or even rooms, I want to know about them. Mia, I'd like you to spend some systematic time in different rooms. Try to open yourself up as much as you can. Alli, could you go with her?"

I glance at Alli, wondering if she'll be disappointed at being asked to hang around with me instead of Lana. But she smiles at me and hooks her hair behind her ears. "Sure."

"I haven't felt anything so far," I warn her.

"Well, a zero outcome is still useful data. Don't worry. Whatever you feel or don't feel will be helpful. I promise."

As soon as breakfast is done, Alli and I head into the dining room.

The shutters are open. The light, which is muted from the scratches and cracks in the windowpanes, shows up all kinds of marks and gouges in the floorboards. Before I can stop myself, I wonder if any of them were made by furniture being moved around when no one was in here.

I go over to take another look at the painting. Rain is lashing down. The mast looks close to breaking.

Alli comes to join me. "The whale fishery, they used to call it. Like they weren't even mammals. My own family was tied right up in it. Three of my ancestors worked whaling ships out of Sag Harbor. They were all wrecked. *Entombed by the sea.* That's what it says in death records all along this coast."

"Do you still have family round here?"

"Not any more. But one of my aunts did spend a summer compiling a list of haunted locations in Suffolk Country. Highlights include the Montauk Point Lighthouse and the Pizza Hut in Centereach."

"Pizza Hut?"

"I know, right? What kind of self-respecting ghost haunts a chain pizza place?" A slight smile lighting her brown eyes, she leans back against the wall by the picture. "So, how're we gonna do this?"

I'm really not sure what to say. "What do you think Regan Martin would do?"

"I have no idea. It was Lana who had a thing about Regan."

"I guess I just stand here. Try to focus on what I'm feeling?"

She nods. "Why don't you take a few moments, focus inwards. Then walk around the room. Tell me if it seems like anything really changes."

I take a deep breath. And I try to home in on the tingling sensations and slight twitches in my arms, my chest and my feet.

Eyes open.

Eyes closed.

Slowly I walk towards the door. Nothing. Only my heart beating harder.

"I'm assuming everything's OK," Alli says quietly. "If it's not, you need to tell me. If it is, you don't have to say anything. Just keep doing what you're doing."

Trying to keep my breathing even, I inch round towards the big bay window. When I'm close enough to touch it, I reach out. The glass is hot, making me shrink back a little.

I close my eyes. Open them again. High in the sky, I notice faint wisps of cloud. The topmost leaves of the plane trees are trembling. A breeze is coming in off the ocean.

I turn back to Alli. "I don't think I feel anything in here."

"That's OK. Like I said, there's no right or wrong in this. Let's move on."

We go through to the crescent-shaped living room. Again Alli waits patiently while I slowly walk around. The room has a definite feel of abandonment, which isn't helped by the smell of dog. But I'm not getting any of the disturbing sensations that I experienced in the lab, or the hospital.

In the kitchen, I don't feel anything, either. We move on to the utility room. I'm a lot more nervous now because of Jetta Amos's story about the washing being flung around.

Slowly, I step through the narrow space, towards the trough sink at the far end.

Now, taking my time in here, I notice that the worktops are coated with a layer of greasy dirt. Shrivelled spider's webs hang in the corners of the window. I can definitely smell dog in here, which I couldn't before. Perhaps it's just because it's so hot, and the air is so still. I can't hear the waves. Just a faint gurgle of water in hidden pipes. Sweat prickles my back and my chest.

"Maybe it's because you're with me?" I say at last, and I glance round at Alli, who's waiting in the doorway.

"I can't leave you alone," she says. "And in theory it shouldn't make any difference."

I jump. My phone just buzzed. I pull it out of my shorts pocket. There's a message from Tamara.

What's happening? OK??

I can picture her so clearly. Like she's in my mind, speaking those words. I wish I could talk to her.

I jerk my top free from my sweaty back. Heat is trying to free itself from my body. Only there's nowhere for it to go.

Alli says, "Look, why don't we take a break? There are some sodas left, I think. We could take them outside?"

*

"Mia! Hey!"

There's loud, rhythmic drumming at Tamara's end and breeze and waves crashing at mine.

"Where are you?" I ask her.

"A trance through dance workshop. Wait."

I wanted somewhere I could talk to Tamara without Alli necessarily overhearing, and the only location I could think of was the beach. The noise of the surf does give me at least some sense of privacy. And, instead of sandals, I'm wearing trainers, which protect me from the sand. And there's a boardwalk, which I'm not straying from.

I glance round. Alli is sitting in the shade of a plane tree, maybe fifteen metres away. Beyond the house, grey-white cloud is definitely massing. But it's like the beach and ocean are fighting back with a blinding glare.

Tamara speaks again, this time without the music. "Gunther asked me to check it out. What's happening?"

How do I answer that question? "We've been surveying the house."

"But you're OK?"

The slam of the door on the terrace sounds again in my mind. I think of the padlock.

"…Yeah," I tell her.

"Have you found anything?"

"Like a ghost anything? No." I feel a little blocked up inside, like what I might want to tell her – *would* tell her if she was here – just won't come out. It's hard over the phone. So I focus on something normal. "How did the lunch go today?"

"They are *loving* it. I helped Mom get it all over there first thing. Then I went to this installation in Green-Wood Cemetery."

I know Green-Wood Cemetery well. On maps of Brooklyn, it's a vast patch of green, veined with a dense network of driveways and paths. "*In* the cemetery?"

"Yeah. It's this white marble obelisk. Like a tombstone. The inscription reads, 'Here lie the secrets of the visitors to Green-Wood Cemetery'. There's a slot in the front. You write down your secrets and you slide them in, down a chute, and they go into this underground repository. It's like giving them a proper burial."

I realize I'm holding my breath, and I let it out. "Did you write something?"

"Of course … or there wouldn't have been much point going."

I turn so the breeze is blowing my hair out of my face rather than into it. Now I'm facing the ocean. The surface is like rippling crystal, dark sapphire where it's in cloud shadow.

"Maybe I should've been telling you about something not to do with a graveyard?" Tamara asks.

"No, I—" Again I glance at Alli. She's resting her arms on her knees, watching me. "But I think I should probably get back to it."

"OK… But, if you decide you want to get out of there, you call me."

I nod into the phone. "I *will*."

25

There's a slow weight to the day. It's like being dragged through water.

We all have lunch together. There's a loaf of sweet, sliced white bread that Jared brought from New York, tomatoes, anaemic mozzarella slices, milk chocolate so thick with cocoa butter I can't eat it, and the cookies. Someone has drawn the blind over the picture window to the garden. To help keep the sun out, I guess. But heat still radiates through the mottled grey fabric.

"Can't we put the AC back on?" Rav asks a little plaintively. Lana frowns.

"Just for now? Mia's not felt anything in here, right?"

He looks at me and I shake my head.

"It's important to keep the environment as natural as possible at all times," Jared says, effectively ending the conversation. "Have you been into Hanna's room yet, Mia?"

The few bites of sandwich I've eaten harden in my stomach. "With Yunoo," I say.

"Yesterday? While you were setting up? Not today?"

"We've been working our way through the ground floor," Alli explains.

Jared nods. "Can you make sure you do it at some point today?"

Alli nods. "Sure."

The conversation moves on. Now Jared's talking to Yunoo about crashing waves as a potential source of infrasound. But all I can think about is the interior of that bedroom. That purple sandal, the strap worn from being done and undone over Hanna's small foot.

I have to move. My legs feeling stiff, I get up, and take my plate and the empty tomato dish to the sink.

"We could probably do with more supplies for tonight," Jared says. "And more basics. There's meant to be a decent grocery store in town. Anyone up for a food run this afternoon?"

"Me," Alli says.

I turn back from the sink. "I'll go with you," I say before anyone else has the chance to.

Jared nods. "You can take my car," he says to Alli. "It's a little more manoeuvrable than the bus."

"I didn't realize the car was on offer!" Yunoo says.

Alli smiles sweetly at him. "Too late."

"But if you could do the first floor before you go?" Jared says.

Alli looks at me. Reluctantly I nod.

We start in the guest rooms off the shorter corridor. Then we move to the landing itself, the longer corridor, the Blue Room, the Pink Room, and into the green one with the sheep, where Rav and I slept.

Nothing… I just don't feel anything.

As I step towards the window, the light darkens. The humidity is getting really intense. I turn back to Alli. She's standing beside Rav's sleeping mat. Her cheeks are pink with the heat. She lifts her hair up off her neck, and her feather and bead bracelet catches my eye.

"It's a beautiful bracelet," I say.

"Thank you. It was a present from Dad for my eighteenth birthday. It's protective."

"Like a talisman?"

"Like a charm, I guess."

Something that I suppose I've been thinking about at the back of my mind flashes to the fore. "Can I ask you something? Back at the library, you said you know ghosts are real."

She nods.

"Why? I mean, what makes you believe that?"

She hesitates. "When Jared or Rav say they don't believe in anything beyond the body, I respect that. But I think that, though the mind and body are connected, the body is not everything. You can call it a ghost or a soul or an energy – it doesn't matter what you call it – but I believe there's something about a consciousness that persists even when the body dies."

"Persists for how long?"

She shrugs. "Forever."

"You mean, what – in other bodies?"

"In other bodies. Out of bodies. Back on a unified level, like a common pool of mental energy that our own individual minds spring from, like water drops. All operating in a way that physicists just haven't grasped because we don't yet have the right tools or the knowledge."

She stands up a little straighter, like the ideas she's talking about are making her stronger. "Humans think that anything that contradicts current scientific ideas about how the world works is wrong, right? How *arrogant* is that? It's typically human. And it's so flawed. Going back in history, we've *always* thought that. And, time after time, our ideas have been forced to change. As they will in future."

She stops. Lets her breath out in one long exhalation. "Look, I don't know what Jared experienced or encountered in this house but it had to be something really significant, or we wouldn't be here. If we can document it … I try not to think about how momentous that would be."

My suddenly tumbling thoughts straighten out. "Wait, you think something happened to *Jared* here?"

She looks surprised that I'd even question it. "Nothing else would have made him so obsessed about coming back. The convergent eyewitness testimony – yeah, it's striking, but there's been eyewitness agreement about hauntings before. This is personal. Something happened to him. That's why we're all here. And it's why I'm, I don't know – *excited* isn't a strong enough word. Whatever he saw or felt, if we could all witness it … there are people whose lives would be totally transformed by that. If the greatest academic sceptic, Jared Robertson, actually confirmed a haunting, it would change so much. Ghost research would shift right to the forefront. Mainstream science couldn't avoid it any more."

The hairs on my arms stand on end.

"But, if something happened to Jared, why does he deny that ghosts exist?" I ask her.

"I guess because just saying something happened to you is never going to convince other parapsychologists. Jared is academically rigorous. Without proof, he's not going to make a claim. He's going to err on the side of doubt – until there's clear evidence to the contrary."

The skin on my right forearm suddenly tingles. Something's moving—

Just a bead of sweat, I realize. Only sweat.

I try to take in what Alli just said about mental energy persisting. And about Jared. My mind jumps back to his talk in the library, and all the interruptions. "When he was married, was his ex hosting poltergeist shows then?"

"Stacey? She's been on the staff at *American Poltergeist* for years. So, yeah, I guess. Lana would know more. She knew Stacey pretty well, I think. Before they split."

"He wasn't, I don't know, *embarrassed* to be married to her? Since he's such a high-profile sceptic?"

Alli shrugs. "I guess he knew what he thought. So, for his work, it didn't matter who he was married to. I do know the split was pretty acrimonious, though. And he certainly got harsher in his criticisms of ghost-hunters afterward."

"He still wears the belt buckle she gave him."

Alli smiles. "And that's Jared for you. No way is he going to let himself feel forced into changing anything. Not his thinking – not even his clothing. I admire him for a lot of things, and that's definitely one of them."

I wipe my forehead. But my fingers are damp, so it's like I'm just moving sweat around on my skin.

Is Alli right? I wonder. *Did* something happen to Jared here in this house? But what? And where?

"It feels like the storm's close," she murmurs.

She picks her way carefully round Rav's and my things, to the window. Peering uncertainly out, she says, "It'll break real soon. We should really go get the food."

"We haven't been in Hanna's room yet," I say.

She nods. "But I'd rather not get soaked. It'll still be there when we get back."

26

Jared's dusty car turns out to be a Ford Mustang. When Alli hits the accelerator, we jump forward, bouncing so hard over a pothole, my bag flies off my knee.

"I hope Jared isn't watching!" she exclaims.

As we head down the drive, I type in the name of the store into the map app on my phone. We go along a couple of streets leading away from the ocean, pass a row of perfect houses with bright cushions on the verandah chairs, then make a short zigzag through to Main Street.

Away from the house, I feel myself start to relax. It's a relief to be focusing not inwards but outwards. I look through my window at mums with blond ponytails, in yoga gear with matching daughters. At older guys in long shorts and sports-team baseball caps, walking fluffy dogs past expensive-looking restaurants with dark awnings.

We pull into a side street, park up by a bike-rental

station, and head into the grocery store. As we grab a trolley, my phone rings. It's Sadie.

I take a breath. With all the bright energy I can summon, I say: "Hey!"

"Mia! What you up to?"

"Actually I'm food shopping. With Alli."

Alli is bending into the trolley, carefully depositing two cartons of eggs.

"So what's the property like?"

"Old," I say. "Almost totally cleared out. No one's living there now."

Alli shoots me a sharp glance. I guess I'm not meant to be talking about Halcyon House. But I really haven't given much away.

"And what does Rav's professor think?" she asks. "I mean, does he think the stories might be true?"

My eyes on Alli, who is still giving me a warning look, I say, "So far, it's just … an old house."

Alli pulls the trolley slowly along, towards shelves piled high with bread. I keep pace with her.

"Are you OK?" Sadie asks. I know that she wants the answer to be yes, which is why it's so easy to give it to her.

"Yeah, I really am."

There's a pause. Then she says, "In that case, I'll let you get on with your shopping. I was just checking in. Love you, *mia cuore*."

"I love you," I tell her. And the line goes dead.

Alli has manoeuvred us over to the hot-food counter. She glances up from the containers of prepared meals.

"Just my aunt," I explain. "Checking everything's OK."

"I'm not criticizing you but ideally it's best not to communicate with anyone about a survey while it's ongoing."

"I get it," I tell her. "I won't mention anything that matters. But, if I don't tell her anything at all, she'll worry about me. And, if she did get worried, she'd probably drive right over."

After a moment, Alli nods. "OK. So what about that jerk chicken for the others? Maybe the cheese ravioli for us? Or the tofu red curry? What would you like?"

After getting a couple of chickens and a large pot of the curry, we find the remaining items on the list back near where we started: bananas and strawberries, bags of salad, cucumbers and new potatoes. We head to the checkout and I bag up the shopping while Alli pays. Then we go back to the car.

The breeze has turned cold and the sky is so dark, it's like dusk, though it can't be much after six.

Alli clicks the boot open and carefully lowers her bags inside. As I lean forwards to do the same, a flash of something makes me freeze.

I spin round. I'm only just in time to see her vanish past the end of the street, riding a yellow bike. Her short hair was vivid red.

There must be countless people with hair that colour. But perhaps my subconscious registered something else, too, because, though we're miles away from New York, where I last saw her, I'm certain it was the girl I met outside the institute.

I hastily put my bags in the boot.

"What's wrong?" Alli asks.

"I saw someone." My heart is racing now. "I need to go after her."

"*Who?*"

I'm already over at the bike-hire terminal. I pull my debit card from my purse and swipe it. The wait feels like forever but the transaction goes through. I snatch up the slip with my release code.

"Mia!"

"Sorry," I call to Alli. "It's someone from New York. I'll get a cab back to the house. You go."

I sling my bag across my chest and release a bike. The seat's too low for me but I'm not going to waste time adjusting it. I push down hard on the pedals and wobble into the road.

Alli starts towards me. "What do I tell Jared? *Mia?*"

But I'm already off.

27

I'm standing up as I ride, pushing hard. As I swerve on to Main Street, I scan the road ahead. A red SUV is about twenty metres in front. A silver coupé, roof up, is coming the other way.

Where is she?

I check the pavements, just in case. Now the storm's close, they're almost empty.

Where is she?

I pedal fast to the next junction but I can't see her.

At a bookstore, I take a left. If Southampton is built in regular blocks, and I'm fast, maybe I can intercept her.

A ringing comes from my bag but I can't talk to anyone right now. I cycle down to a dentist's surgery, pass a row of detached homes, then turn right at a tall hedge, and pedal back in the direction of Main Street

There's no sign of her. I let out a frustrated sigh.

This plan is half crazy. She could be anywhere by now. Inside one of the houses down here – or the next street – or the next. I'm annoyed with myself. And disappointed at losing her again.

Slowly now I cycle along Main Street. It's tough going. The wind's so strong that even the leaves are being whipped from the trees. Again my phone rings, and I ignore it.

I feel a pulse on my shoulder. Then another on my head. Rain. An even bigger drop splats on to my right thigh. From the direction of the ocean comes a flash of white light, followed by a bursting crack of thunder.

This is pointless. And I'm just going to get drenched. Reluctantly, I cut across the street, to reverse my direction and head back towards the hire terminal. As the rain picks up pace, so do I. I just have to make sure I don't miss the side street with the bank on the corner—

My neck twists. I squeeze the brakes so hard, I jerk up off the seat.

I've just seen a bike rack, with a single bike in it – banana yellow, like the one she was riding. The rack's to the side of a stone-fronted building marked with a circular black-and-white sign with a logo of a burning flame. The sign reads:

The Well
Welcome to our Spiritualist Church

What did she tell me back at the institute? That she was talking to a spiritualist.

It's an extremely long shot.

But it's worth a try.

28

The front door has opaque glass panels. I can see nothing through them except light.

I try the handle. It turns easily. I step on to a brush mat that gives way to the polished oak floorboards of an otherwise white hallway. Coming from an open door towards the end of the hall is a woman's voice. It's too quiet for me to make out any words. Carefully, I wipe my trainers on the mat – and a poster on the wall by my head catches my eye.

EVENTS

Monday, Friday. Spiritual healing. 6 p.m.
Tuesday, Saturday, Sunday. Open circle. 6 p.m.
Wednesday. Practical spirituality for dynamic living. 7 p.m.
Thursday. Join Rev. Karen Griminger for a medium reading. 6.30 p.m.

OPEN TO ALL

DONATIONS GRATEFULLY RECEIVED

It's Thursday. So it must be the voice of Rev. Karen Griminger that I can hear. Quickly, I flick my phone to silent without even checking who's been calling. My heart thrumming as fast as the rain on the roof, I head for the open door.

Through the gap, I see an airy hall lit with dozens of candles. A circle of around twelve people are sitting on wooden chairs. In the centre of the circle is a white table holding a thick pillar candle, its flame burning steady. A woman dressed in a white linen shirt and white trousers is talking. She has long, tousled, beach-blond hair. Her voice is relaxed, even musical.

A few of the people notice me but they quickly turn their attention back to her. I scan their faces, hoping, hoping— And there she is.

Her head is lowered, showing her black roots. Her hands are clasped in her lap. She's wearing long black shorts and a loose grey jersey top, dark in places from the rain. The silver butterfly pendant rests on her collarbone, glinting in the candlelight.

I feel dizzy suddenly. Even on the verge of tears. I wanted to find her but why should my emotions be so strong? Then it occurs to me that maybe, at the back of my mind,

I've been worried that she wasn't real. That I'd imagined her.

But, unmistakably, it's her here in this room.

My next thoughts are, *Why? What* is she doing here?

I know Southampton's a popular holiday destination for wealthy New Yorkers. Could it be coincidence, and she's just here on holiday with friends, or family? But what are the odds of seeing her at the institute, then at Jared's talk, and now also *here*?

Another crack of thunder jolts through me. And I realize that Rev. Griminger is looking at me. Her expression is curious but warm.

"Please," she says softly, "come in. Sit with us. There's a space right here." She gestures towards a vacant chair four down from the girl.

Most people look up as my trainers squeak across the floor. But not the girl.

I'm so tense, I'm not sure at first that my knees will bend. But I manage to sit down. Griminger nods at me, then resumes talking.

"There are no masters, my friends. Only messengers, teachers and lovers, and tonight I will be a messenger from the world of the spirits. We are here this evening to learn what we need to learn. We believe that eternal progress is open to every human soul. Let us together affirm that the existence of the individual continues after the change called death, and that communication with the so-called dead is a fact."

A quiet murmuring goes round the circle. The girl unclasps her hands then interlocks her fingers again. She seems tense, too. Nervous.

Griminger closes her eyes. After placing her hands, which gleam with silver rings, flat on her thighs, she takes a long, deep breath. Her eyes flicker open. In a gentle, almost dreamy voice, she says, "I have a daughter figure with me, and the number eight. Does this mean anything to anyone?"

Silence, apart from the rain on the windows. Then a woman two to my left sits up a little more in her chair. "My first miscarriage was a little girl. Eight years ago."

Griminger's expression suggests that this is what she'd expected. "Your daughter wants to tell you that she's at peace. She's content and she wishes for you to feel peace also. She says there's someone with her. An older man." The rings flash as her hands move to her chest. "He had trouble with his heart. His favourite chair was by the window, looking on to a beautiful garden."

The same woman takes in a sharp breath. "My grandfather."

"Your daughter wants to tell you that he's with her and that she feels safe," Griminger says, then her brow creases. "I'm getting another message now. Wait, you will have to take turns... I have a woman who passed while she was still quite young. She says there's someone here who grew up beside a park, and whose red kite got caught in a tree..."

Silence.

"That doesn't mean anything to anyone? ...Let me see. I have another child spirit. A girl again. I'm getting the number six this time. I know this spirit. A local girl." She splays her hands wider on her thighs. The furrow between her eyes deepens. "She's troubled because she senses that her family is not at peace. There has been upset, change. Her home is under some kind of threat. Does this mean anything to anyone?"

I stare at Griminger, my heart pounding, my fingers gripping my thighs so tightly, they hurt. Surely she can't be talking about Hanna? About Halcyon House? Should I say something?

But the red-haired girl looks up. With a dropping weight in my stomach, I suddenly know what she's going to say.

"That must be my sister," she whispers.

29

I want to ask so many questions. Some of the girl: Didn't you go to live in *Canada*? What are you doing *here*? But mostly of the so-called spirit Griminger claims to be communicating with.

How did you fall from that window? Were you ever aware of a supernatural presence in your home?

But for those questions – or their answers – to mean anything, I'd have to believe, like Alli believes, that some essence of Hanna is still intact and out there – that what Griminger is claiming is true. And, if it's true for Hanna, why wouldn't it be true for Holly, too?

I'm trembling. My thoughts are slipping over and around each other. I can't make sense of them. Griminger's talking but, to my frustration, it's not about Hanna or Halcyon House any more.

She's communicating with a spirit who loved Burmese

cats and Nina Simone. Then to someone who wants to pass on a message about a box buried beneath a lilac tree.

The girl is focusing on her hands again. As far as I can tell, she hasn't noticed me. I'm focusing on her, and hoping desperately that the session will soon be over.

But now Griminger fixes her warm gaze on me. "Welcome. Is there somebody you would like me to try to contact?"

My palms suddenly sweat. My heart races. Should I mention Holly?

It wasn't remotely on my mind when I walked into this church. But it occurs to me: what, exactly, do I have to lose?

My voice shaky and over-loud, I say, "I lost a friend. Five years ago."

"You were close?" Griminger asks. "You and this – girl?"

"Yes."

"Why don't you call to her? Ask her to come forward?"

Call to her?

"Use her name. Ask her to hear you."

The woman beside me nods.

Though I can hardly believe it, I hear myself say, "Holly?"

The shaking gets worse. I feel almost like I might fall from the chair. Just saying her name out loud in this group seems like a kind of betrayal. What if she doesn't want to be called?

"Try again," Griminger says, her eyes closed.

Tears roll suddenly down my cheeks. Surprised,

embarrassed, I hurriedly wipe them away. I take the deepest breath I can. "Holly? It's me... Mia."

Griminger's frowning. In concentration, I think. "Holly?" she says. "A friend would like to talk to you. Are you there?"

A few moments pass. It feels like forever. She shakes her head. "I'm sorry, Mia, I can't hear her. So many others. Yes, you will have your turn... But not tonight."

She folds her hands. Straightens her back. Composes herself. "I'm sorry, everyone. As you know, each session is unpredictable. Sometimes we can remain in this circle for hours, but sometimes the intensity of the contact deeply saps me... It's time for me to draw our evening to a close."

My head drops. Did Holly hear me but not want to communicate? Or is there nothing out there to communicate with?

After last night, talking to Rav, I was definitely feeling better. Now I feel hideously worse.

People are murmuring their thanks, and the circle begins to break up. While some head straight for the exit, others hang back to talk.

The girl's still sitting, head down, knees pressed together. I wish I hadn't brought up Holly. But at least, against the odds, I've found her.

Unsteadily I walk over. I stand right in front of her until, eventually, she looks up. I watch recognition dawn.

"Your sister was Hanna James?" I say as I slump down hard on the chair beside her.

I touch her arm and she pulls back. From behind us comes a soft voice. "Everything OK?" Reverend Griminger asks. "Eloise? Mia?"

Quietly, so Griminger can't hear, and quickly, because I know I'm breaking the investigation rules, I murmur: "I'm with the group from the institute staying at Halcyon House. Amy – your aunt – she asked for a medium."

Her dark brown eyes narrow. "*You?*"

I can't blame her for being confused, not least because I just asked Griminger to try to contact my dead friend. She looks over at Griminger, who's blowing out the candles near the window. Her hand jumps to her butterfly pendant. "Have you found anything?" she whispers.

Glancing at Griminger, I say, "Let's talk outside."

We're silent in the hallway as we head for the front door. Outside the light is dim and the rain is falling in sheets but at least no one will overhear us. She faces me. "Have you found anything?" she asks again.

I know what Alli said, in the supermarket, but this is Hanna's sister. "We only got here yesterday."

Her eyes search mine. "Not even in Hanna's room?"

"Not yet…"

She wipes her face with her hand. "I *have* to know if she's still in that house." She looks at me, her face wet with rain, and also with tears. "I don't want to hear it from Amy or that other woman. I want *you* to tell me."

"Me?"

"You're the medium?"

Feeling like a fraud, I nod. Then I process what she just said. "What other woman? Why don't you want Amy to tell you?"

But she's already talking again. "If anything happens at the house, you have to call me. I'm staying with a friend close by. I can come straight over. Any time. You have to promise." Her tone is urgent.

She's staying *nearby*? "Did you come to the house last night? Through the pine wood by the boardwalk?"

Shaking her head, she pulls her phone from her bag. "Give me your number."

"What other woman?" I ask her again. "And why don't you want to hear about the investigation from Amy?"

She blinks at me, looking upset. "I don't know her name… The woman who told Amy to go to Jared Robertson. I agreed with that. Dad trusted Jared Robertson. I know because my uncle told me. But he has to report to Amy, and I don't trust her. That's why I wanted to talk to him. But he didn't reply to my emails, and I couldn't get into the institute, and at that talk he was always with other people. Please," she says, "just tell me your number."

And so I give it to her. She calls it. I find my phone – and see that the missed calls were all from Rav. I take it off silent so she can hear that it's ringing. She ends the call. Then she manoeuvres her bike out of the rack.

"I thought you lived in Canada," I say.

"I came back for my mother's *funeral*," she says, making me instantly feel bad about not realizing. "Then I heard what Amy wanted to do…"

She jumps on to the saddle, and now she's pushing her way into the driving rain.

I can't do anything but stand there, watching her go. And I'm left feeling strange. Hollow and nervy.

30

"The *younger sister*?" Jared says. "And you're sure you also saw her at the institute? And at the talk?"

I nod. I'm standing in the kitchen, a stiff white towel draped round my shoulders. Lana, Rav, Alli and Yunoo are here, too. I cycled back, and left the bike out in the garden. I'll have to return it tomorrow. Beyond the picture window, rain is still falling steadily through the late dusk, but it's drizzle compared with before.

Glancing at Yunoo, Jared says, "Maybe it was her we saw last night."

"She said it wasn't," I tell him. "I asked her."

"But what does she want?" Jared asks. "Why was she even at the institute? Why's she here?"

I relay everything that Eloise told me.

"She has to be, what – seventeen now?" he says, half to himself. "Eighteen, maybe. Who's she staying with in Southampton?"

"I don't know. She just said a friend."

"How did you recognize her?" Lana asks. "She was at the end of the street on a bike."

"Her hair. It's red. Like bright red. And short. And, I don't know, she's tiny. Petite."

Alli frowns suddenly. "…I might've seen her. At the institute last week. Short red hair, and she was wearing boots, a floaty skirt? I was going in, and she was right outside. When I got out my pass, she asked if this was where Jared Robertson's office was. I asked if she had a meeting, and she shook her head and asked how to get one, so I told her to email him. You." She looks at Jared. "I thought she was just a student wanting to do something at the institute."

"*Did* she email?" Rav asks.

"If she did, I didn't notice it," Jared says, shaking his head. "But I get a lot of email. Rav, you know where my laptop is. Can you check later?"

Rav nods.

"Why do you think she doesn't trust Amy?" I ask. "What other woman do you think she was talking about?"

Jared shrugs. Shakes his head.

Alli says, "So it sounds like Eloise is close enough to Amy to know about the investigation. But they don't seem to be on great terms?"

"Perhaps Eloise isn't happy that her mother's house has gone to her aunt and not to her," Lana says pointedly.

"Right now, the relationship between Amy and Eloise

is not relevant to us," Jared says, looking round at everyone in turn. "We need to concentrate on the investigation in hand." He fixes his pale gaze on me. "Mia, there must be no contact with Eloise without clearance from all of us. If she calls you, please tell her that you can't comment on the ongoing investigation. It's not that I'm insensitive to how she must be feeling. But if she were to learn any details of anything we might uncover here, it could leak out. Then we'd have every ghost-hunter from here to Hollywood descending on us."

I nod.

"OK, then we need to get on. Mia, I suggest you get yourself dry and grab something to eat. I'm afraid you missed dinner."

I glance over at the kitchen table behind him. There's a foil bag, torn open, only chicken bones left inside. And the plastic tub of red curry and rice, still three-quarters full. But there's no way I want to eat. My stomach is knotted up tight.

"As soon as you're ready, I need you in any rooms you haven't surveyed," Jared continues. "Alli says you still need to do Hanna's. So please start there. And then repeat. The entire house. Bottom to top, inside out. Rav, will you go with her?"

Rav nods.

"Yunoo, I need you back with me in the garage. Alli and Lana, I'd like a full equipment scan of the attic. Every inch."

"But—" Lana starts.

"I know," he interrupts. "You've already done it. Let's do it again."

Lana doesn't look happy. But she says, "Right."

On her way out of the kitchen, Alli pauses beside me. "I'm glad you're back OK. I was worried."

"I'm sorry I rushed off—" I start but she holds up a hand to stop me.

"I'd have done the same. It was important." Then to Lana she says, "Actually I'm gonna take a quick shower first."

"Sure," she says. "I'll wait right outside."

*

As we go back through to the hall and climb the stairs, I wonder about telling Rav that I asked Reverend Griminger about Holly. But somehow I can't quite bring myself to.

Back in the sheep room, Rav switches on the LED lantern and sits down on his sleeping mat.

I grab some clean clothes and take them and my torch through to the bathroom. My thoughts are jumping from Eloise to Holly, to Eloise.

When Hanna died, Franca effectively lost both her daughters, and her husband. And Eloise lost her family, too. What must it have been like to grow up, knowing her mother was alive, but that she'd rather live alone in the place where Hanna died than take care of the daughter who was still living?

302

I find it hard to get my head around. But I also struggle to understand how, when Holly's stepdad became violent – I'd seen the bruises on her mum's face, and even once on Holly, though she pretended they came from falling off her bike – her mum didn't make him leave, or leave with Holly, if that's what it took.

I don't often feel angry. When I think about Holly, it's usually with a mixture of fear and guilt and love. But anger's what I'm feeling while I take a scalding shower.

I twist off the tap, step out on to the bare tiles and rub the towel over my reddened skin and through my hair. Then I change into black leggings and a Drenge T-shirt that Freja gave me. Freja. Back in my other world.

After grabbing my torch from the sink, I step back into Eloise's old bedroom. Rav's doing something with his phone. He gets up, and pockets it as I hang my towel over the corner of the bathroom door.

"What's she like – Eloise?" he asks.

I think for a moment about how to answer. "She … is upset." I drag my brush hard through my hair, twist it back and secure it with a band. "I think she really just wants to know if the haunting stories are true."

"When you met her at the institute, that's when she said she'd lost her sister?"

I nod.

"But she didn't mention her mother – who'd only just died?"

"I guess her mother died of natural causes but her sister's death is still a mystery. Add to that stories of a poltergeist and paranormal activity and is it any wonder she's focused on that? I think she's really hoping we'll give her answers."

He bends to pick up his torch and lantern. "So are you ready to have another go at finding some?"

I don't have any choice. Eloise and me – we both need them.

I'm first out into the corridor. Franca's bedroom door is open. Maybe Lana hears the floorboards creaking because she steps out. "Where're you two going to start?"

Rav looks at me. "Hanna's room," I say, about as firmly as I can.

I don't *want* to go in there. But I have to. And so I make myself walk towards it, stopping just short of the door. "But I think I should go in alone."

Rav immediately says, "Jared's first rule—"

I interrupt him. "There's a camera in there, isn't there?" I call to Lana. "You could watch me on your phone? You could even call me, and we could keep the call open."

Glancing uncertainly at Rav, Lana steps further into the corridor. "Why exactly would you *want* to go in alone?"

I steel myself to explain, to try to force the issue. "How many of the stories involve two people seeing something together? That figure of light in this corridor – that was seen by Jetta and Jon James and Amy Ambler, but never together. Hanna at the window, a girl laughing, lights in the attic – separate sightings by individual people."

"Mia, you're here because you're sensitive to physical factors," Rav says in a low voice. "It wouldn't matter—"

"But it *might*." I don't spell out what I'm thinking: *if* ghosts do exist, and I really have seen Holly, and *if* there is a poltergeist in this house and *if* Hanna does haunt it, my environmental sensitivities won't matter. They only matter to Jared – for potential identification of links between environmental factors and the locations of witness statements. But I've been in almost all the rooms now, and so far I've felt nothing. "What if they only appear when people are on their own? Why don't I just try?"

Rav looks deeply uncertain. "Jared would say no."

"Lana can watch me on the video. You'll be right by the door, and we can talk on the phone."

Lana doesn't look convinced but she shrugs her agreement.

It's hard advocating for something that I'm really scared of doing. But if I don't try everything I can to get to the bottom of this house, and I'm left without answers, only more uncertainty, I know I'll regret it.

Rav swivels back to Lana. "What about Alli?"

"I could stand right here, with the door open," Lana says. "She's still in the shower. Wait." She swipes the screen of her phone. Taps a couple of times. "So, I have the camera feed up. Whenever you're ready."

305

"Don't take your eyes off your phone," Rav tells her.

She flashes him an annoyed look.

"No, even if I irritate you, don't take your eyes—"

"I'm watching!" she says, focusing her gaze back on the screen.

"I'll be right outside the door," he says to me, pulling his phone from a pocket of his cargo shorts. He calls me and I answer.

"You really sure about this?" Rav's double voice comes from my phone, as well. His black eyes still look unsure.

I nod. Then I switch on my torch and, with my phone in my other hand, I grab the worn brass handle, and step inside.

As I shut the door behind me, Lana calls, "I see you, Mia." And then I'm alone.

*

My breathing comes fast and shallow. I search first for the red flash of the camera. There it is. Up above the door frame. I put the phone on to loudspeaker. Then I wave at the camera, hoping it won't show that my arm is trembling.

Rav says, "Hey. Lana says she can see you."

"Can you hear me?" I whisper.

"I can hear you," he replies.

Now I have to make myself move the beam round the room.

My heart hammering, I pick out the ladybird bed.

The black dots on the headboard aren't perfectly round, I realize. Maybe Franca or Jon painted them.

Then I move to the shelves of stuffed animals. A long pink fabric tongue dangles from the mouth of a felt snake. The torchlight makes the silver glittery eyes of a polar bear seem to move.

I force myself to take a step, and another, until I'm beside the circular green rug. The frantic *rush-rush* of my blood and the coarse quickness of my breathing seem so overwhelming, I'm not sure I'll be able to feel anything beyond my own fear.

Keeping my arm as steady as I can, I search out the photos that I saw tacked to the wall. I'm close enough now to take in the detail. There's Hanna, with huge dark eyes, a mass of curly hair, silver glitter sandals and a huge grin, Mickey Mouse looming behind her, and—

My arm wavers. A silver butterfly pendant hangs from a chain, over Hanna's heart. It's *Eloise's* necklace now.

The next picture was taken on a dazzling beach. Franca Ambler is tanned, wearing a loose coral dress, her feet buried in sand, Hanna on her hip, Jon James beside her, his arm draped protectively round her shoulder.

The third is of a baby with just a nappy on, smiling in a pink rocker, Hanna, in a green dress, bending over it, holding a dummy. Hanna and Eloise, surely.

Jerkily I shift the beam, and it catches the purple sandal. I freeze.

My heart's suddenly racing so fast, I can't separate the beats. Something's moving behind my left shoulder. I spin round – and it's gone.

Rav's voice comes out of my phone, "Mia?"

The camera's behind me. They can't see my face. Forcing my breathing under control, I manage to whisper: "I'm OK."

I stumble towards the window, and my body is gripped. A freezing-hot shiver burns from deep in my chest, to my throat, rolling over my face, to my scalp. A cold hole opens in my stomach, and spreads. There can't be some kind of entity inside me. There *can't* be.

My neck twists— This time it doesn't vanish. It's over my shoulder, a patch of shifting black energy. Like nothing I've seen or felt before.

I want to run. I'm desperate to get out but I *have* to do this. I force my feet into a shuffling step towards the little bed. Holding my phone as far away from my mouth as I can, I whisper, hoping Rav won't hear: "I want to meet you." My voice breaking, I make myself whisper, "You should show yourself to me."

I twitch the torch beam to the chest of drawers, which I imagine still holds Hanna's clothes, then to the globe, and the plastic castle – and there's a sudden stabbing, like a fistful of needles, inside my chest. My phone drops to the carpet. My hand rushes to my heart. I can't feel a beat.

I can't see the energy any more, but something's pressing in on me. I'm still breathing but it's coming in on all sides.

My eyes hurt. I want to close them but I don't dare. I have to try to see what's coming, if it's coming – but it's already here because I can feel it, and raw fear tears through me. I don't think I can stand—

Then two things happen, a fraction of a second between them.

The door behind me slams open and from down the hall comes a panicked yell.

*

"Mia?" Rav's gripping my shoulder. I flinch. The beam of his torch is in my face. "What's happened? What's happening?"

As though from outside myself, I realize I'm still standing. And as I force myself to focus on Rav – on his face, sharp with fear – I also realize that the shivering, the pressure, the cold have vanished. My heart's beating in rapid, solid thuds.

"Something was here," I whisper. "But it's gone. I heard a shout?"

"Yeah. We need to check it out, OK?" He takes my arm, and we go into the corridor together.

Immediately I hear raised voices coming from Franca's bedroom.

As we hurry in, Lana's exclaiming, "It must be there!"

Alli's standing in a white towel, her hair dripping on to the carpet. "It's *gone!*" Lana darts past her into the bathroom.

"What's wrong?" Rav asks. "What's gone?"

"My bracelet," Alli says. "I left it by the basin when I got in the shower."

"So it fell on to the floor!" he says.

"I checked! It's not there!"

Lana comes back out of the bathroom and shakes her head. "It's not."

Rav stares at her. "But that makes no sense. Maybe it slipped down the plughole?"

Alli shakes her head. "It was *by* the basin, on the little shelf."

"Are you sure?" he says. "Perhaps you were gonna put it there but you were distracted, and you put it somewhere else."

"I know where I left it!" Alli says. Turning back to Lana, her gaze hits me. Stops. Uncertainly she says, "Mia, what's wrong?"

I swallow. "There was something in Hanna's room."

Lana spins to face me, and everything about the way she's standing, the way she's looking at me, seems aggressive. Doesn't she believe me?

"I saw it." My voice wavers. "And I felt it inside me. Freezing cold. It moved through me."

In a challenging voice, Lana says, "You felt something *inside* you?"

"Rav?" Alli sounds like she's doing her best not to sound scared. "Did you feel it?"

His eyes stay fixed on me. "Like in the lab?" I shake my head.

310

"We did a thorough equipment check of the room yesterday," Lana says briskly. "Alli did. There was no infrasound, no unusual EMFs."

"No, nothing," Alli says, shaking her head in agreement. "But Rav—"

"Did you see anything on the video?" Rav interrupts, addressing Lana, I guess, because he doesn't want to admit to Alli that I was in there alone.

Her cool gaze on me, she says, "I saw you turn your head twice. I saw you walk towards the window and the bed. A couple of times, you turned. I didn't see anything around you. Then Alli shouted."

"We need to update Jared," Rav says.

Lana already has her phone out. She swipes and taps the screen and lifts it to her ear. "…Voicemail." She ends the call, scrolls, taps, waits. "And voicemail for Yunoo."

"They were going to the garage," Rav says. "Check the video. If they're still there, I'll go find them."

"I'm already checking," Lana says irritably, focusing on her phone. After a few more moments of keying and swiping, she frowns.

"What?" Rav demands.

"I don't know – I—" Her face looks suddenly drained. "There's some problem with the video feed from the garage. I'm getting distortion. It's too blurry to see anything."

"But they are in there?" I ask.

"…I can't tell."

Rav says urgently, "Mia, we need to go find them." I nod.

"Stay together," he says to Alli and Lana.

I expect Lana to say something like who is he to order them around and point out the obvious. But she doesn't. She looks worried, too.

*

Rav and I are side by side all the way down the stairs. My head is full of Hanna's room. That burning-cold pain, the patch of complete blackness in the air.

We reach the entrance hall, and my phone starts buzzing. I fumble for it.

"Jared?" Rav says hopefully.

"…Tamara." I reject the call.

We hurry on into the crescent-shaped room. Strips of moonlight cut across the bare floor. What was it in Hanna's room? It didn't feel like a child. Jetta Amos talked about a figure of light. There was no light in what I saw. Another wave of cold runs through me, like an aftershock.

My phone rings again. If I don't answer, she might call Sadie. "I have to talk to her," I tell Rav, and accept the call.

"Mia!" Tamara sounds happy. Upbeat music's playing in the background. "How's it going?"

Rav's at the door to the kitchen, frowning at me. I hold up a finger, to tell him I'll just be a minute. I do my best to sound normal. "Hey."

"Mia? What's up?"

I guess my best is not great.

I swallow. "We're just at the house. Everything's OK."

"*Mia?*"

"It's just we're in the middle of something. Tamara, really—"

"Mia?" That was Rav. Impatient.

"What's wrong?" Tamara demands.

"Nothing," I say but I can hear my voice shaking. "Just something's happening. Can I call you back later?"

"No—" she starts. But I end the call.

I handled that so badly, I expect her to call again right away. But as I follow Rav into the kitchen, and on towards the utility room, my phone stays silent. Rav's silent, too. Why hasn't he asked me more about what just happened in Hanna's room? I guess he wants Jared to be there.

The light in the utility room is off. He feels for the switch. Flicks it. Nothing. Flicks it the other way. Then back again.

"Bulb must have gone," he says firmly. He pulls out his torch.

I walk in behind him. In the powerful torchlight, the dust on the worktops seems thicker than before. The straggly cobwebs in the window look greyer, more matted.

Rav takes another step, and freezes. I don't need to ask why. A clamp of dizziness has just gripped my skull. Now it's spreading out, into my blood.

I can't see Rav's face but I can smell his fear. Or mine.

"You feel that?" I whisper.

Without answering, he goes to grab the handle of the far exit door. Twists it. Pushes. It rattles. But it doesn't open.

Hot sparks of panic ignite inside me. My arms are tingling. It feels like something's moving through my flesh, into my bone. I get the distinct sense of a presence in here with us, even merging with my own body.

"Let me try." I wipe my trembling palm on my leggings, and twist the handle. The door won't open. Another wave of dizziness pushes through me, so strong I'm worried I'm going to fall. Rav glances sharply over his shoulder, into the shadows.

"What? Can you see something? *Rav?*"

Jaw clenched, he says, "We have to find Jared!"

He takes my hand. Together, we run back through the kitchen and the living room to the entrance hall. The intense dizziness and the sense of something inside me have gone, but my nausea's back. I'm moving. Rocking. Or the house is.

Rav yanks open the front door, letting in damp, warm air. I catch the stench of rot from the dune. My arms and legs erupt in goosebumps. A creaking of the floorboards above makes both our heads jerk up.

"They'll be looking for the bracelet," Rav says.

But it sounded like the creaks came from further down the corridor. Near Hanna's room.

He strides out on to the verandah. I go after him.

Every groan of the warped planks sends a fresh rush of adrenalin through me. It's a relief when we reach the grass, which is still soaking from the storm.

We keep our torches aimed on the ground immediately ahead. As we reach the corner of the house, I glance back. And I stop. Lights are flickering behind the attic windows.

I look at Rav, and he's watching, too. "Jared did ask them to survey up there."

But I think: *Lights in the attic windows when no one was home.*

And Rav just felt what I felt in the utility room. I know he did.

We round the corner of the house. There's the garage, looking small against the pines. The roller door is shut. Rav jogs over and bangs his fist against it once, twice. The clangs rock my skull.

"Jared!" he shouts. "Yunoo? *Jared!* Are you in there?"

31

There's a clunk, and the roller door judders upwards. It seems to take forever to rise just a few centimetres. But now I can see black trainers. Black jeans, as far as the knee.

Jared squats. He peers up at us, through the widening gap. "Rav?" He looks surprised but not alarmed.

"You OK?" Rav demands, sounding worried.

Jared's pale eyes narrow. "What's happened?"

As soon as the door's high enough for us to duck under, we stumble inside and flick off our torches. Light from two electric lanterns placed on waist-high cardboard boxes shows that the back half of the garage is stacked with boxes – the kind you can get from self-storage companies – as well as piles of other stuff, loosely covered by fraying black tarpaulins.

I spot two bikes leaning against the far wall. Just beyond them is a double child trailer. The plastic windows of the trailer's pink canvas cover are blotted with greenish-grey blooms of mould.

Yunoo's sitting on a camp chair, peering at an iPad. When he sees my face and Rav's, he lowers it. "What?" he says, getting up.

Rav explains about Alli's bracelet vanishing, and the problems with the camera feed. We all look up, searching for the telltale red flash. There it is, high up, to the right of the door roller mechanism.

"Could you check the hardware?" Jared says to Yunoo. "Might be dirt on the lens."

Yunoo goes over behind the trailer, in among the boxes. Then he drags out an aluminium stepladder, the frame and rungs plastered in dark trails of dirt and web.

"And something happened in Hanna's room," Rav says quietly.

Jared has been peering up at the camera. Now both he and Yunoo look sharply at Rav, who turns to me.

Quickly I describe what I saw and felt. I don't mention that Rav was outside the room.

Jared's gaze is locked on me so tightly, it's almost unnerving. Like he's trying to see past my words, get inside my head, feel what I felt.

"When you saw the shadow, what other impressions did you get?" he asks, and I sense that he's working hard to contain his emotions. "Human? Adult? Child?"

"I don't know," I tell him honestly.

"But it was a feeling of presence."

"Alli surveyed for infrasound and EMFs yesterday," Rav reminds him. "There was nothing in there."

"You see or feel any of this in the room?" Jared asks him. Rav shakes his head.

"Is there anything on the video?"

"Unfortunately … no."

"And the dizzy feeling in the utility room," Jared says to me. "Like confusion, or weakness?"

Rav says, "Like something inside your skull."

Jared frowns. "You just said—"

"Not in Hanna's room," Rav says, and his voice catches. "But I felt it in the utility room."

Jared's eyes flick to me. Back to Rav. "You *both* did? Together?"

"It was like something was moving into my body and my brain didn't like it," I tell him. "Similar to Hanna's room but different somehow. Less mean."

Jared swivels to Yunoo, who's stopped halfway up the ladder to listen. "Check the lens! Please! And can you review the temperature data from Hanna's room and the utility room?" To us, he says urgently, "You *see* anything in the utility room? Hear anything?"

"I thought maybe," Rav says haltingly. "I think I felt something, saw something in the shadows. It didn't feel like we were alone."

"And the door out to the garden was locked," I say.

"Did you do it?"

"Locked?" Jared says. "Or stuck?"

"It wouldn't open," I say. "We both tried it."

"Jared?" Yunoo's at the top of the stepladder. He's got the camera cupped in one huge hand, and he's aiming his torch at it. "The lens is clear. That's about all I can tell you. Lana might be able to uncover a potential hardware issue if she checks the function read-outs. Or it might be a software problem."

"Where are Lana and Alli now?" Jared asks.

Glancing at Rav, I say, "I think they went up to the attic… I saw lights up there."

It might be my imagination but I think anxiety flickers in his eyes.

"So now what do we do?" I ask Jared.

Before he can answer, Yunoo says, "*Guys*," his voice taut with warning.

He's still up the ladder but he's leaning into it, one arm wrapped round a rung, to stabilize himself while he checks something on his phone. "Lana has direct access to the live feeds from all our cameras, but I've got them up through our server. Something's not right." Swipe. Tap. *Tap*. His brow furrows. "There's some kind of interference in the signal from the attic."

"What interference?" Rav asks.

"A problem with the camera or the data… It's distorting."

"Like for the garage earlier," Rav says, half under his breath.

"Are they up there?" I ask.

"I can't tell."

Yunoo slips his phone into his pocket and descends the ladder rapidly, jumping the last few rungs. "I think we need to find them. We should all be together now."

Jared is watching him. He looks unsure what to do. But Rav's already gone back out to the garden – and now I'm racing after him.

*

The front door's wide open. I guess we didn't close it properly. Or at all.

Jared and Yunoo have caught up with us. As we run back into the house, Jared calls, "*Wait.*"

Rav doesn't look like he wants to. But we stand in the entrance hall together, our breathing loud.

"What—?" Rav starts. Jared waves a hand to silence him.

Though the wind has eased, I can hear leaves rustling in the plane tree right outside. I can also hear drops of water falling from gutters or branches on to the wooden roof of the verandah. Then there's a faint creak overhead. And a bang, loud enough to make us all jump.

Bang.

Jared's first on to the stairs, calling, "*Alli? Lana?*"

Yunoo, then I, then Rav follow right behind. Jared stops on the landing, by the recessed window. Jagged silhouettes of branches wave behind his head. "Alli? Lana?"

"Jared?"

That was Alli's voice, scared. It came through the narrow door to the attic stairs. Jared grabs the handle. Shakes it.

"It won't open!" Alli shouts.

"Where's Lana?" Yunoo yells.

"Trying to get the roof door open! Get us out!"

Yunoo grasps Jared's arm and gently but swiftly moves him aside. He backs up to the far end of the landing. Then he runs, surprisingly quickly given his size, and slams his battering ram of a shoulder against the door. It buckles. But, when Jared tries the handle, it still won't open.

"Alli, get back up the stairs!" Rav shouts. "Yunoo's trying to break the lock!" He says to Yunoo: "Try kicking it?"

Yunoo backs up again. This time, as he powers forward, he pivots, to raise his leg, and smashes the heel of his trainer just above the handle. The wood splinters but the door holds firm. He repeats the manoeuvre, just below the lock, and there's a loud crack.

Rav hauls the door open. A few moments later, Alli's practically falling out of the stairway. Her hands and arms are smeared with cobwebs and dust. She's shaking violently. Jared holds her by the shoulders, Rav aiming his torch at them. "Alli, it's OK, you're back with us. It's OK."

Rav yells up the stairs: *"Lana!"*

No answer. Then we hear her voice, scared, distant: "Alli?"

We all look up. A creaking is moving from the direction

of the roof terrace towards us. Then there's a slipping sound and, a few moments later, Lana emerges from the stairwell, dirty and sweaty. She looks shaken.

"What happened up there?" Rav asks.

"We were locked in!" she exclaims.

Trembling, Lana puts her arms round Alli. They hug each other tightly.

"I think it might be time to get out of here," Yunoo says, turning to Jared, who doesn't respond. He's standing by the window seat, shoulders hunched, face drawn.

"They were *locked in*." Yunoo's voice is loud, even for him. "Doors are being locked. Things are being taken. *Rav* felt something in the utility room. Mia encountered a presence in Hanna's room. This has become dangerous."

Jared stirs. Takes a deep breath. "It's also become our best chance yet to document a haunting."

Yunoo stares at him.

Lana lifts her head from Alli's shoulder. She looks totally drained, all her fierceness gone. "And I found this."

She's reaching into the pocket of her shorts. When she pulls the object out, I stumble back against the wall. It's a small purple leather sandal, with a worn sole. The match to the one on the carpet in Hanna's bedroom.

"Where was it?" Rav asks, his voice rough.

"In the attic," Lana whispers.

Somehow, I make my way past Jared, to kneel heavily on the window seat. I need more than the wall to keep me up.

"I take it that the sandal was not in the attic earlier?" Jared says.

"No," Lana whispers.

I bring my forehead close to the window, and stop. In the reflection, I can see Lana, still holding that sandal. I try hard to control my runaway breathing. What exactly does it mean? That there's a poltergeist in the house and it moved the sandal from where – from a drawer, or from under the bed? Or that Hanna put it there? That she really does haunt the house?

Bang.

For a split second, I'm frozen, then I twist to face the others. It's obvious from their alarmed expressions that they all heard it, too. It was different to the thud of Alli's fist on the locked door. More like something slamming. And it came from downstairs.

Bang.

My entire body judders.

Bang. Bang.

Yunoo looks stricken. Rav's hand is over his mouth, gripping his cheekbones. Alli and Lana aren't moving. Jared lets his breath out in one sharp exhalation. I feel dizzy. I'm remembering what Jetta Amos said about doors banging.

"We go down together," Rav says quietly, his voice wavering.

Bang.

Lana whispers, "Perhaps we should wait."

Bang.

Bang.

Bang, bang.

Bang.

"Sounds like it's the dining-room door," Lana breathes.

"Jetta Amos heard it, too," Alli murmurs, voicing my thoughts. "The dining-room door—"

Bang.

Bang.

Pause.

Bang.

A faint scraping sound comes up the stairs.

Bang.

Jared's moving to the top of the staircase. "We go down together, in pairs, in physical contact."

"We should be recording this," Lana says. She's already tapping the screen of her phone.

Bang.

Bang. Bang.

Jared whispers loudly, "Yunoo, you're next to me. Then Lana and Alli. Then Rav and Mia. *Now*."

Jared and Yunoo set off cautiously – the first stair, pause, then the second. I wonder if Jared's hoping to see something, or if he thinks our presence will make it stop. I drag my left hand down the banister, needing something to help with the weakness in my legs. *Bang*. We all jump. Then Jared and Yunoo take another step. And another…

Rav and I are about halfway down, and I realize that it *has* stopped. It's been at least a few seconds since the last bang.

In the entrance hall, we stay clustered together, as though human contact can somehow protect us. The door to the dining room is slightly open. In the gap, I see darkness.

I expect Jared to give some kind of instruction but he's silent.

It's Lana who eventually breaks away. She walks with her right arm outstretched, her back very straight, her palm flat. Rav trains his torch on her. At the moment that she makes contact with the door, I flinch and she shoves it so hard that it slams against the inside wall.

I still see nothing: only textures of darkness.

Lana says, "Hello…? Why are you showing yourself now? Why not earlier? Why not yesterday? Where've you been?"

Her voice reverberates inside my pounding head.

…*Where've you been? Where've you been?*

"*Lana.*" This is Jared talking. "You're recording?" She nods.

"Then keep doing it but don't go in. Not yet."

He glances at Alli whose face has gone white. Then at Yunoo, Rav and me. "I'm not going to try to force anyone to stay. If you want to leave, go now. But this—" He takes a quick breath. "I *can't* leave. I'm staying to see what plays out, no matter what. Who's with me?"

"I'm not going," Lana whispers hoarsely.

Alli looks scared but she nods.

Shaking his head, like he's deeply uncertain, Yunoo says tightly: "OK. For now."

Rav looks at me. I'm shaking. I'm not sure I can speak. I'd begun to think it was all in my head. *Our best chance yet to document a haunting...*

I want to go. I also hear Tamara's voice in my mind: *I truly believe that power comes through knowledge, and you need power over this situation.* What do I know now? That ghosts are real ... that Holly is real? What power does that give me? I feel like I'm swaying.

"Mia." Alli comes over to where I'm standing. Takes my hands. Tries to focus her gaze on me but it's jumpy. "We're stronger together."

From the doorway, Lana says, "Alli, if Mia wants to leave, she should go. Rav, you should go with her. But we can't wait. I need to do another equipment scan in here right now." She looks at Jared.

He nods. "You and Alli go together. I'm going back to the attic. Yunoo?"

Yunoo rubs a massive hand across his face. At last he says, "OK."

Again Rav looks at me.

"If the camera feeds in the garage and attic distorted for a technical reason, I also need to know about it," Jared adds. "That could be done on the laptop in the kitchen..."

"What if we go do that?" Rav says to me. "Nothing's happened in the kitchen."

Not yet, I think. But I can see that he wants to stay. And, while I can drive, no way do I want to be driving off by myself. So, reluctantly, I nod.

"They should help us do another equipment scan," Lana says, glancing warily up the slanting staircase. "It's better if we check all the rooms that experienced activity as soon as possible."

"Yeah," Jared says. "But I also need that technical check on the video distortion. So that first, then Rav and Mia, you find me." His gaze, tense and animated, shifts to take us all in, one by one. "I don't think I need to spell out the significance of what's happened tonight. It's extraordinary. This could change everything. But we have to do it right. Now *go*."

*

Rav and I head back through the living room into the kitchen. I'm on high alert, expecting something to happen at any moment. Another rush of cold. A bang. A glimpse of something behind me. Whenever I've felt Holly, it's been fleeting. This house – Hanna's room, the utility room – is different. I've never been so afraid.

Rav grabs the Ghostbusters laptop from the worktop and opens the lid. He glances up at me. "OK?" I shake my head.

"So the best thing is to focus on checking our data. We can worry about the significance of it all later. When we're back in New York."

I want to say: *How can I wait?*

How can I not be thinking that, after what's happened tonight, Holly really is still with me – and maybe she'll never leave?

Still, I scrape a chair back and sit stiffly beside him, my body rigid, my pulse still throbbing in my ears.

Jared's name appears on the login window. Rav enters a password.

"I just need to get into the cloud account, and the camera files should all be there…" He brings up the home page. Jared's disguised, asterisked ID fills the box. Rav clicks to sign in.

Immediately a page full of files appears. Some appear to have date- and time-stamped names. He sends the cursor scuttling across the page. I try hard to focus on what he's doing, rather than my runaway pulse, and the thoughts running wild through my head. But something occurs to me.

"Eloise made me promise to call if we found anything," I whisper.

Rav's hands hover over the keyboard. He turns to look at me properly. "I know this is tough but you just can't right now. Partly because we don't even know exactly what we've found. We have to sort through the evidence.

Let's look at the camera in the attic first. We'll start at three this afternoon and move forward."

His fingers resettle. After a few clicks, a window opens. It shows the attic. Though the camera angle covers most of the space pretty well, and I can see Yunoo and Jared easily, the door at the far end is pixelated. Lana was right. You can't tell whether there's a padlock there or not.

A digital clock at the top right-hand corner of the frozen image shows the time, down to hundredths of a second. Rav clicks on it and enters 15.00.00. The image shifts. Now the room is empty. He clicks on fast-forward. The numerals on the clock start spinning, but the image doesn't change ... until suddenly it does.

Rav quickly stops the video. He rewinds to the moment the picture blurred. "That's when it changes. Seven forty-six p.m." He pulls out his phone from his pocket.

"What're you doing?"

"Checking the time of my call to you, when you went into Hanna's room. So I can work out roughly when we got to the garage – when Yunoo checked the attic feed and found it was blurry." He brings up his recent calls list. And he frowns. "The signal from the attic degrades well before Yunoo checked it. Right before I opened that call to you, in fact."

I wrap my arms tightly round my chest. "You think it knew I was going into Hanna's room? What about the other cameras? Was it watching us somehow?"

He rakes a hand through his hair. Shakes his head. "I don't know." Then he clicks back into the cloud account and brings up another video file. "This is footage from Hanna's room." He starts at 6 p.m. this time, and fast-forwards, stopping again when the image blurs. "Yeah – look. It's just like from the attic. The distortion in here starts right before you walk into her room."

A kind of physical echo of the freezing-hot shiver rolls through me. "It didn't want us to video it?" I whisper.

"Maybe." He sits back a little in his chair. "But we have to consider all the possibilities, right? That's my job." He frowns. "Hanna's room has to be under the camera in the attic... I've seen something a bit like this once before."

Our heads shoot up. Lana just shouted something from out in the entrance hall.

"What did you see?" I ask. But Rav isn't paying attention. He's busy finding and clicking on an icon titled ENTRANCE. A new window opens, showing Lana and Alli at the foot of the stairs.

"Jared?" Lana's strained voice is clear on the audio. "Nothing here. Everything OK?"

A few more clicks, and up comes the attic feed. It shows Jared turning towards the door. Yunoo's behind him, iPad in hand. Jared's voice bursts from the laptop's speaker: "We're OK." He's calling down the stairs to Lana.

Quickly now Rav opens yet another video feed. It's for the utility room this time. He adjusts the start time and clicks play. For the third time, the picture starts out clear, then suddenly jumps and fades. I can just about see a line of black worktop. But the rest is murky.

"This must be right around the time we went in," Rav says, his voice low. "It's badly distorted."

I remember the awful dizziness, and the haziness in my vision. Then my body tightens another notch. On the screen, two shadowy outlines have just entered the room.

"They must be *us*," Rav whispers. "Look." The figures move to the door. After a few moments, they quickly back out of the room. "That's when we found we couldn't get out."

He hits slow fast-forward. The footage stays blurry until a couple of minutes after we leave, then it clears.

"This is evidence," I say quietly, my voice shaking.

"It's certainly evidence of *something*. There's a possibility…" He shakes his head. "I'm probably wrong but we have to go back in there."

I'm staring at him. "Possibility of what?"

He gets up, pulls his torch from his pocket and picks up the laptop. "I saw something in an SCC investigation once. A bit like this distortion, only nowhere near so clear-cut. The homeowner reported occasional sudden flickering of her TV, her radio going and off. She thought a poltergeist was responsible." He heads towards the utility room. "Mia, I need you with me for corroboration."

He grabs the door handle. When it clicks, my flesh

shrinks, remembering what I felt in there. But I don't want to be alone so I make myself follow Rav. He aims his torch inside. The beam picks out grimy black granite. Shadows over the ceiling.

"What was responsible for that woman's TV and radio flickering?" I whisper.

He replies under his breath: "I traced the electrical interference to a faulty insulator in a high-voltage power line." And takes two more cautious steps.

I put one hand on his back, partly to steady myself, mostly for the contact. "There's no power line here," I murmur.

Rav darts the beam all round the room. Over the worktops, and the trough sink, and the dark windows. At last it comes to rest on the old washing machine. He goes to put the laptop down on the worktop beside it. After glancing up towards the tiny red flash of the camera in the far, high corner of the room, he clicks on the touchpad to return to the feed. And there we are. Clear in the image. My face looks so drawn, so pale.

"You have to be my witness, too," he says.

"Witness to what?" I manage to whisper.

"Here goes."

With one hand, Rav jerkily raises the lid of the washer. With the other, he aims the torch beam inside. I smell musty clothing. In the bottom is what looks like a purple rag. Rav reaches inside. My breath short and fast, I watch.

332

Carefully he lifts it out and shakes it. It's a wrinkled pillowcase. Then he aims the beam back inside.

I sense the sudden contraction of the muscles in his arm. Afraid to look, but unable not to, I peer in, and see a rectangular slate-grey metal box.

Rav's pocket starts ringing, making us both jump. He ignores it.

"What is it?" I ask.

He plunges his other arm inside, and I hear a tiny click. Instantly a throbbing dizziness expands in my head. Alarm rolls hard through me. Another click – and the throbbing stops. My body's left pulsating with fear.

"*That*," Rav says, his voice shaking, "is an EMP generator."

"A what?"

His face is grim. "An electromagnetic pulse generator. We use them in the lab, to induce feelings of presence and hallucinations that can be interpreted as ghost encounters. They have a switch. But they can also be operated remotely."

My brain feels thick. I can't quite work out what he's saying. "What's it doing here?"

"*Right*. What's it doing here?" He looks like he can't quite believe it himself.

"Alli surveyed the entire house yesterday," I say. "She didn't find any infrasound or strong electromagnetic fields."

"No. But, like I said, it can be operated remotely."

Again his phone starts ringing. Without even checking it, he lets it ring off.

"An EMP can also disrupt devices," he goes on, "especially if they're not protected by a metal shield. The lens mechanism in the cameras would be vulnerable. EMP distortions could explain the blurring video *and* what we felt in here." He takes a quick, deep breath. "Someone put it in here and used it. Which means someone is *deceiving* us."

My head spins. "Someone used it? What do you mean?"

"Someone wanted us to feel those sensations – to think we were having a supernatural encounter. When we weren't."

I stare at him. What I felt in here wasn't *real*?

"But who—?"

"Yeah, who?"

"But what about the banging? And Hanna's room?"

"There could be another device in there," Rav says darkly, turning back to the laptop.

I try to get a grip on the trembling through my body. It wasn't real…

"But it was different in Hanna's room. I really felt something. A bit like in the lab but on a totally different level."

Rav glances up from the screen. "EMFs *and* infrasound? I don't know. We'll need to check it." He swipes and clicks, swipes and clicks.

"What are you doing?"

"Backing up the video footage of us finding the device to a separate account."

I glance over to the door. It was locked. That couldn't have been faked. "Maybe the box was just left here by accident – I don't know – and maybe no one's deceiving us," I say. It all felt so real. "Rav?"

He's clicking to close the file, and a notification box suddenly appears in the top right-hand corner of the screen. It's a message.

> This is insane... I knew you could do this. The medium video's poor quality but it's also INCREDIBLE. Prepare to MAKE HISTORY 👻

My heart's pace rises to a whole new level. And the name of the sender is just as astonishing.

Stacey Disaranno.

*

Rav instantly swipes to view the message properly. It's not part of an exchange. It's a lone message.

"No way," he says, shaking his head. "*No way* – not Jared."

I stare at him. "You're logged in as him," I point out.

"Yeah, but he and Stacey don't even talk! He wouldn't send footage to her!"

"But look at the message."

He blinks. Rubs a hand over his face.

"He was here before we arrived," I whisper. "He could have planted that then." I'm looking at the EMP generator. "And whatever else."

Rav looks at me, confusion and disbelief in his black eyes. "Other parapsychologists would kill for Jared's reputation. He wouldn't risk it by staging a haunting. And anyway *why* would he?"

"But look at the message," I repeat. "Look what you just found… What's the evidence telling you?"

My thoughts are whirling but something suddenly strikes me. I pull out my phone from my pocket. Tap on the last number called.

After two rings, Eloise answers. "Mia? What's happened?"

"The other woman you were talking about – the one you didn't want to hear from, either. I need to know what she looks like."

Pause. "Tall. Long hair, thin…"

"Tall," I repeat. "Thin. Long reddish hair?"

"Yes. Why? Have you found something?"

"I'll call you back. I promise."

"Wait—"

After I end the call, Rav says "*Stacey?*" He exhales hard. "Jared knows I know his logins. Why would he let me use his laptop if he was setting this up? I just can't believe he would give footage to her."

"But he *has*."

I think: *First Lana secretly videoed me, and shared it with Rav and Jared, Alli and Yunoo. Now this. But was the banging faked? And what about the locks?*

Rav's phone rings again. This time he answers it, his mouth twitching. "Jared."

I hear Jared's voice clearly. "Why weren't you answering? Anything from the camera footage?"

Rav's face crumples into a frown. Eyes fixed on me, he says, "I need to show you something. Can you meet us in the kitchen?"

*

Somehow I expect Jared to come alone. But Lana, Alli and Yunoo are with him. Alli looks tense but hyped. Lana seems anxious, her mouth trembling. Like Alli, Jared seems wired – like he's only just containing high emotions.

Yunoo squares his broad shoulders. "Rav, what is it?"

Rav has put the laptop back on the table. He swivels it round to face them. "Jared, I'm sorry," he says. This must be tough for him. He's even apologizing. "I'm logged in as you. This message just came through."

They crowd round to read it. There's a stunned silence.

It's Lana who reacts first: "Stacey...?" She looks at Jared. "You're giving footage to *Stacey*?"

"We found this in the washing machine in the utility room," I say. The EMP generator, which Rav cut from its mains wiring using kitchen scissors, is on the chair beside me. I pick it up. Put it on the table.

"But that's—" Yunoo stops, like the words have got stuck in his mouth. "We have them in the lab!"

I'm watching Jared. He's frowning hard at the box. "In the *washing machine*?"

"Jared!" Rav says hotly. "What's going on?"

"I told Stacey not to contact me while I was here!" He looks angry. But his expression quickly changes. I see a flash of pure bewilderment, and then an even darker cloud building.

Rav's staring at him. I realize he'd been hoping that somehow there would be another explanation for the message.

"Jared!" Lana sounds scandalized. She takes a step back, like this news has literally pushed her away from him.

"I had no choice about contact with Stacey." Jared's voice is hard and clipped. "After Amy Ambler inherited the house, she went to *Stacey* first and Stacey got in touch with me. She said she could arrange for me to be brought in as the investigator, but in return she wanted access to whatever footage I got from the house. She signed a legal document. She can't publish anything until three months after the investigation is concluded – and even then she has to disguise the identities of anyone in the footage. I had no choice. It was either that or Stacey was going to lead the survey, and I wouldn't even be allowed in!"

Silence.

"Why would Amy go to Stacey?" Lana whispers.

"And why would Stacey want *you* to do it instead?" I say.

"Because of his *reputation*." Yunoo almost spits the word out. He fixes a hard, betrayed gaze on Jared's face. "If *Jared Robertson* found something – well then, the world would believe it!"

"All I did was agree to release the footage," Jared insists. "I had nothing to do with that." He points at the EMP generator.

"Stacey wouldn't leave it to chance!" Rav says. "She wouldn't risk bringing you in and you not finding anything – better if you agreed together to plant devices that you *know* generate feelings of presence."

"No!" Jared says, his voice cold. "You really believe I'd do that? You're accusing me of fraud!"

"But you can see how it looks!" Lana exclaims.

"You want to know why she'd risk it?" Jared says hotly. "Because she knows what I witnessed here all those years ago." He shakes his head, and his eyes half close, like he's being drawn into the past. "I was in Hanna's room. The photographs on the wall by her bed… One dropped to the ground. The other didn't fall, not at first. It floated up, and up, and then it swooped down, hard, on to the rug. It was the photo of Hanna with Eloise." He blinks, and fixes a steady gaze on Rav. "The window was shut. There was no breeze. It's the only time something like that has happened to me. Stacey and I were married then. I told her about it."

Silence. In the deep, far distance, I hear waves on the beach. Breaking, changing, re-forming. Our eyes are all on Jared.

"And she made extra certain you'd find something by planting EMP devices," Rav says, his voice low.

Jared raises a warning finger. "*Think*. Even if she somehow planted this device, and maybe others, how did she control them?"

"Stacey has access to the camera footage!" Rav says. "She knew where we all were. She could track us. Those devices can be operated remotely via a phone. She didn't need to be anywhere close by."

Jared's gaze takes in every one of us. The muscles in his cheeks twitch. "Except that she didn't have real-time access. It was easier to set it up so that she got the regular back-up dumps every twenty minutes. Mia was in and out of Hanna's room in well under twenty minutes. She couldn't have coordinated that."

"And how did she lock and unlock doors?" Yunoo says. "How did she make the dining-room door bang?"

"Then maybe it's actually real!" Alli says keenly. She turns to Jared. "She couldn't have known when Mia and Rav were in the utility room. What they felt could have been genuinely caused by a spirit presence."

It's with a scrutinizing expression that Jared says, "Alli, I know you'd like that to be true."

She looks stunned. Then her face contracts. I remember her excited expression when she imagined Jared Robertson actually documenting a haunting.

"You're setting up with your dad soon," Yunoo says accusingly. "What incredible publicity this would be for your new venture."

"No! I would never do that!"

"But everything suggests that somebody has!" Yunoo exclaims. "And the banging – we never *saw* a door close, remember. We were on the landing, on the stairs. A recording would have worked. We just didn't suspect it for a second because we *trusted* each other! And one of us is a liar!"

I jump. My pocket is ringing. Unsteadily, I pull out my phone, ready to silence it, expecting it to be Tamara. It isn't. I quickly swipe to answer.

"Mia? I didn't see her properly." It's Eloise. She sounds worried. "When I was in New York, I was staying with Amy, and she came by. I wasn't feeling well. They were whispering at the front door. I don't think it was really reddish. Tall, thin, young, long hair – but it was blond. Light blond. And she had an accent. European. What's happening?"

My hand grips my phone so tightly that it hurts. "I'm going to call you back as soon as I can." I end the call, my heart hammering.

"Mia, what?" Alli asks. "Who was that?"

I swallow. Lick my lips. Eyes on Jared, I say, "Eloise.

I asked her again about the woman she didn't want to hear from about the investigation. She just told me this woman was tall, thin, with long hair—

"Stacey Disaranno," Yunoo interrupts. "We know."

"Tall," I repeat firmly, my throat tight. "Thin. Long hair. Young… Blond. European accent."

There's an intense silence. Everyone's eyes immediately turn to Lana. Then there's an eruption of noise all around me.

I hardly hear it. It's like I'm wrapped up inside my head, and it feels like everything else is happening beyond a heavy curtain.

Lana's talking, her voice raised. "It could be anyone!"

"Hardly," Jared says quietly.

"*Someone* has set us up," Yunoo exclaims. "Someone on the inside! Who else fits the physical description? *Me?*"

Suddenly Lana's flashing me a look. It's ice-cold, vehement. She's striding out of the kitchen, and the others are following her.

I start to go after them but the sole of my trainer grinds on something, making me look down. When I realize what it is, I feel like I'm going to black out.

Sand.

No.

My clammy hands squeeze into fists. *Lana* may have somehow created the events in this house but I heard Holly's voice. Is she here?

I have to get out. I force my legs to move. Now I'm stumbling through the crescent-shaped room into the entrance hall. And then I'm on the verandah, and down on the grass.

Somewhere in the near background, over by the plane tree, I hear Rav shouting, calling to Lana to stop. But I see only shadows and snatches of images. Rain. No, not rain. Spray. Sand. A spreading, blinding pool of glistening sand.

In my head, I hear Lana's voice in the kitchen and in the dark doorway of the dining room. *Where've you been?*

And on the roof, right after that door slammed shut.

Not Lana's voice now. *Holly's.*

Mia, where have you been?

I'm breathing so fast, I'm dizzy.

In my mind, through a cloud of water spray on a hot day, I see all the colours of the rainbow.

Washington Square Park…? *No.* This is not New York.

A little boy is howling behind me. I hear a slosh of water, then a click, and a happy cry. Someone's just hooked a plastic duck. My fingertips feel rough. Traces of candyfloss have hardened on my skin. Now I'm looking up again through the spray from the fountain. The colours are shimmering right in front of my eyes—

There's *Holly*. She's kneeling on a bench up the steps, by the main road. Her back is sandy, her pink top smeared with melted chocolate, or dirt. A boy in the foreground wanders off – and I realize that someone else is holding her

343

up. White T-shirt, wiry arms. Her stepdad.

He's gripping her shoulder. That's why she's kneeling like that. He's swaying. Now he's bending to talk in her ear. She's trying to twist away. She's pulling hard.

I start up the steps. Her head turns and her scared eyes meet mine. She shouts: "*Mia*, where've you been?"

In the background of my mind, I know I'm in Southampton, in Long Island, and that the scene playing out in my mind is from thousands of miles and five years away.

Where've you been?

When he came for her, *I wasn't there*.

Where was I?

Why wasn't I there?

I was on the bench with her. I shouted for help. I *tried* to stop him.

…Didn't I?

Cold sweat's trickling down my back. I press my hands to my head. I need to remember.

We bought candyfloss and lemonades with money Mum had given me. We rode on the swingchairs. She sweet-talked the attendant to let us on. Then she stood up, though he'd warned us not to. I said maybe she should sit down. Suddenly there was a wild look in her eyes, a different expression to any I'd seen in them before.

In the deep, far distance, I think I hear a voice in the present calling my name. But I tune it out.

"Mia, stop being so scared all the time. What have you got to be scared of?"

That's what she said… All she said.

But this was *Holly*, my protector, my defender, my best friend. This was the first time she'd given me even the slightest criticism. And it wasn't just that. It was the look in her eyes. Like she saw things more clearly than I did, that I was still a kid, and she had crossed a threshold, though we were both still just thirteen…

That's why, when we got down from the swingchairs, I walked off. She called to me not to be mad, to come with her for chips. But I wasn't quite ready to swallow my pride.

Instead of going after her, I went and sat near the fountain, and I watched the glittering rainbows form and vanish. Then I realized how silly I was being, stomping off like a little kid.

When I first spotted her on the bench, I felt a warm welling of anticipation at making up. But then I saw her stepdad was grabbing at her. She turned her head and saw me. *"Mia, where've you been?"*

Even if I couldn't have got him off her, I could have stopped her from running into the road—

Something's tickling my leg. In the present, I realize. A blade of grass. I'm on the drive. I can smell the sharp freshness of the pines. I can hear waves rolling and crashing. I can just about make out the outline of Jared's Mustang.

I feel like I'm seeing things clearly for the first time.

I *wasn't* there. I wasn't with Holly.

I didn't try to help her. I didn't do anything.

She'd spoken the truth. I *was* scared, of so many things, but the people around me loved me. I wasn't threatened. Not in the way she was. As soon as I realized he was grabbing her, I wanted to run to her. But, even before I took my first stride, I was already too late.

Again I feel my own horrible inertia. I hear the jarring screech as the bus tried to brake—

"Mia!"

The voice is very close. Here, in the present.

"Mia, I was looking for you. Lana's admitted to Alli she was paid by Amy! Now she's run!"

Rav. But suddenly his head swivels. He's blinking through the jagged treeline of the drive. I can hear it, too. A noisy engine. It's rapidly getting closer, headlights jerking. Has Lana called Amy to pick her up? If so, she was lying about going to Manhattan. But then she's lied about so much more than that.

"Stacey must have introduced Lana to Amy," Rav's saying. "They knew each other pretty well."

Amy – who wanted to set up the presence of her own niece's ghost. At least Eloise knew not to trust her.

Amy … lying.

Lana … lying.

And I've been lying to myself about exactly where I was and what I did, or didn't do, when Holly died.

The incoming vehicle stops in a cloud of dust. After a moment, I hear the tinny sound of a car door being slammed shut. Then a familiar voice shouts: "Mia? *Mia!*"

I try to wave the dust cloud from my face.

There, by her mum's old yellow Datsun, wearing a green maxi-dress and gold flip-flops, is Tamara. She coughs and grins, first at Rav, then at me.

"Hey!" she says. "You sounded so worried, and, as I kinda pushed you into all this, I thought I'd better come. And I actually made it!" I guess she finally clocks our expressions because she says, "Have I missed something?"

I stumble towards her. She opens her arms at once. As she wraps them tightly round me, her bangles dig into my back and the sharp smell of her hair dye gets me right in the heart. *Tamara is really here*, I find myself thinking.

She's here, and she, at least, is undeniably real.

32

Tamara and I are sitting in her car.

When Jared, Alli and Yunoo came back to the house, Jared asked if Tamara would mind not being present while what just happened was discussed.

I wanted to stay with her, and didn't want to go back into the house, or near the beach, either. Or into the wood. So I said we'd sit in the car. But, with my window open, we can hear their voices from the verandah pretty clearly.

I hear Alli saying it's too hard to believe – that Lana's work meant everything to her.

"And she needed money to return to studying!" Yunoo says. "And she's run because she knows we can prove what she's done!"

"If she placed signal distorters all over the house, she could have coordinated blurring and image failure whenever it suited her," Rav puts in. "And she could have taken your bracelet, Alli, and manipulated padlocks, and even taken the other sandal from Hanna's room, to use later. Or Amy could have taken it while she was here first, and given it to Lana when she arrived."

"*And* she could have controlled the infrasound and EMP machine from her phone," Yunoo says. "But, Alli, how did you not notice any of this? It would make most sense if you were working together."

I can't see Alli's face but I can hear the horror in her voice. "No! And we were in pairs so we could corroborate if anything happened, not to watch each other all the time! I was doing my own thing while she did hers. I *trusted* her."

"Lana found Mia," Jared says. "I thought Mia was exactly what we needed. But she suited Lana's purposes even more perfectly."

Tamara frowns at me. "*What?*" she mouths.

"She scored highest on the goat scale…" Rav's saying as if in response. "And what she was made to feel in this house was overwhelming. Here's a medium who, as far as Lana knows, doesn't even believe in ghosts – but look what she felt. And here's the biggest academic sceptic in the entire field – and just look at the footage. It would seem totally compelling."

Jared says quietly, "Stacey may have known nothing about all this."

"I wouldn't bet on that!" Yunoo says.

Alli says, "But why would Amy Ambler want to pay

someone to make the house seem haunted?"

It's Jared who answers. "Same reason as Lana. For *money*."

"And what a spectacular way for Lana to get back on the academic track," Rav says, shaking his head.

"But so risky," Yunoo says. "To hide devices."

"You did infrasound and EMF searches with her," Rav says to Alli. "At those times, obviously, she had whatever she'd placed switched off. Like you said, we trusted each other. She relied on that totally. No doubt she meant to remove the devices tonight – and then we'd never have known."

Tamara's eyes widen even further. She whispers, "Mia, you need to tell me, like, everything. In total detail. Right now."

And so I do. While the others continue talking and debating, I tell her about every event since I arrived at Halcyon House. My resurfacing memories about Holly come last.

She listens carefully. When I've finished, it's the house that she asks about first.

"So there's no actual evidence of any poltergeist – or Hanna's ghost, right?"

"I don't think so. There are all the eyewitness stories, though."

"What, like the one about the washing?" I nod.

"So the back door was open and a cat got in while the

housekeeper was taking the delivery and jumped on the pile, knocking it down."

"That sounds really unlikely," I tell her.

"But what's *more* unlikely? A cat, or some other animal, got in. Or there was this spirit force that no one understands that decided throwing washing around was the thing to be doing. Once. Then it went off that idea and started banging doors… Or there's a draught somewhere, and it was the wind."

"And Jared—"

"And Jared was young and spooked, and there *was* a breeze."

I shake my head. "He was sure."

But she's already talking again. "And Holly—" She stops. "You see what you're telling me, right?" Her eyes seem almost to be burning with energy.

"You just freed yourself, Mia. You see that? This house, this is the one place that still worried Jared Robertson. The only one in all his years of investigating ghost reports that made him afraid that ghosts might be real. Right? That's what Rav said. And there's *nothing* here. And you fell out with Holly right before she died, so you weren't with her. You were so upset with yourself, you couldn't even let yourself remember what actually happened that day. But you've been punishing yourself for it all this time."

I press the heels of my palms to my eyes. It's not that I want to blot her out, I just need to try to work out what

I think, and Tamara's conviction is making that hard.

She says, "You also have these sensitivities to things like infrasound, magnetic fields, which you didn't know about, so you couldn't guard against them. When they make you feel strange, your brain tries to come up with some kind of explanation – any explanation. You see how all this is making sense to me? Mia, this is *good*. What Lana's done is terrible, I totally get that. But I think maybe, in some ways, it was the best thing that could have happened to you."

I let my hands drop. Stare at her with what must be obvious disbelief.

"I mean it! When you get over the shock of all this, I think you'll agree with me." She sighs. "You know what I think? I think we get out of here. Go home. Let them sort out whatever they have to do."

Realizing their voices have gone silent, I turn to look for them but they've disappeared inside.

"I promised I'd tell Eloise if we found anything."

"You could call her on the way home?"

"I feel like I have to see her." I meet Tamara's gaze. Hold it. "If that's OK?"

"You know where she is?"

"I know she's close."

I get out my phone and call her. It goes straight to voicemail. I message her:

Can we meet? I have news. Mia

I glance round again at the house. "I should tell Rav and the others. And get my stuff."

"You want me to come in with you?"

I shake my head. "But thanks… And thank you. For coming."

"Of course," she says, with feeling. "Anyway, after I burned the onions *twice*, Mom wasn't that crazy about me helping with the cooking again tonight." She smiles.

I don't quite manage a smile back. But I get pretty close.

*

It's odd – going back inside Halcyon House.

I feel different, I realize. I'm still nervous but the entrance hall doesn't seem so forbidding. All the black paint doesn't feel intimidating so much as just old. Shabby. And something else has changed… Then I realize that a bright light is coming from the upstairs landing. Someone must have got the electricity back on. I guess the circuit board wasn't in as bad a state as Lana claimed.

"Rav?" I call.

After a moment, he shouts down the stairs. "Mia? Up here."

I take the steps slowly, resting my hand gently on the worn banister, allowing myself to feel … nothing.

Up on the landing, the glow from the bare bulb shows the scattering of splinters from the attic door. I think of the plastic knight that I found in the dust. Hanna played up there.

She was a little kid, and she wasn't scared to be in the attic.

"Hey."

I swivel in the direction of the voice. Rav is down the corridor, in the doorway to Hanna's bedroom. He looks totally dishevelled, his hair half down, his shirt crumpled and dirty. He also looks exhausted. Like finding out about Lana has sucked all the remaining energy out of him.

"I'm going to go back with Tamara," I tell him.

There's a pause before he says, "I think that's a great idea. Look, I was gonna apologize for getting you dragged into all this, but I'll do that properly later. Before you go, there's something in here you'll probably want to see."

"In Hanna's room?"

He nods. "It's OK. Come on."

I take a few steps but as I reach the end of the landing – the start of the corridor – I stop suddenly. My gaze is focused on the foreground, near the wall.

"Mia?"

"Rav," I say quietly, "come here."

"What is it?"

I don't take my eyes off it, for fear I'll lose it. "You have to come."

He walks quickly to me.

"Here, stand next to me," I tell him. "Can you see it?"

"…What?"

"Try taking a step back. Just there." I point towards the wall.

"Mia, I don't—" and he breaks off. He turns his head towards the window, then back.

"You see it?"

"It's a reflection off the window," he says softly.

When the electricity wasn't on up here, we couldn't have seen it. Now some of the light from the bulb is bouncing off the window, then the far wall of the corridor. Though it's faint, it's definitely there: a slight haze of light.

"But it would have been there all the time," I say. "When the light was on."

"Not all the time," he says. "In daylight, you wouldn't see it. At night, the phase of the moon could make a difference."

"You think Lana made sure the electricity was off up here?"

"I don't know for sure but, if she did, it had all kinds of advantages for her. She might not even have known about this… I'll show Jared when we're done in Hanna's room. Come on."

Memories of what happened last time I was in here make my heart race. And, when I follow Rav inside, I'm startled. But just because of the light: the decorative perforations in the metal shade are scattering it around, like confetti.

My gaze jerks round the room. The plastic knights on their sides catch again at my gut, but it's the poignancy of it all – this child's bedroom left untouched for all these years – that's the cause this time.

Jared's at the window. Yunoo is kneeling by the little

bed. They both look round. Alli's sitting on the floor in the corner, talking quietly into her phone. Her body is hunched over, her face drained.

"Hey, Mia," Yunoo says. On the duvet in front of him is a device that looks like a small fan. "Rotary subwoofer… Like the kind we use in the lab to generate infrasound. I found it under the bed." He shakes his head, like he still can't believe it. "And, in the dining room, a wireless speaker tucked inside the case for a spare pillow. *And*, in a bag with Lana's dirty washing, another EMF device."

"We could be here for a while, checking the house over again," Jared says grimly. "If you want to stay, you're welcome. You deserve to know every detail of what's been happening here. But, if you want to go home, you should."

"I'm going to go," I tell him. I don't mention Eloise because, while this has been his investigation, he wasn't honest with us, and I feel like I owe her, and I don't want her to have to wait to learn what's happened.

"It will sound totally inadequate after what you've been through," Jared says, "but I am sorry."

His voice is flat. But I don't think that's because he doesn't mean what he's saying. Like Rav and Yunoo, he looks shattered, emptied out. And it occurs to me that it's probably more than Lana's betrayal. Just as I think he became sure that this house *was* haunted, that conviction was yanked out from under his feet.

And me? I was sure, too. But now, standing here in

this room, Hanna's things all around me, Tamara's voice echoing in my head, I think maybe she's right.

All these years, I've been carrying Holly in my own reality, because of my guilt, my caution, my fears, my sensitivities, my beliefs.

I can't comment on what Jared experienced here all those years ago. Or what Jetta Amos saw and heard.

But in my case all along, I think, it's been me. Just me.

33

As I'm sliding the holdall I borrowed from Sadie on to the back seat of Tamara's car, Eloise texts an address. It turns out to belong to a small, two-storey house on the outskirts of town. The porch light is on, showing a bare bench and a neat rectangle of lawn.

Peering out at it, Tamara says, "You want to talk to her alone, right?"

"I think I'd better. I'm sorry. I'll be quick."

"I came to help, right? So, if I'm helping, I'm happy." She stifles a yawn. "Go."

Even before I'm up the porch steps, I hear a TV on in the house, blaring. I wonder whether I should just call Eloise to tell her I'm here, but I press the little white bell. A rapid outburst of barking comes in response.

After a woman calls out, and the barking dies down, I hear a heavy tread in the hallway. Then the door opens.

The woman standing there in red slippers and a scarlet cotton dressing gown, a white terrier of some kind by her feet, looks familiar. But then Eloise suddenly appears behind her, saying it's a friend of hers, who's only in town for the evening, which is why she's here so late, and we'll talk outside.

So it's only when she's shuffled back inside with the dog, and Eloise has come out to sit with me on the top step of the porch, that I realize with surprise who the woman is.

"You're staying with Jetta Amos?"

"I used to see her most times my uncle brought me out to visit Mom. They kept close. She used to go round every few days – check on Mom. When I saw her at the funeral, she invited me to stay." She fixes me with a cautious gaze. "You said there's news?"

On the drive over, I tried to think through what to tell her. I decided that though no doubt it will hurt to hear that her mother's sister paid someone to make it seem like Halcyon House was haunted by a poltergeist and perhaps even by Hanna, she deserves to know everything.

So that's what I tell her.

The fingers of her right hand clasp the little silver butterfly. "You're saying you *don't* think Hanna's still in there?"

"I can't tell you she definitely isn't. But we didn't find anything to suggest that she is."

"People saw her at the window," Eloise whispers. "They heard her."

"People remembered seeing her at her window, and those memories, mixed with all that emotion, influenced what they saw and heard." This could be Rav speaking. But I think I actually believe it now.

"I *knew* Amy wanted Hanna to be there." There's hurt but also anger in her voice. "I didn't live with Mom, right? But my uncle used to bring me to visit her. Every month. The last time I was with Mom, she said Amy was talking about the sightings again."

"Did your mum talk about seeing Hanna ever?" I ask.

Eloise shakes her head. "Not literally seeing her. But she said she felt like when she was in the house, Hanna was close." She pauses. "I thought maybe Hanna wouldn't show herself to Mom because it would upset her. To think she wasn't at peace."

Before tonight, I hadn't realized that Eloise and Franca still saw each other. And I think of that comment Lana made about Amy inheriting the house. "Why do you think she left the house to her sister?" I ask her. "Rather than to you?"

"I have shares held in trust till I'm twenty-one. The fund's done well. That's what my uncle's lawyer says. The house was all Mom had to leave, and Amy lost her business last year. She's been borrowing to cover her home loan and her car payments. She's even been asking my uncle for money."

I let this information sink in. "If Jared's investigation concluded that the house *was* haunted—"

"What would that be worth?" Eloise finishes, with a surprising lack of bitterness. "She'd be on every TV show. She'd get someone to write a book about it." She fixes me with an intense gaze. I get the impression she's trying to make a decision. She takes a quick breath. "Maybe you should know that Mom told me what might have happened. When Hanna died."

I'd been feeling like my body would find it impossible to respond to any more shocks today. But somehow it manages to react yet again. My heart suddenly racing, I wait for her to go on.

"I think Dad knew. Or he suspected. Only a couple of summers ago, she told me. They'd had guests for the weekend. They'd been partying hard and it had been really hot. A heatwave. The day everyone went home, the heat broke. Mom always used to swear the window was locked in Hanna's room. Then she told me she wasn't actually sure. She might have opened it to air the room. Forgotten to lock it back up."

Before I can stop myself, I say, "Your parents took the company to court."

Eloise looks directly at me. "Well, is it better to think that a window company's to blame for Hanna falling? Or Mom?" Tears well in her eyes. She quickly wipes them away. "I just wanted to know – I wasn't sure – I wanted to know that *she* wasn't still there. The spiritualist says she talks to her. You heard her."

I try to remember Griminger's exact words. "She talked about the number six. A house under threat. Change. It's so vague. It doesn't have to be Hanna… After your mother died, maybe there were stories about the house in the local paper? She could have read about it?"

And my thoughts race on. I can't help wondering, if this is true, if Franca stayed in the house because she couldn't bear to leave, because deep down she felt so guilty, even though it was an accident. Because she couldn't forgive herself – she just couldn't move on.

Something else occurs to me, and this thought I do voice out loud: "Do you think maybe, after they lost the court case, Amy, even your dad, maybe even Jetta Amos encouraged the idea that a poltergeist was involved to try to *help* your mum? Maybe they did whatever they could think of to make her feel it wasn't her fault?"

Eloise hugs her knees. She frowns into the darkness of the street.

"They didn't ever say they saw *Hanna*, right?" I go on. "That was other people. After the poltergeist stories came out."

Still she doesn't speak. I become aware again of the canned laughter from Jetta's TV. Now it feels like it's battering at my skull. A deep ache buds between my eyes.

"I don't know," Eloise whispers at last. "Maybe." She looks tired suddenly and I realize just how worn out I am, too.

"I'm going back to my aunt's place now," I tell her. "And I'll be back in England in August. But you can call me any time."

I stand almost groggily, my legs heavy, my head now really hurting.

"I honestly don't think Hanna's there," I say, trying to condense all the belief I now feel into my words. "I think you can go home and feel that she's at peace."

Eloise doesn't look up but she slowly nods.

As I walk back to Tamara, I almost feel like I'm floating. Somehow, my body manages to clamber into the passenger seat, and I collapse into it.

Tamara's holding her phone. She flicks it off and drops it in her lap. "Is she OK? You ready to go home now?"

I think of my cramped room with the rattling AC, the view along Manhattan from the roof, Marlowe soft against my leg, Sadie's enthusiastic hugs. I am so ready to go home, it's untrue.

"I think so – and totally," I tell her, and I feel the remaining tension start to seep right out of me.

Tamara twists the key in the ignition. There's a clicking but that's all. She lets it go. Twists it. Once again, the car vibrates to the sound of the unresponsive starter motor.

"OK." Tamara looks at me with a mixture of sheepishness and frustration. "Emergency person extraction in Mom's ancient car was maybe not my best idea, after all."

34

I have no idea what time it is when we get back to Brooklyn.

Rav and Yunoo came to collect us in the minibus. Jared's taking Alli directly back to her place, Rav explains, in case Lana goes back there.

During the drive, I've been thinking about everything that's happened, and what Tamara said to me in the car. I don't quite feel free. But maybe there's something that would help.

As we draw up outside her building, Tamara turns to hug me.

"Can you meet me tomorrow?" I whisper in her ear. "Ten a.m., my place, with your bike?"

Pulling back slightly, she gives me a puzzled look.

"I'll explain everything in the morning," I promise her.

She gives me another squeeze. "OK."

Outside Sadie's place, we're all too shattered for anything

more than quick goodbyes. Rav tells Yunoo that he'll call him first thing, and we trek up the steps with our bags.

Just after we set off from Southampton, I called Sadie to let her know Jared had decided to call off the investigation because there were problems with the equipment. It was the only thing I could think of at the time, and it was kind of true, in a way.

Even before my key is out of the lock, she's there at the door, tying the cord of her fuchsia silk kimono. "Mia! Rav. Hey, welcome home!"

She gives me a tight hug. "What happened with the equipment? What a shame."

Rav glances at me. "Yeah," he says. "It was."

Marlowe comes slinking out from her bedroom. I snatch him up, and bury my face in the silky fur at the back of his neck. He smells of ginger and jasmine, with undertones of musty cat.

"But interesting?" Sadie asks.

"Really interesting," I tell her, trying my best to put some feeling into it.

"Though also totally exhausting," Rav says. "You have to stay up at night. It's hard to get much sleep."

Sadie looks from Rav to me, then back to Rav. "You look like you haven't slept at *all*. You want something to eat before you go to bed? That mango should be ripe now. How does mango, Galaxy and a ginger cranberry mocktail on the roof sound?"

I smile. It feels unfamiliar – like it's been so long.

I feel like I could fall into bed and sleep for a year. But I want to hear Sadie's voice, and be up on the roof, here, in this familiar world that now somehow seems even safer, even more like home. I guess Rav feels something similar because he manages a tired smile, too, and nods.

"It sounds perfect," I tell her.

35

Friday morning, I wake to the gentle sound of the AC rattling away in the corner. I scrabble blearily on the floor for my phone. First I register that it's 9.12 a.m. Then I notice that I have three messages. One each from Mum, Dad and Freja.

I tell Mum and Dad everything's great. Freja's reads:

Don't want to pressure you but need to book Airbnb. What you think?

I shove my pillow behind my back, and shuffle up, so I can lean against the wall. I rub sleep from my eyes and send:

I'm so sorry. Definitely. Yes. If it's not too late?

Instantly I see the flashing dots of Freja replying.

Of course not too late! Great!!

There's a broad smile on my face as I write back.

Can't wait!

Italian or Japanese? What you think?

Whatever you'd like best. Either amazing xx

Excited!!

Me too! xx

Got to go. Let's talk later.

I can hear someone moving around in the kitchen already. From the tread, I'm guessing it's Rav.

I'm about to get up in search of breakfast but then my phone rings. It seems too soon for Freja to be calling.

"Expected-but-still-good news or new-and-totally-unexpected-good news first?" Tamara asks.

"Expected," I say, smiling.

"Gunther just called. The embroidery hoops have arrived. We're all set to start tomorrow morning. He is, I quote, deliriously excited about our imminent arrival."

"Deliriously? Really?"

"Which brings me to the other good news. Though, I don't know—" Her tone changes. She sounds doubtful. "I should maybe challenge it because I know it's not fair."

"What?"

"Jared Robertson rang me, right before Gunther. He says he's had the car taken to a mechanic in Southampton and when it's fixed up they'll have it driven back here. He says the institute will pay the bill."

I sit up straight. "Are you serious?"

"I knew the car had issues. I chose to drive it out there."

I think about how he shared video of me from Halcyon House with his ex-wife. He had his reasons but still. "It's a private university," I say. "He's offering. If he wants to pay, I think you should let him."

There's a pause. "But, if he's really going to cover that, we will be at least, like, seven hundred bucks up on where I thought we'd be after we do the job for Gunther."

"Road-trip slush fund."

"Road-trip spa motel fund! I'm going off right now to plot every spa motel between here and Nevada! Then I'm getting on my bike. See you in half an hour-ish."

She ends the call and I go through to the kitchen, where I find Rav scraping out the last of a jar of Sadie's strawberry jam to smear on half a bagel. He waves good morning. "How'd you sleep?"

"Really incredibly well, thank you. You?"

"Like I just got home from climbing the entire Himalayas."

Smiling, I go to the fridge in search of juice, and find a note from Sadie under the pina colada magnet:

Day of classes...
TACOS LATER xxx

"Any news?" I ask him.

He finishes a mouthful of bagel. "No one can get hold of Lana. Or Amy Ambler. But Jared and Yunoo looked back at their photos and they think it could have been Amy who was outside the house – waiting to meet Lana, maybe. Lana certainly managed to make sure she went off by herself, without Alli…"

"I guess Lana didn't go home?"

"There's no sign she did. But she did message Alli, to say she was sorry. And that she'll send her bracelet back."

I close the fridge door. "She only apologized to Alli?"

"Apparently. Not that it's made much difference. Alli's really cut up. I mean, I find it hard to believe what Lana did but they were close."

I take a glass from the shelf and fill it with orange juice. "Has Jared called the police?"

"To say what?"

I stare at him over the rim of my glass. "To report the fraud. Obviously."

"Conspiracy to deceive a ghost investigator? You think that would stand up in court?" He sighs. "Look, Lana has *zero* chance of an academic future now. Not in the States, anyway. Given everything she hoped for, maybe that's a harsh enough punishment."

"But what about the video and the audio? Stacey has it."

"Jared's already been on to his lawyer about that. No way will she be allowed to use any of it. If she tried to, he'd expose her for using material she knew was part of a set-up. He's got no proof that she was involved in that, but we're all pretty certain she was."

I drain my glass of juice. "Are you going into the institute?"

"We've been officially instructed to take some time off. I think Alli's gonna go stay with her folks. Yunoo's talking about maybe even going home to Seoul." He sits up straight on his stool. Stretches. "What are you up to?"

Thinking about what I have planned makes me wonder if it would be good for him, too.

"I'm meeting Tamara. You want to come?"

"Where?"

"Not far. There's that other bike in the basement that no one seems to own any more. You could take that."

"But you're not telling me where we're going because, what, you feel like I need more surprises in my life right now?"

Smiling, I say, "I could tell you. But I'd rather show you."

He looks totally unconvinced. "So long as it's not some

place that's got anything to do with hauntings. OK?"

I wonder how to respond to that. "*Kinda* OK," I tell him.

*

It must be nearly eleven, and the air is buzzing with heat. Having locked up our bikes, Rav, Tamara and I walk along a driveway through a stone entrance gate that is so extremely high Gothic, it's practically a caricature.

Rav gives me a pointed look. "What exactly are we doing here?"

"It's just up here," Tamara says.

She leads the way off the drive and up a narrow set of stone steps cut into a grassy hill.

Already, the traffic back on 5th Avenue sounds a long way distant. From a nearby tree comes a cooing sound.

The steps lead up to a path, with graves to either side. Everything from simple headstones to ornate stone columns. I don't actively want to read the inscriptions, but I can't seem to stop myself. The sparest of them hit me the hardest.

ELICIA
MOTHER

JOSEPH
FATHER

Like anything else would only muddy the elemental loss.

As we climb on, I pause to look at a crypt in the form of a little house, with green copper windows. Two sleek doves are pecking in the grass outside.

"Mia, what are we doing here?" Rav asks.

I'm about to tell him to wait, he'll find out shortly, but from further up the hill, off the path, Tamara calls: "Over here!"

When Rav and I catch up with her, she's standing beside a long rectangle of grass that's much darker and thicker than the grass all around it. At the head of the grave stands a pure white marble obelisk. I go closer, to read the inscription.

HERE
LIE
THE
SECRETS
OF THE
VISITORS
OF
GREEN-WOOD
CEMETERY

"What exactly is this?" Rav asks doubtfully.

"It's an installation," Tamara says. "You write down

your secrets. You post them. And you leave them here. Acknowledged. And buried."

I sit down on paler, more raggedy grass to the side of the grave, my eyes on that inscription. Rav and Tamara sit down, too, on the other side.

"I've done it already," Tamara says. "So here." Unzipping her bag, she pulls out a black-bound A5 notepad and a red pen.

I listen to the cooing of doves back near the path, and the trickle of water from a fountain somewhere off behind me.

Write down my secrets?

Post them into a tomb?

Bury them?

…Can I?

I feel Rav's eyes on me. "I could go first," he says quietly.

Tamara passes him the pad and pen. While he writes, we both focus on the ground.

At last he tears out two sheets and folds them in half together. He kneels, to push them into the slot. They slip over the ledge and away, underground. After a moment, he reaches over the grave of secrets, and hands me the pad and pen.

For a few minutes, I just sit with them on my lap, half listening to the doves, and trying to organize my thoughts. I know Holly's never going to read this. But it has to be right.

After wiping my damp palm on my shorts, I grip the pen.

Holly, I'm not sure exactly what to say - except that I'm so sorry. I couldn't say it before, because of all the things I was trying to keep secret from myself... I wasn't there. I didn't do anything. I didn't even try to stop him. I didn't scream when I saw him. I wasn't there to stop you running into the road. I loved you so much. I'm so sorry.

Tears are running down my cheeks now. I twist my neck, so they drop to the grass rather than the page.

I know you wouldn't hate me. Because that's not who you were. And you know I love you.

The pen slips from my hand to the ground. My fingers trembling, I tear out the single page. I fold it in half, lean towards the obelisk and I place it into the slot. For a moment, it wavers on the ledge, and I'm afraid it's not going to drop. Then a breeze makes the leaves of the trees behind me rustle … and it's gone.

ACKNOWLEDGEMENTS

Huge thanks to Jane Harris, my editor, who has made this book better in so many ways. Thanks also to Julia Churchill, my wonderful agent at AM Heath. Heartfelt thanks to Rosa and Ben for all your hospitality and New York knowhow. And to Kate for climbing that fire escape, and so much more in New York, and at home; you are a special friend.

I learned a lot about academic ghost research from interviews I conducted for magazine articles with leading scientists in the field, including Ciarán O'Keeffe, a parapsychologist and professor of psychology at Buckinghamshire New University, and Professor Chris French, head of the Anomalistic Psychology Research Unit at Goldsmiths, University of London. The VR experiment is partly based on a research project being supervised by O'Keeffe (minus the infrasound and EMFs).

Some of the criticisms of modern populist ghost-hunting methods come from a presentation by the rigorous parapsychologist Steve Parsons at a meeting of the Society for Psychical Research in London. Parsons is the co-author of *Paracoustics: Sound & the Paranormal*, among other books, and the man behind the loose torch battery ruse. (He also wore a Ghostbusters belt buckle while giving his talk.)

But most thanks go to James – as always, without your support, this book would not have been possible.

Two final notes: Here Lie the Secrets of the Visitors of Green-Wood Cemetery is a 2017 installation by the French artist Sophie Calle, which will remain in place for twenty-five years. Information on hearing voices is available here: https://www.hearing-voices.org and here: https://www.dur.ac.uk/hearingthevoice/

ABOUT THE AUTHOR

Emma Young is an award-winning science and health journalist who has written for the *Guardian*, the *Sydney Morning Herald*, *BBC Online*, *The Atlantic*, *Mosaic* and *New Scientist*. She has also written fiction and non-fiction for adults and children. Her books include the Storm series of science-based thrillers for 9-11 year olds under the name E. L. Young and the YA novel *She, Myself and I*. Emma lives in Sheffield with her husband and two children.

@EmmaELYoung